PRIMEVAL

THE LOST ISLAND

Also available in the *Primeval* series:

SHADOW OF THE JAGUAR
By Steven Savile

Coming soon:

EXTINCTION EVENT
By Dan Abnett

FIRE AND WATER
By Simon Guerrier

PRIMEVAL

THE LOST ISLAND

PAUL KEARNEY

TITAN BOOKS

Primeval: The Lost Island
ISBN: 9781845766948

Published by
Titan Books
A division of
Titan Publishing Group Ltd
144 Southwark St
London
SE1 0UP

First edition October 2008
1 3 5 7 9 10 8 6 4 2
Primeval © 2008 Impossible Pictures.
Cover imagery: A big wave breaks the foam and spray
highlighted by the sun © Shutterstock.

Visit our website:
www.titanbooks.com

Did you enjoy this book? We love to hear from our readers.
Please email us at readerfeedback@titanemail.com or write to us at
Reader Feedback at the above address.

To receive advance information, news, competitions, and exclusive Titan offers
online, please register as a member by clicking the "sign up" button on our
website: www.titanbooks.com

A CIP catalogue record for this title is available from the British Library.

Printed and bound in Great Britain by CPI Group UK Ltd.

For Marie

ONE

With a cough and a mutter, the engine died. They were 300 nautical miles out into the North Atlantic.

"Damn it, Michael; see to that. Did you clean the plugs?"

"I cleaned the plugs, Da," Michael replied, shouting to be heard over the din of the storm. "It's the bloody engine."

"There's nothing wrong with that engine, boy."

"Aye, apart from it being forty years old."

"Don't you backchat me now. We're wallowing. Get down there."

They stood glaring at each other across the wheelhouse. Michael Mackey, black-haired and six-feet tall in his socks, thumped one broad fist into the binnacle console, then turned and went down the hatch behind them.

His father, James, puffed on his roll-up until the tip glowed yellow in the murky dimness of the dusk. One hand light on the ships wheel, he leaned forward and stared through the salt-streaked glass of the wheelhouse windows. Under him, the big, broad-beamed trawler rose and fell like a toy duck in a bathtub. The *Cormorant* was sixty-feet long, wooden-built. It had been his father's boat, and one day it would be Michael's, unless the Atlantic had its say first.

James rubbed his hand over a grey-stubbled chin, and then thumbed the intercom.

"Kieran, are you awake?"

After a moment the intercom crackled back at him.

"Aye — who wouldn't be? We're being thrown about like a baby's rattle down here."

"Get down to the engine, give Michael a hand. It's quit on us again."

"Jesus, Skipper."

"Get on with it. And get the rest up. Survival suits, the whole heap. Best be careful."

"Right-ho. She's picked a hell of a night to give up on us."

James lifted his thumb.

"She's not given up on us yet," he snarled aloud.

The roar of the gale was deafening, the merciless thunder of the waves. The *Cormorant* was running for home with the wind on her starboard quarter — just behind James's left ear. All around her the sea was a vast rolling landscape of broken hills fringed with white foam. That was a twenty-five-foot swell out there, the wave tops higher than the boat's antenna.

The trawler fought her way up the steep sliding back of each wave, the bow plunging as she came over the crest. The wind struck her stern at the top, so she slewed round a little, and James fought stubbornly, swearing and praying together as he wrenched at the wheel and the boat came sliding and plunging down the far side of the wave. The wind cut off, and the course was running true again. If the wind were to push her broadside-on at the crest of any wave, then the one behind it would swamp her, catch her beam-on and likely capsize her.

"After such a catch, too," James said bitterly, his cigarette spitting sparks as he sucked on it. The hold was full, good-sized cod and haddock, the best catch they'd taken in months. They were paying for it now, though.

Without propulsion, there was little they could do but set the trawler before the wind and hope to ride out the gale until Michael got the engines started again. The gale was hammering them off course, south and east, towards the Bay of Biscay. It was damn near as bad as the Atlantic for storms.

Kieran Fitzsimon lurched into the wheeldeck, hauling himself up the companionway. He was grinning, his freckled face white under a shock of ginger hair.

"It's fifty knots out there, or I'm a Dutchman," he shouted. "You ever been out in one like this before, Skipper?"

James smiled unwillingly. Kieran's simple-headed enthusiasm was impossible to resist. "Too many. I'm too old now to see the funny side of it."

"Ah, sure, where's your sense of adventure? You were right, so you were, about the cod run. We hit them right where you thought. When we get home we'll be rich."

"Rich," James said dubiously. He grunted, tugging on the wheel, resisting the battery of sea and wave as the trawler rose up another crest to be slammed by the full force of the storm. The boat tilted to port thirty degrees. An empty coffee mug flew off the console and shattered on the deck.

Kieran, bright red hair in a bright orange survival suit, went tumbling into the bulkhead, landing with a dull thud, and clung there looking even more dazed than usual. James stood like a planted stone, teeth bared, his cigarette champed in two. Profanities hissed through his teeth as he fought with the wheel.

The ship slewed round, then back again, like a car skidding on an oily road, only thirty tons heavier. Then they were in the calm of the leeward side, with the bow pointed down into a dark abyss of raging water, the trough of the wave.

James stared into it with the sweat beading on his face, and for a second he could have sworn that he saw a light there, deep in the dark heart of the water. Just a momentary glitter.

He wiped his eyes, breathing heavily.

"Kieran, you all right?"

"Fine Skipper." He was rubbing the side of his face ruefully.

"Get down below and see how Michael's getting on. Tell him we need power soon, or we're —" He paused. "Just tell him."

"I will." Shaking his head like a boxer who'd received a shrewd blow, Kieran navigated the companionway aft.

James Mackey spat out the mangled remains of his roll-up. He longed to light another, but there was no letting go of the wheel now, not for a second. He swore under his breath, cursing his bitch of a ship, yet praising her, and cajoling her as though she were a woman he was trying to seduce.

Outside, the North Atlantic widow-maker raged on. He glanced to the side, at the bright, flickering screen of the weather map. There was a great, whirling white funnel west of Ireland; he was standing in the middle of it, like a bug caught in the gyrations of a washing machine.

"We're too far out," he whispered. The *Cormorant* wasn't made for these seas. She'd been built for the coastal fishing grounds to the west of Bantry Bay. James had deliberately set out to try the further grounds. The East Thulean Rise was an undersea shelf that rose up some four hundred miles west of Cork. The cod had been there, in the slightly shallower waters of the shelf where there was an abundance of food for them. The *Cormorant* had filled her hold in a matter of hours, and had been motoring back at full speed when the storm hit. The system had been too big to skirt around, so James had plunged his boat and her crew into the middle of it, trusting to his skill, to luck, and the well-made timbers of his father's vessel.

There was a thumping growl from below aft as the diesels began to churn for a minute, sounding like bad-tempered beasts. Then they stopped again, followed by a distant curse and the clang of metal thumping on metal. Michael was a wizard with anything mechanical, but he had his mother's temper.

Never again, James thought to himself as the cold sweat slimed his spine. *Never again. It's inshore work for me from now on. I'm too old for this.*

As the boat shuddered under his feet, bucking up and then crashing down again, James thought for an instant he had seen something in the arc of the bridge lights, something which wasn't water or the explosive spray of the great waves. It seemed to roll over in the sea to his front, a momentary glistening glimpse of some huge shape. He clenched shut his tired eyes for a few seconds, and the light spangled red behind his eyelids.

When he opened them again there was just the black and white fury of the sea, the bow of the trawler rising and falling before him, crashing through it, the water flooding aft as though seeking to bury her.

God, I'm tired, James thought. *Tiredness does things to you.*

He peered at the radar, but it was a fuzzy mess: fish, currents of warm and cold water, even containers washed off the decks of cargo ships.

The sea was full of life, the depths of it as populated as any city that man had made, and, at the same time, it was more of a wilderness than the most remote icecap. There were vast swathes of the seabed around the world that had never been sounded or mapped, where man had never gone and would never go. James remembered his own father telling him that, at home by the peat fire while a widow-maker like this one had lashed the thatch of the house around their heads.

"The sea will give up its riches freely," he had said. "But it always exacts payment for them in the end."

The engines farted, muttered, and then began a full-throated snarling. There was a *halloo* from down below, a shout of triumph. Even up here, James could hear Kieran's chortled laughter. He grinned and hit the throttles.

Under him, the *Cormorant* came to life again. She began to power forward into the waves, no longer a bathtub duck, but a thing with force and strength in her. The hull creaked and groaned as James tilted the spokes of the wheel to starboard, fighting to get back on course.

The waves seemed to resent this impertinence. They slammed into the trawler like angry monsters, and cannoned up the ship's side in white explosions of spray, drenching the foredeck and streaming along the wheelhouse windows. Grimly, James fought the wheel, feeling the rudder bite astern, feeling the thrum of the overworked engines as they cranked around the propeller shaft.

A clanking on the deck, and Michael was back at his side, pale face smeared with grease, hands black with it. He stank of diesel and old seawater and his hair was dripping into his eyes.

"The seams are opening. I've got the bilge pumps at full blast, but the water's pouring in. She won't take this course. The engine won't either. Da, we have to ride this one out."

"The hell we do," James grunted. "This thing could blow us all the way to France. If we don't fight it, we'll be a week at sea, and the fish'll be rotten."

"Better the fish than us."

"I know what I'm doing Mike. Leave me to it. You just keep that bloody engine running."

A huge impact slammed the ship aside. Down below they could hear the three other crewmen cursing and shouting. Michael and his father clung to the binnacle as the *Cormorant* seemed to stop in her tracks for a moment, before swinging round to port. She was near the crest of a wave, and for a few moments her rudder was out of the water and the wheel circled freely whilst the engines whined at the prop shaft.

Then she came down again, hammering into the trough of the wave like a toy boat dropped by a bored child. The bow went under, green water foaming up six-feet deep to the very wheelhouse windows. The ship groaned around them, her timbers screaming, bending, the sea pummelling them. The wheelhouse door burst open and in came the North Atlantic, foaming and hungry. In a second they were knee-deep.

"She's going!" Michael yelled, his face a mask of white terror.

"*No she won't,*" his father bellowed, and he stood at the wheel again. He yanked back on the throttle, gunning the engines to bursting point. "Close that bloody door!"

The trawler whirled round in the broken fury of the waves. Michael charged the door and managed to push it shut on the hungry water. He turned the bolt and hung on to it as the *Cormorant* bucked like an angry horse and his father stood fixed at the wheel, almost a part of the ship itself.

The bow rose slowly, slowly, tons of water streaming aft. They were going up the back of the next wave.

They were afloat.

They were alive.

"What the hell was that?" Michael rasped. "It felt like a collision." From below, the rest of the crew were shouting at one another. The intercom crackled. "Skipper, we've a hull-timber stove-in and half cracked. What in the world hit us?"

"The *sea* hit us," James Mackey said through grinding teeth. "The sea and all that's in it. Michael, rig the spare pumps, and see what can be done to plug her side. Quickly now."

"Maybe it was a submarine," Michael offered. "I've heard of things like that happening." He hauled himself to the radio, and clicked it on again. At once, the hiss of static filled the wheelhouse.

"You think there's a sub on the surface, on a night like this? I don't know what it was, a drifting container most likely. We were lucky." He glanced at his son. "For God's sake stop twiddling with that thing.

We must have damaged the aerial. I already tried, and got nothing out of it at all."

"The aerial's fine; I checked not ten minutes ago. Maybe it's the storm, the waves."

"You know better than that. We're on our own Michael, no one can hear us out here, and there's only ourselves to pull us through it. Get below now, and keep this bitch afloat for me."

"Da," Michael said. He looked very young now, washed out and frightened. "Da, do you think —"

"Get below son. We'll be all right. It'll be dawn soon. This thing'll blow itself out, you'll see."

Michael left the wheelhouse. His father stared out at the sea before him, that pathless wilderness. He flicked on every exterior light the boat possessed, but all they illuminated was a wrack of broken, foaming water, and the slate-grey backs of the immense waves as they coursed endlessly before the wind. There was nothing out there, nothing but the angry Atlantic.

And in the lurching wheelhouse of the boat, the useless crackle of the radio went on and on.

TWO

"Why don't you leave it alone?" Abby asked, her voice exasperated. She ran a hand through her spiky bob of platinum-blonde hair. She looked, Connor thought, like an angry dandelion. The thought made him grin. Lying on the steel-plated floor, he pushed further into the casing of the anomaly detector so she wouldn't see, and blinked as the forest of wires came scratching round his face.

"I can do it; just leave me to it. It won't be long."

"We're offline, Connor. Lester will go through the roof, to say nothing of Cutter." She folded her arms, tapping her foot impatiently, but he didn't reply. There was a grunt, then the sound of wires being snipped.

"Connor?"

"Hand me the soldering iron will you, Abby? I'm nearly done, promise."

Deep in the bowels of the machine he had created, Connor extended his hand out, opened wide in fingerless gloves. The soldering iron slapped into his palm.

"Ah, thanks Abs."

"You're welcome," a man's voice said in a low Scottish brogue.

Connor froze, blinked, then extricated himself from the wiring compartment, with his best sheepish grin on his face.

"Professor, I didn't know you were —" but the older man didn't give him a chance.

"Connor, what the *hell* are you doing?" Cutter snapped. He and Abby stood under the harsh lights of the Anomaly Research Centre, both in exactly the same pose; arms folded, heads down, eyes glaring at Connor as he lay there with fragments of circuit boards and snips of multi-coloured wire surrounding him, and a smell of burning as the forgotten soldering iron scorched a hole in his waistcoat.

Connor stood up hurriedly, yelped as the soldering iron stung his fingers, and slapped at the thin line of smoke proceeding from his clothes.

"I have a theory," he said quickly, glancing at the hole in his vest and brushing away smoldering fragments of cloth. "It's like this —"

"How long has it been offline?" Cutter asked Abby, pointedly ignoring Connor's protests.

"About an hour."

Cutter stared at her.

"An hour and a half," she admitted.

"This had best be a very quick theory, Connor," Cutter said.

"You see, I think I can improve the accuracy, periodically, temporarily," Connor said, tripping over the words. His hands were extended towards Cutter, like those of a supplicant. His absurd porkpie hat was planted firmly on his head, and below it his stringy black hair looked in need of a wash.

"Go on, quick now," Cutter pressed him.

"I've redirected a few of the console energy sources, the ones which are just jam really; they make the lights blink and whatnot. I can pulse the mainframe for short bursts and —" He hesitated. "Well, I won't really know if it'll make much difference until I try it. But in theory —"

"This is not a Meccano set, Connor," Cutter said. "This thing is important."

"But it'll work, I *know* it will. I'm nearly done here, Professor. A few more minutes and I can give the mainframe a pulse. Just one shot — that's all I ask."

"This pulse of augmented energy —"

"Well, it's not just juice. I've rewritten the basic code to compensate for it, electronically. Simple, really. You just —"

"You've rewritten the basic software of the detector?" Cutter's ginger eyebrows shot up his forehead.

"Well, just a little," he admitted awkwardly.

Cutter turned away, and stared back at the great plate-glass windows that surrounded the well in which the anomaly detector rested. The detector itself looked like the most desirable home-cinema system ever invented, married to a block of grey steel cupboards which concealed the thing's innards. No one in the surrounding offices was looking their way; no one had yet noticed that the usually blue flickering screens of the detector were now black.

Cutter turned back, his jaw set, the ever-present lines under his eyes accentuated by the harsh lighting.

"Connor, I don't suppose you've ever heard of the saying, 'If it ain't broke, don't fix it'?" Cutter asked.

"Aw Professor, how can we make progress if we don't tinker with things, see what they're capable of? Where would the fun be?"

Cutter looked back at the detector. It appeared as though a fair tranche of its guts had been yanked out, chopped up, and scattered over the floor in fragments of copper wiring, discarded transistors, and brightly coloured rubber insulation.

"God Almighty, Connor, if you've broken this thing, Lester will have you banged up for life."

Thus encouraged, Connor dropped to his knees, one hand scrabbling for the smoking soldering iron.

"Ten minutes, Professor — fifteen at most. And then I'll have her up and running again. Honest."

"Get on with it," Cutter said with an unwilling smile, and when Connor grinned up at him, he snapped, "Well, go on!"

Connor disappeared back into the belly of the machine. Abby shook her head.

"Can't we just put him in a room with some Lego?"

"He built it," Cutter replied, his voice low, careful not to let the younger man hear him. "He knows what it can do."

The wind had dropped a little, James thought, and there was a grey light in the sky that hadn't been there a half hour before. Dawn wasn't far off.

"Long night," his son said, braced against the wheelhouse door with water still swirling ankle-deep about him. He had donned his orange survival suit, as had all of the crew. Kieran liked to joke that it went with his hair, while the two Murnahan brothers were too small to properly fill theirs out.

"Long night," James agreed. His eyes were stinging with salt and tiredness. "Light me up one, will you Michael?"

His son extracted a bruised roll-up from the tin on the binnacle and lit it with a plastic lighter, puffing blue smoke and grimacing.

"These things'll kill you," he said to his father as he set it between the older man's lips.

"Not today they won't," James Mackey answered, sucking down the smoke gratefully.

Under them, the *Cormorant* was moving more like a rational thing now. The waves she rode upon were still monsters, but the wind no longer threatened to broach them every time they came up upon the crests. It was still pulling thirty knots, but that was nothing sensational for the North Atlantic at this time of year. The shriek of it, the roar of the sea, now competed with the snarling rattle of the engines and the dull thud of the bilge pumps working nonstop.

The ship was alive. She was fighting the water and the wind with a valour that warmed James Mackey's heart.

Kieran came up the companionway, splashing through the water.

"We're holding our own," he said. He no longer had to shout so loud to be heard. "The extra pumps did the trick, though Liam and Sean are about to have their arms drop off with the pumping."

"What do we have?" James asked him.

"There's a foot still in her down there, but we're keeping pace with it. What's our position, Skipper?"

James nodded to Michael. But he didn't take his eyes off the great swells breaking before him, the bow powering up them as though the ship were climbing the black, shining back of some vast beast. His son bent over the GPS screen, tapping it with an impatient forefinger.

"We're 240 miles out, south-southwest of Bantry." He checked the weather on the other screen; the meteorological station at Cork Coastguard updated it every few minutes. "Guns Island is twenty-five miles to the northwest of us."

"Thank God we missed that," James said, puffing. "I've heard tell of ships than ran full tilt upon it with a northeaster at their backs. It's so black you can't see it at night."

"I thought it had a beacon," Kieran said.

"It did, but it's been out of commission for months now. They're arguing over who owns it, us or the French, so no one's allowed to go out and fix it until it's settled in Brussels. So I hear anyway."

"I heard the Brits took it during the war, and made a secret base on it," Michael said.

"Don't believe all you hear. There's nothing on it now but about a million gannets, and it has thousand-foot cliffs all around. Whoever wants it can have it, as far as I'm concerned."

"Two forty miles," Kieran said. "What speed are we pulling, Skipper?"

"Twenty knots."

"Will we make it in before the catch spoils?"

"With a little luck, and if —"

Suddenly a massive concussion knocked them all off their feet. The ship shuddered, and groaned like a living thing, slewing round in the water. From below, the voices of the Murnahan brothers sounded out in fear and pain.

"What the *hell*?" Michael yelled, splashing around in the flooded wheelhouse on his hands and knees.

Another crash, this time deep in the hull. It was as though something was butting against the timbers of the ship, like a bull charging a gate. The *Cormorant* was shoved side-on through the water, and the angry waves she rode upon fountained up in explosive geysers of spray as the keel smashed through them.

The trawler canted to starboard, and in the wheelhouse James, Michael and Kieran tumbled over each other like sacks, cannoning into the bulkhead. James's head struck a stanchion hard, and it was opened up in a red flower of blood, a spray that painted his son's face scarlet in a second.

"Da!" Michael screamed.

Another crash, this time on the bows. The stern of the ship rose out of the water and foaming green seas swallowed up her bow. Above the chaotic bellow of the storm another sound arose — an animal roar.

The windows of the wheelhouse were smashed in and the sea rushed through, a white fury of surging water. In seconds the wheelhouse was waist-deep, then chest-deep. The water poured down the companionway and flooded the lower compartments, the engine room. It filled the ship, killing the diesels, drowning the batteries.

The lights went out. The *Cormorant*, groaning in protest, tilted further to starboard, like a tired animal laying down its head.

Michael Mackey reared his head up above the water.

"Da! Kieran!" A body in a survival suit was floating face down before him in the dim grey light of the shattered wheelhouse. He grabbed at it, but then something huge and dark came crashing clear through the bulkhead, smashing through the nine-inch timbers as though they were kindling; something like a black missile. With it came a noisome smell, like that of ancient, rotting seaweed, or fish left in the sun.

Michael saw teeth like spearheads, a glimpse of a red maw, and then it withdrew again. He stared, frozen in shock, and the water rose up to cover his head.

The *Cormorant* rolled over with a long, rending groan of laboured timber, capsizing as the hundreds of tons of water within her finally dragged her down. A great wave washed over her upturned hull, and the hole which had been smashed through it.

As the ship went down, Michael scrambled out of the broken wheelhouse, lungs bursting, mind white and empty with the shock of it all. The survival suit lifted him, and his life jacket inflated about his shoulders, drawing him upwards, away from the wrecked carcass of the doomed trawler. He gave a great whoop as he broke surface, sucking in air and spray, coughing as the salt water fouled his mouth.

He bobbed there in the grim grey light of the hour before dawn, the strobe on his life jacket blinking, the cold of the Atlantic penetrating even the rubber confines of his suit.

"Da!" he screamed to the racing sky. "Kieran!" But there was no answer.

And then something broke the surface beside him. So vast was it that for a second he thought the trawler was coming up again. A sleek black shape, forty, fifty — perhaps sixty feet long, black as a submarine. Michael stared wide-eyed and frozen at it in the spray-lashed morning. Even as he watched, it submerged again. He caught a glimpse of a blunt tail. There were no flukes on it — this was not a whale — and then it was gone.

He floated alone again in the middle of the desolate Atlantic, the cold water slowly taking him to his death, his mind as numb as his freezing limbs. *Why wouldn't the radio work?*

It was the last conscious thought of his life.

THREE

"Do I have to ask what's going on, or is someone going to be good enough to tell me?" James Lester demanded. He stood twiddling the signet ring on his little finger, his Dunhill suit hanging impeccably from his shoulders.

"I see the cleaners have been doing their usual bang-up job," he added, peering at the jumble of wire and plastic circuit boards that littered the floor.

"We've been adjusting the anomaly detector," Cutter told him. "Just some fine-tuning. Everything's fine."

"Fine," Connor repeated, grinning nervously.

Lester looked at the blue screens of the detector, pursing his lips.

"What a meaningless word that is. Everything's *fine* nowadays, when it's not *okay*. Yet it looks to me — a layman — like our little programmer here has been playing with a toy which doesn't belong to him..."

"I built this — I made — I mean, I wasn't doing anything wrong." Connor started out indignant, but at the look on Lester's face, he subsided to a mutter.

"So long as it's working," Lester said with a touch of weariness edging his voice. "Is this all you brought me down here for, to look at the litter on the floor?"

"We're about to try something," Cutter said. "We thought you should be here. Clau..." He paused for an instant. "Jenny and Stephen are on their way."

Lester caught the verbal slip, and stared at Cutter, his pale face intent for a moment.

"I trust you're feeling well, Cutter? No mindstorms, no little lapses of rationality?"

"I'm fine — perfectly in the pink," Cutter responded with a snarl in his voice.

"Glad to hear it." Turning away, Lester beckoned over a white-clad technician who had been hovering in the background, clipboard at the ready. "Make yourself useful, man. Bring me a coffee. Black, no sugar." And when he hesitated, Lester snapped, "Run along now. I pay your wages you know."

The man sped off.

"Well, I send in appropriations at any rate," Lester said with a shrug. Then he smiled a little. He had a gift for it, smiling without humour. He leaned forward and stared at the cluster of flat, flickering screens that were the displays of the anomaly detector. Upon them, maps of the United Kingdom wheeled back and forth, and tables of figures and graphs of undulating frequencies came and went. "It looks just the same as always to me."

"There's a new button on the console," Connor volunteered. "The red one, just there — but don't touch it!"

"I have no intention of doing so," Lester said, straightening. "Civil servants and red buttons do not go well together. I shall be perfectly happy to leave it to you." He looked at his watch. "But not for much longer. Cutter, I'm a busy man —"

The clack of heels on concrete made him turn his head. Jenny Lewis came walking down the reinforced ramp which led to the central well of the ARC. She was wearing a short skirt, an ivory-coloured blouse and a string of pearls. Her dark hair was tied up in a bun and she strode down the ramp as though it were a catwalk, head held high, eyes flashing. All three men standing around the detector paused to watch her, their gaze travelling from her legs to her face and back again.

Abby rolled her eyes.

"I was in a meeting," Jenny said. "What's so all-fired important?" Behind her Stephen Hart jogged down the ramp, t-shirt sticking to his lean torso, sweat shining his smooth, clean-shaven face. His eyes were bright beneath dark brows.

"And I was out for a run," he said. Behind him, at the top of the ramp, the technician reappeared.

"You carry your mobile when you're running?" Abby asked him.

He held it up, breathing heavily.

"Of course. You never know when some enthusiastic person is going to call you and tell you to drop everything," he said tartly. "So what's the rush? There's no alarm is there?"

"We're here to watch Connor press a red button," Lester said dryly. He accepted his coffee, waved the technician away without thanks, and grimaced as he tasted it. "All right Professor, we're all here, so dazzle us."

Cutter looked at Connor and raised an eyebrow.

"She's your baby," he said, not sounding entirely confident.

"Try not to electrocute yourself," Abby said.

"Very funny," Connor retorted. He licked his lips and set a finger on the red button. "Now what's going to happen here is that —"

"Just do it, Connor," Cutter snapped.

Connor pressed the button.

And around them, all hell broke loose.

The Sea King bulled its way through the storm like an angry dragon. Painted a bright red-pink, the helicopter belonged to the Irish Coast Guard, and was on the last leg of its search box, snarling its way across the North Atlantic at 200 feet, the pilot swearing as he fought to keep the aircraft straight and level.

"Eleven minutes to PONR," the copilot's voice crackled, and the pilot nodded, scalp sweating under the heavy helmet, his flying gloves soaking up more perspiration as they grasped the cyclic and collective. He turned his wrist a little, and the massive Rolls Royce Gnome turbines roared harder as the throttle was opened. The wind was trying to force the helicopter's nose up, and the pilot was continually inching the cyclic down to maintain forward flight.

"Windspeed fifty-six knots," the copilot said.

"I need a beer," Jeff, the pilot, told him, grinning weakly while his eyes were fixed out of the rain-lashed windows.

"We get home from this one, and I'm buying." This was the voice of the third member of the crew, the winchman. There was a pause as the three men concentrated on their jobs. Finally the copilot spoke.

"Skipper, we're six minutes to PONR," he said. "Suggest we make return heading of —"

"I see something!" It was the winchman. Despite the chaos outside, he was leaning out of the open side door of the aircraft, securely tethered in his harness, and he was wiping the rain and spray from his goggles. "Jeff, I see a body in the water, broad on our port side. I see a survival suit. Maybe 300 metres away."

"Coming round. Dave, best get in back."

"Roger that." The copilot unstrapped himself from his seat and made his way aft, staggering as the heavy aircraft was thrown around by the storm. "Will this bloody wind ever drop?" he muttered, his words coming through the headset.

"The low systems are coming in from the west, a whole rugby team of them. It'll be like this for days yet; weeks maybe," the pilot replied. The strain was audible in his voice.

"I'm at the winch," the copilot said. "Mike, you ready?"

The winchman slapped him on the shoulder. "Just tell me when to jump Dave, and hang around to pick me up." They both looked down at the raging surface below.

"Where'd he go?" the copilot shouted. "Christ, yes, I see him. Now Mike, go go *go*!"

The winchman jumped, feet first, arms folded around his torso. He arrowed into the sea and disappeared.

"Hold hover here," the copilot shouted into his comms. "We're in the water. I see him. We are making our — *damn* —" Suddenly the helicopter was shunted aside by a fist of wind that caught it broadside-on.

"Sorry about that Dave," the pilot said. "It's playing with us. Coming back on station."

"Port twenty metres" the copilot said. "He's waving. Dropping winch now." He hit the button and the heavy cable with its harness attached began to unwind towards the sea below.

"Starboard five metres. Hold it. Hold here — hold hover Jeff. He's attaching harness. He's having trouble. Christ, Mike, hurry up."

"Fuel is in red. Bingo fuel in eighteen minutes. We have to move on this one Dave," the pilot warned.

"There's a problem. He's attaching the harness. He's — damn it, he's lost it again. What the hell is his problem? He's faffing about like an old man. Wait, wait — I have thumbs-up. Raising winch now." The copilot thumbed the winch control and the cable began to wind in on its drum, raising the winchman and his catch to the helicopter's open door.

"My God, my God," the copilot said as the cable came up from the sea.

"Dave, what is it?"

"Maintain position. He's at the door now."

The pilot blinked the sweat from his eyes and tried not to look at the blinking red of the fuel warning light. He could still make it in; they would have this wind behind them on the way back. They would be all right.

"Talk to me!" he grated into his helmet. "Dave, are we secured?"

His copilot's voice sounded extremely odd as he replied. "All secure, Skipper. Take us home. Returning to cockpit."

The nose of the Sea King lifted and it barrelled away to the east with the wind behind it. The airspeed climbed and the turbines roared. They would make it. The Irish coast was less than a hundred miles away. They would make it.

"Bantry, this is alpha one zero," the pilot said, his voice clipped and professional now. "We are returning to base with one casualty recovered. Request medical assistance on landing. Wait out for word on casualty's condition, over."

A hissing, faraway voice came back to him.

"Alpha one zero, roger your last. Will stand by for further sitrep, out."

The copilot made his way into the cockpit and strapped himself in. Then he sat wordlessly for a moment, staring sightlessly out of the Perspex of the cockpit windows.

"He didn't make it, did he?" the pilot said heavily.

"No Jeff, he didn't." The copilot wiped his face with one gloved hand. "Jesus Christ, he was — he was cut in half, Skipper."

"What? God Almighty. Poor bloke. Must have been caught by the prop blades."

"I guess." The copilot hesitated, and then said quietly, "Between you and me Jeff, it looks more like he was bitten in two. By bloody great teeth."

The pilot was silent a moment before he responded.

"Well, I don't know about that, but it's for the medics to figure out. Or the coroner. Any ID?"

"He was from the *Cormorant* all right. The name on the suit was Mackey. He was young — must have been the son."

"Well, at least now his mother will have something to bury."

"Not much, Jeff. There's not much left of him to fill a coffin."

The Sea King roared off before the storm, its three crewmembers all silent now. The winchman sat on the pitching deck of the rear compartment and stared at the severed torso which lay before him. Then he leaned out of the open hatch and was sick into the wind.

FOUR

They turned off the blaring Klaxon, but the red warning lights set around the well of the ARC continued to flick on and off, bathing them all in bloody, garish light.

"Come on Connor," Cutter was saying, eyes wide with urgency. "Clamp it down — *find it.*"

"I'm trying, I'm trying," Connor replied. His fingers flew over the keyboard. He frantically scanned the blue screens before him, while Lester, Jenny, Abby and Stephen stood nearby, rapt and silent.

"It's not mainland UK, Professor. It's out to the west."

"It's in the sea," Stephen said. "In the Atlantic. This is a first."

"Yes, how marvellous," Lester drawled. "At least we don't have to worry about the general public chancing across it. Seagulls perhaps. The odd school of cod."

"I have it!" Then Connor was almost bouncing up and down in his chair. "Professor, I have it! It's southwest of Ireland, 200 miles or so out in the sea, it's — it's —" he stopped.

"What is it?" Lester demanded testily.

"It's more than one," Connor told him. "It's two, three, four — my God, Professor, there's at least half a dozen open anomalies out there."

"Let me see." Cutter leaned close, jaw set, pale-blue eyes wide and intent on the screen before him. After a minute he straightened. "Can you up the resolution on this thing?"

"I'll try. She's creaking a bit already. This is so awesome!"

Lester looked away, impatient and coldly angry.

"This is a nightmare," he said. "Then Peru wasn't a coincidence — it's really gone international. Inevitable I suppose. Jenny, you realise what this means?"

Jenny nodded, "Things get complicated."

"That's a restrained way of putting it."

Cutter looked up from the monitor.

"They're not in the sea, not all of them anyway."

"What do you mean?" Abby asked him. "That's just a big ocean out there, the whole Atlantic."

"He's right guys," Connor said. "With all the clutter on this screen, it's hard to make out, but I think there's an island of some sort out there, and the anomalies are clustered around it."

"Get out of the way." Lester pushed Connor aside and stared hard at the detector screen. After a moment he said, "We need maps and charts for the whole of the North Atlantic. Jenny, I want a line opened up to our friends in the Royal Navy." He straightened and sighed. "By the look of this, we'll be dealing with the Irish on this one."

There was a fizzing sound, a gentle pop, and the anomaly detector went dead for a second. Then the screens flickered into life again.

"Connor?" Cutter asked. The young man just shrugged.

"It was just a temporary pulse. I haven't yet been able to wire the thing up permanent, like. Shouldn't have done any damage. Might need to go offline again just to make sure, though."

"At times like this, the term *idiot savant* comes to mind," Lester said grimly. "Cutter, what are the implications of an undersea anomaly?"

Cutter blew out his cheeks.

"Huge," he said. "In a way, it's far worse than a land-based one. As long as the anomaly stays open, water will be travelling through it, and whatever is in that water will make its way into our oceans. Our only consolation is that the North Atlantic is very cold at this time of year — colder than the ocean of most ancient epochs. If warm-water creatures come through, they shouldn't last long, not long enough to cause any large-scale ecological damage anyway."

"Well, that's reassuring, for once. And if the land-based ones are all on this little island, then the problem is at least contained." Lester took out his mobile phone, stared at it, then raised his head and glared at the white-coated technician who was still hovering, fascinated, behind them, holding a pot of cooling coffee in his hand. "I believe I asked for some maps, some charts. Do you think you can handle that, or shall I just go and start rooting through cupboards myself?"

As the man hurried off he pursed his lips.

"International waters perhaps," he said in a low tone. He tapped his phone against his upper lip. "That could be interesting."

"I've got it," Connor said.

"Got what? Haven't you got enough for one day, Temple?"

Connor had opened up his personal laptop and propped it on the console of the anomaly detector. There was a map on the screen, and Cutter leaned over Connor's shoulder.

"It's called Guns Island," he said. "Scroll down a bit. Yes, fifteen hectares in size, surrounded by sea cliffs. An important nesting colony for gannets..."

"Gannets. Wonderful," Lester said. "Let's hope all we have to worry about is the RSPB getting their knickers in a twist over a few dead birds."

Now Jenny was leaning in close to the laptop, as well.

"Google Earth," she said. "Brilliant."

Cutter shot her a sidelong glance. Her face was quite close to his, and he could smell her perfume, the scent of her hair.

"We have a problem, James," she said, and straightened up again. Cutter found himself staring not at Jenny's exquisite ear but at Connor Temple's shiny face. Connor smiled nervously, his Adam's apple convulsing up and down his throat.

Cutter frowned.

"The island's sovereignty is disputed between Ireland and France," she continued. "Apparently there are large natural gas reserves in the seabed around it, so whoever claims the island gets the gas."

"In other words," Stephen said, striding forward, "our presence there would take a bit of explaining."

"It gets better," Connor said. "Look at this, guys."

"Wikipedia?" Abby said scornfully. "Do you know how much of what's on that thing is rubbish?"

"A lot of it's pretty accurate," Connor protested. "Including this, I think."

Cutter read out the scrolling text on the screen.

"During World War Two, Guns Island had a small observation post built on it to look out for German U-boats. In the early years of the Cold War, Britain expanded this post into a small base, and it was rumoured that biological weapons tests were performed on the site. When the Cold War ended, the issue of the island's sovereignty was handed over to international arbitration. Britain has given up all claims to Guns Island, and now the ownership of the place is being debated through the international courts, the two claimants being —"

"France and Ireland," Lester interrupted him. "So now we have our European partners involved. This just keeps getting better."

"The Foreign Office —" Jenny began.

"Don't worry about them. They'll be at their clubs, reading the paper and bemoaning the loss of the Empire," Lester said with a bleak smile. He tapped the screen of his mobile and set it to his ear. "Yes, Sir Charles Morley please," he said, looking off into the air. "James Lester speaking, Home Office. Yes, I'll hold."

He looked around at the rest of them.

"I suggest you wrap up warm," he said to Cutter. "The North Atlantic can be bitter at this time of year. Or so I'm told."

The Quartermaster's stores of the ARC were a white-painted concrete sepulchre with iron doors. The team filed inside and Cutter banged the heavy door shut behind them. Connor at once walked down the aisles of shelves and racks with a wide grin on his face, his hands running over the mass of neatly arranged equipment and weaponry. He looked like a toddler let loose in a toyshop.

"I love this place," he said. "It's like that scene in the Matrix, when Neo says, 'We'll need guns, lots of guns.'"

"James Bond, eat your heart out," Stephen said. "Even Q would have been impressed by this lot."

Connor lifted up a gleaming black rifle from its rack. "Can I have this?"

Stephen walked over to him, a smile on his face.

"That is an M4 carbine with folding stock and a SUSAT scope, 5.56mm calibre. It's nice and light, isn't it?"

"Yeah!" Connor said happily, hefting the black rifle in his hands.

"You can't have it," Stephen said. He took it out of Connor's grasp, replacing it in the rack.

"Aw, guys," Connor complained, "even Abby gets to have a gun."

"Even Abby?" Abby said. She blew a blonde hair from in front of her face. "That, Connor, is because *Abby* can use a firearm to hit what she aims at. She does not fire wildly, she does not treat these things as toys — and she tends not to shoot her friends!"

Connor bent his head.

"That was just the once," he muttered.

"Think small," Cutter said, walking up and down the shelves. "We're flying into a foreign country on this one, so we can't go wild."

"We're also going to a deserted island hundreds of miles from anywhere," Stephen told him. "We'll need to load up on survival gear, prepare for the worst."

"I'm *always* prepared for the worst," Cutter told him sharply. The two men looked directly at each other, and the air between them seemed almost to fizzle with tension. They were both thinking of Helen — Cutter was certain of it — though neither would say her name.

"Sleeping bags, karrimats, stoves, mess-tins, boil in the bag stuff. It'll be like going camping," Abby said brightly, interrupting the face-off and hauling a huge black rucksack out of a locker. She walked up and down the stores humming to herself and stuffing things into the sack like a shoplifter with nothing to fear.

"More like a safari," Connor said. He picked up a long-bladed hunting knife, looked at it with wide eyes. When he thought no one was looking, he tucked it into its sheath and down the back of his trousers.

"How will we get there?" Stephen asked. He, too, was pulling out a rucksack and a set of webbing from a locker. He was careful to avoid Cutter's eyes.

"That's Lester's problem," Cutter said. "He and Claudia should be seeing to all the diplomatic niceties."

The other three stopped and stared at him. He glared back.

"What?"

"Boss," Connor said diffidently, "it's just that —"

"I did it again, didn't I? Damn. All right, all right. Don't worry about it.

Slip of the tongue." Cutter ran his hands through his red-gold hair, spiking it up so that he looked like a deranged punk rocker. He began slamming equipment into his own Bergen with unnecessary force.

"It's all right, Professor," Abby said, and he glanced her way. She almost put a hand on his shoulder, then thought better of it.

"No it's not all right," Cutter snarled. "I had a life, before; we all did. A life that was different, before we mucked it up with all these anomalies, all this running from world to world. The only thing is, I *remember* the life before, what it was like, who was in it." He paused, looked at Abby. "I'm quite sane, you know." He smiled at her. She smiled back, uncertain, and now she did grasp his shoulder and gave it a squeeze.

"Do we go there to trap, or to kill?" Stephen asked. He was holding an L-96 sniper rifle with infrared scope and integral bipod, a heavy, serious-looking piece of kit.

Cutter looked at him. "There are at least five anomalies on that island. God only knows what has come through them, or what eras they lead back to. Guns Island is at this moment potentially the deadliest place on earth. We go there to protect our own lives, and to try to limit the inter-species swapping as much as possible. We go there to kill them, this time."

Stephen nodded.

"I never thought of it like that," Connor said, his expression aghast. "Five anomalies, all on one little island! It'll be like *Jurassic Park*."

"It could make *Jurassic Park* look like Disneyland," Abby told him. She lifted up an MP5, a small, light, elegant machine-pistol, and sighted down the barrel thoughtfully. "I think I'll take this. It's more ladylike."

"Ladylike!" Connor sputtered.

Cutter's phone went off. He stared at it, looking suddenly tired.

"We have an update. It seems the Atlantic may not have been as empty as we had thought. I have to go and see —"

He stopped. With their eyes on him, he stomped out of the stores, glowering.

Jenny Lewis's office in the ARC was a small cubicle with a window out onto the corridor. She had made it her own with a pair of potted ferns and a photograph of her fiancé, a muscular, handsome, smiling man.

Cutter disliked him on sight, but smiled at Jenny as she sat behind her desk, sipping coffee, and waved him in. He shook his head when she offered him the pot.

"So tell me the good news," he said. He felt large, awkward and clumsy in this neat and trim little office — it was entirely too constricted a space for him to be in with her. He could smell her perfume again. Maddeningly, it was the same one Claudia had used. Claudia Brown, who was no longer here — who had now never existed. And yet her twin sat sleek and lipsticked in front of him, with her eyes, her voice, even her smile.

It was enough to drive a man mad.

"Bad weather in the North Atlantic," Jenny said. "That's not exactly news, but this is a succession of storms which are rolling east, becoming more violent as they come. We may already have our first casualties." She handed Cutter a sheet of shiny fax paper.

Cutter scanned it, then raised his head.

"Not necessarily," he said. "Trawlers are lost at sea all the time. These poor guys were probably just swamped by a freak wave."

"They brought back a body this morning from the area where the boat went down," Jenny told him, looking suddenly grim. "Irish Coast Guard helicopter. It's not generally known yet, but the body had been badly mutilated."

Cutter stood and rubbed his chin with one hand.

"How big do trawlers get?" he asked absently, his mind turning over.

"They're not small. This was a coastal vessel, too far out for its own good. It had a crew of five though, so it was no cockleshell. Cutter, what could sink a boat like that — what kind of creature?"

Despite himself, Cutter felt a thrill of excitement as his mind ranged over the possibilities. It was like this every time — it was what kept him here. What would it be? What would they encounter? With Helen off on her insane sojourn through the anomalies, and with Claudia gone, lost to him, all he had for a life was this frisson, these walls and the promise of what was going to pop into their world next.

It was all he had left.

"Some kind of Mosasaur perhaps, or a Pliosaur, like a Liopleurodon. Even a large Ichthyosaur."

"Terrific," Jenny sighed.

"Until we get out there, speculation isn't worth much," Cutter said. He smiled at her. She looked strained, a tenseness lurking behind the carefully coiffured façade she presented to the world. "Lester getting to you?" he asked kindly.

"What? No, no." She seemed to pull herself out of some momentary reverie. She looked at the photograph on her desk, and a frown seemed to flit across her face for a second. Then she smiled brightly. "No — just the nature of the job in hand. This will be a complex one. Lester is calling in every favour he is owed, and pulling strings I never knew existed. We're trying to keep this thing under wraps from two governments this time, and that's not the same as fooling Joe Public."

Cutter nodded.

"We'll need backup on this one," he said. "Military."

Jenny leaned back in her chair. "It's not like you to go asking for an armed escort. Usually you like to steer clear of them."

"This is different. There are several anomalies on that island. The place could be swarming with God knows what kind of predators. And there's nowhere to run to, once we're there. This time around, I want firepower with me."

Jenny nodded. "I see your point. Very well, I'll call Hereford. We have a sabre team on standby twenty-four/seven."

"Try to pick some with brains, as well as muscle," Cutter said.

Jenny glared at him. "You don't much like the army, do you Cutter?"

"It has its uses. It's not soldiers I dislike; it's those who give them the orders. I lead this expedition. I want that made clear — to Lester, to the men you're giving me. There will be no agendas except my own. Do you understand me?"

"Perfectly," Jenny said, raising an eyebrow.

"You and Lester can take care of the diplomatic shitstorm, if it happens. For me, all I want is to get my people out there, and then bring them all back alive."

FIVE

Regent's Park in winter was as bleak and grey as some moor, and beyond the fringe of trees the roar of the city rose up interminably, a wall of endless noise. Lester loved London. He would never tire of it, but at this time of year it did not present much of a friendly face to the world. It was a bellowing metropolis without pity, a great animal that created and consumed men.

He strode up and down alongside the rain-slick park bench. There was no way he was going to sit upon its scarred, slimy slats in his bespoke Ozwald Boateng coat. Irritably, he looked at his watch again. This cloak and dagger stuff was all very well, but they might just as well have met in a decent hotel.

Stopping for a moment, he looked up at the blank sky. At least the rain had stopped.

There were few people in the park on this winter's afternoon. Dog-walkers, tramps, a woman pushing one child in a wheeled contrivance and hauling another by its raw little hand, swearing all the while. Then a man appeared in a dark overcoat, striding in his direction, tapping the ground with an umbrella as he came.

He was an older man, his collar turned up against the wind and his florid face reddened further by the cold. Lester held out a hand and he shook it. His fingers felt like ice in Lester's grasp.

"Thomas — so sorry to get you out here like this, on such a bloody day."

The older man shrugged a little, turned and surveyed what he could of London, and the dreary expanse of the winter-emptied park.

"My own apologies are in order for the *sotto voce* meeting," he replied, his voice deep. "I just thought —"

"You were quite right," Lester said smoothly. "And I am exceedingly grateful. Thomas, I have to call in a favour."

The older man sat down on the bench, careless of his similarly immaculate overcoat. After a pause, Lester joined him, grimacing a little.

"I owe you one, then?" Thomas asked, smiling a little. Like Lester, he had a gift for smiling without humour. His eyes were set hard as glass in the heavy-set crannies of his face.

"You know you do. I won't mention why."

"I was just being flippant, James. I have no arguments. So what is it you need?"

Lester drew a deep breath. "A diplomatic bag — a very large one."

"Indeed? And where is it to be sent?"

"The Republic of Ireland."

Lester's companion frowned. "It's been a while since we tried anything there. Last time I heard, James, the war was over and we were all friends together, citizens of the EU sitting round the campfire and singing 'Michael Rowed the Boat Ashore'."

"There's been a development. It must be dealt with outside of normal channels," Lester told him.

"How major a development?"

"Of international consequence, possibly — if it blows up."

"And that's all you're going to tell me."

"And that's all I'm going to tell you. Believe me, Thomas, I would say more if I could, but my hands are tied." *And I wouldn't trust you with so much as a racing tip*, Lester thought, but he kept his face neutral and solemn.

The older man sat in thought for a while, punctuating the silence with the tap of his umbrella point on the ground.

"We know that the term 'Diplomatic Bag' is an elastic one, James, but there are limits. How big are we talking?"

Lester cleared his throat.

"Something in the order of several hundredweight, and the size of a large tea chest." He had no idea, really, but it sounded about right. How much could a small but lethal arsenal of modern small arms weigh?

His companion nodded slightly.

"Just like the old days," he said with a grunt.

"Believe me, Thomas, it's nothing like the old days. Your mind can be put at rest on that score."

Thomas stood up then, leaning so heavily on his umbrella that it creaked.

"The rain's coming on," he said. He opened the umbrella and raised it over his head. "Very well, James, you shall have your bag. I'm a man of my word, always have been. This sets us even, I believe. Do you concur?"

Lester stood up and proffered his hand once more.

"I do. Thank you, Thomas." The other man shook his hand firmly. His bloodshot eyes were cold as the afternoon that surrounded them.

"And if it all goes tits-up, I shall denounce you as volubly as I am able," he said in a matter-of-fact way. "You know that, don"t you?"

"I do," Lester said, and he smiled, a genuine smile this time, tinged with respect.

Without another word Thomas turned on his heel and strode off, the wind batting at the umbrella above his head. Lester watched him grow smaller across the park. Then he remembered, felt the back of his overcoat, and gritted his teeth as the green-slimed residue of the park bench smeared his hand.

Captain John Willoby looked around in wonder as he entered the central well of the ARC. He was dressed in jeans and a pale blue shirt, and carried a green army holdall. Behind him, four more men and one woman trooped in single file, similarly burdened. They all had the angular features and ruddy skin of athletes, and there was a certain poise about them which Cutter, looking on, found himself envying. For a forty-something academic, he was in pretty good shape — not as good as Stephen, but pretty good. Compared to these newcomers though, he felt about as fit as a sack of lard.

Willoby strode right up to him and stuck out his hand.

"Professor Cutter, I presume?"

The man's hand felt as though it was made of muscle and steel wire. Willoby met Cutter's eyes. He was of average height, sandy-haired and square-jawed, with a crescent-shaped scar running from the corner of his left eye. *Action Man in person*, Cutter thought wearily. He had read the file. Originally a Greenjacket, Willoby had made Selection three years before, and had two more to go with a Sabre Squadron before he would return to his parent unit. He volunteered a lot — he volunteered for bloody everything: Iraq, Afghanistan and some murky visits to Central and South America.

But did he have a brain in that heroic head of his? It remained to be seen. Lester's cronies in the MOD and the Home Office had cleared Willoby and his team for this operation. Cutter would need to rub along with them all as best he could, because he very much doubted if he would be able to replace any of them.

"Let me introduce my team," Willoby said, stepping aside as the remainder of the soldiers lined up behind him.

"Corporal Peter Farnsworth, demo expert." A small, well-made up, shaven-headed man with a humourless face, Farnsworth nodded curtly as he was introduced.

"Demo?" Cutter asked.

"Demolitions. Explosives," Willoby explained.

"Ah."

"Private David Doody, team medic," the Captain continued. Doody was a young black man with a badly broken nose and a broad smile. Cutter liked him instinctively.

"Sergeant Calum Fox, our mountaineering expert. Another Scot, you'll be glad to hear."

A tall, rangy, dark-haired fellow with grey eyes.

"Whereabouts?" Cutter asked him.

"Skye, sir."

"You'll know the Cuillins, then."

"I was brought up at their feet, sir." He was about to continue when Willoby interrupted.

"Private Joe Bristow, our heavy weapons expert," he went on. Bristow was a small, squat man who looked as though he was a professional weightlifter.

His scalp gleamed in the overhead lights and he had the guarded, arrogant air of a man who is supremely confident in his own physical abilities. His gaze slid over Cutter as though dismissing him, and Cutter felt a flare of wordless anger rise up in him, but quickly smothered it.

"Lastly, our communications expert, seconded to us from the Royal Signals. Lance Corporal Anita Watts."

Watts was a slim, dark-haired young woman, extremely pretty, pale-skinned and rather waifish-looking standing next to the hulking Bristow.

"How'd you get mixed up with this lot?" Cutter asked her, smiling.

"I earned it," she said coldly. Out of the corner of his eye, Cutter saw Bristow smirk. He turned away. "Very good, Captain. Now I suppose I'll introduce my own team."

Sitting in plastic chairs around the anomaly detector, Connor, Abby and Stephen lounged amid a welter of tumbled rucksacks. Stephen had on a rumpled t-shirt, his dark hair spiking up as though it had not been brushed in days. He was yawning. Abby was looking on with folded arms, her taut, pierced midriff showing above a pair of frayed jeans that were cut at the knee. Connor was grinning, his ridiculous little porkpie hat perched on his head, a singed hole in his waistcoat and threads hanging from the chopped ends of his fingerless gloves.

Cutter sighed heavily.

"Perhaps introductions can wait until later. We have a plane to catch."

"We can get them as far as Cork."

Lester was perched on the edge of Jenny's desk with his legs crossed and his hands clasped about his knee.

"All their equipment and the diplomatic bag are already in the air aboard a freight carrier bound for Shannon. I want you to fly out today and get there to organise its transport onwards to Cork itself. Once the team and their gear are reunited, it's up to you and Cutter to make your way out to the island without causing a diplomatic incident. Is that perfectly clear, Jenny?"

"Absolutely," she said, her mind turning over the problems and the possibilities. She loved things like this; logistical details to be unsnarled, people to direct, timetables to be kept. During her early days in public relations she had organised parties for lazy, famous, rich people. In a sense, she was still doing it. Making sure the band turned up on time, as it were.

Lester looked at his watch. He seemed tired, less urbane than usual, with less sarcasm and more genuine irritability.

"The odds are, by the time you finally get out to this blasted little island, the anomalies will all have disappeared anyway."

"Yes, we can be thankful for that. But any creatures that came through will still be running around."

"Not for long; not with Willoby and his team on board," Lester said with a small, satisfied smile.

"What about the bodies?"

Lester started. "What? Oh, the creatures. They'll be tossed into the sea. Yes, we can thank God this has happened where it did. Can you imagine half a dozen anomalies opening almost simultaneously in central London? Or even in the provinces. It's a scenario from a bad B-movie."

"They always are," Jenny replied, arching an eyebrow. Lester sighed and stood up.

"In any case, if we can keep this quick, quiet and efficient, then there's no reason for either the Irish or the French to ever suspect a thing. That's our goal, Jenny."

"I know, James."

"That's your job, in other words. We've had a few circuses in the past; this must be different. Don't let Cutter grandstand. If it comes to the crunch, make sure Captain Willoby knows he has my authority to take over command of the expedition. Is that clear?"

Jenny shifted a little uncomfortably in her chair.

"Cutter's a responsible man. I'm sure it won't be necessary."

Lester snorted.

"Cutter is an unstable, idealistic train wreck," he said, without a hint of humour. "Your job is to keep him on the rails, or make sure someone else can. Understood?"

"Understood."

"Good. Have a pleasant flight. If things go to plan, all this talk will soon be academic."

She watched his retreating back in the immaculately cut suit. He shot his cuffs and strode out of her office as though he were monarch of all he surveyed. In some ways, he was. Jenny didn't know whether to loathe him or admire him.

SIX

The minibus inched its way through the rain-congealed traffic on its way to the harbour. Inside the ten members of the team — Connor had dubbed them the Dirty Ten — sat scrunched up together with their luggage at their feet and resting on their laps, looking out at the ancient city of Cork as it ambled drearily past them in the downpour.

"Looks just like England," Connor said, disappointed.

"What did you expect, Leprechauns and rainbows?" Abby asked him.

"I wonder if we can slip in a pint of Guinness. I hear it's phenomenal here," Connor continued, ignoring her.

"No!" both Abby and Stephen said in unison.

The driver called back at them. "You're quite a crowd. Here for a break are you?"

The soldiers all stiffened, and their faces closed. Cutter was half-dozing, not listening. Connor spoke up.

"It's a stag weekend," he said, just before Abby's elbow caught his ribcage.

"A stag weekend? And you brought the girls along with you?"

There was a momentary silence, until Connor spoke up again.

"They're the strippers," he said, and swallowed convulsively. They could all see the driver's wide eyes in the rearview mirror. There was a chorus of smothered laughter from the male soldiers, and even Willoby had to turn his face to the window to hide his smile.

"Well, I never," the driver said. "I tell you what, how about —"

"Don't even think about it," Abby snapped.

The minibus deposited them by the quayside. Above them, white-winged gulls were calling raucously, stark against a shifting slate-grey sky, and the late-morning rain poured relentlessly down. A line of pubs, hotels and B&Bs ran up from the waterside, and all along the stone-built docks there stretched a line of Atlantic trawlers, some shining with well-kept paint, others streaked with rust. A few men were pottering about the decks of the boats, but otherwise the quayside was relatively deserted.

"So this is Cork Harbour," Connor said.

"Technically, it's Crosshaven," Willoby told him. "This is where the fishing boats and ferries come in. Cork has half a dozen good harbours, but a lot of them are for container ships and tankers. We're south of Cork City now, south of Cobh, where the Port Operations Offices are — and the headquarters of the Irish Navy, I might add. We're out from under the heels of officialdom. Now we just want a boat and a skipper who doesn't ask too many questions."

"And one who'll take his boat out in a storm," Cutter added, looking doubtfully up at the sky.

"It doesn't look so bad," Abby offered.

"We're sheltered here, in the estuary of the River Lee," Willoby informed her gravely. "It's miles out past the promontory to the south before we hit the open ocean. It's blowing a gale out there, and has been for days."

"Fishermen can handle the odd gale," Cutter said. He looked around him. The ten of them were standing in a pile of their baggage, black rucksacks and holdalls that were not military, but didn't look civilian either.

"Short-haired chaps with English accents don't go down well here," Willoby said, as if reading his thoughts. "When is Miss Lewis due to arrive with the balance of the gear?"

"Late this afternoon," Cutter told him. "Too late to get our feet wet. We'll have to stay the night here and leave in the morning."

"Very well. But let's get this stuff out of sight. We're attracting attention already."

To Connor's delight, they repaired to a nearby pub, piling their gear up in a corner with Private Bristow sat balefully beside it while the rest of them leaned up against the bar. As a long line of Guinness pint glasses were filled slowly and surely by the barmaid, Cutter's mobile rang. "You can't stand in a bar and not drink something," Connor had said, quite reasonably, and so they were rationed to a pint apiece.

Cutter stepped to the side, murmuring into the phone, then slapped it closed and returned to the bar.

"Jenny's on her way with a privately hired truck containing the rest of the gear. No questions asked at Shannon. They waved through the crates."

"Lester was true to his word," Willoby said. He sipped his Guinness and closed his eyes for a second. "My word, that's good." He looked at Cutter. "You're not drinking?"

Cutter raised a small glass filled with honey-coloured liquid. "I prefer a different brand of poison. It's not Scotch, but it's not bad."

The two men looked at each other. Willoby lowered his voice. "Do you have any idea what we're in for out there?"

Cutter shrugged.

"We never do. That's part of the fun. I take it Lester has informed you as to the... unique nature of our job."

"Yes. Though I confess that I'll have to see it to believe it. It all sounds like Roswell to me."

"You'll believe it," Cutter said heavily, and gulped whisky from his glass. He looked into the bottom of it. "This won't be like big-game hunting, Willoby. There are things that..." he lowered his voice, "things that come through the anomalies which are entirely more deadly than anything you could hope to encounter in our world today."

"We'll handle them," Willoby said.

"You're not the first man I've heard say that," Cutter responded moodily. "And I'm willing to bet you won't be the last." He drained the last drop of whisky from his glass.

Cronin's Bar rented rooms upstairs, and since it was the middle of winter, they were all vacant. The team rented five doubles and lugged their bags upstairs, then sat in their rooms to avoid the inevitable curiosity of the locals as the day drew on. Cutter and Willoby went out for a while, asking around for a boat they might hire, but they soon returned.

It was dark early, and when the truck pulled up on the quayside Cutter and Willoby met it with the hoods of their parkas pulled up against the unending downpour. Willoby and the truck driver shook hands; they knew each other from Hereford. Jenny clambered out of the cab looking drawn and tired. She nodded to Cutter.

"Nice trip?" Cutter asked her. He'd had more than one whisky, and the bright fire of the alcohol had banished the cold from his system. *God*, he thought, looking at her, *she's beautiful*.

"Interesting," she told him, keeping her voice low. "Strange to think that with the connivance of the British establishment, I've now become an international gunrunner."

"What about getting them back afterwards?" Cutter queried, smiling.

"We don't. When the thing is done, they all get tossed in the sea. Simpler that way."

"We seem to have a generous budget," Cutter said.

"You don't know the half of it. Have you hired a boat yet?"

"We've been making enquiries."

"Before or after the pub?" she asked, frowning.

"This is Ireland. Half the time the enquiries can only be made *in* the pub."

"We have to talk, Cutter."

Jenny took his arm and led him away from the truck. Willoby and his driver friend had climbed into the back and were examining the crates stacked within. The rain shone in Jenny's hair. Cutter felt like kissing her, and realised that he had drunk more than he had intended.

He did not greatly care.

"I've had word from Lester at the ARC," Jenny said.

"Let me guess; the anomalies have gone."

"Yes and no. They've disappeared within the usual timeframe, but then others have taken their place. They're flicking on and off like cheap Christmas tree lights, but the hub is always on the island. At least four seem to be coming and going upon it, and two or three more in the sea within fifty nautical miles. Something odd is going on out there."

"Odder than the opening of holes within the space-time continuum?" Cutter asked, then realised it sounded more flippant than he had meant.

"Odd as in we haven't seen the like before. Lester wants your team on the island as soon as is practicable. He wants you to use a helicopter, if possible."

Cutter shook his head. "We looked into that; they've all been grounded by the storm. Even the Coast Guard isn't flying the North Atlantic right now. It'll have to be a boat."

"Then it has to be tonight. We've no time to lose."

"You won't get a reputable captain at such short notice. Willoby and I were talking to a chap who thought he could get us out there in a day or two."

"Then we go with disreputable. Speed is of the essence."

Surprised by the intensity of her words, Cutter's head cleared.

"There's something else. Something you're not telling me."

Jenny looked away. "It's not important."

"I don't believe you."

She went to protest but he interrupted.

"Jenny, please will you tell me what's going on? Because in a day or two, maybe less, I'm going to be sitting on that island with my life in my hands, and the lives of others depending on what I know and how I respond to it. So please, tell me."

It was Jenny's turn to be surprised, and she relented.

"All right, it seems as if our little diplomatic bag raised a few eyebrows in Dublin. It was tracked to Shannon, and may well have been followed here. Lester tells me that the Irish Special Branch are on their way to interview you and your team. We can't let that happen."

Cutter blew air out through his cheeks.

"They think the old enemy is up to something, eh?"

"Something like that. Your cover hasn't yet been blown, but the operation is in danger of becoming compromised. You need to be at sea tonight."

"Charming. Just charming." Cutter rubbed his eyes. "All right then, we'll do it your way. Any boat we can get, so long as it floats — and may God help us."

***

Any boat, so long as it floats, Cutter thought. *Luke Skywalker's first impression of the* Millennium Falcon; *that about sums it up*. And then he caught himself.

I've been spending way too much time with Connor.

The *Polar Star* was an aged, steel-hulled stern trawler. At one time she had been painted red along her waterline and white on her superstructure, but the rust had so streaked her steel that there was no real colour scheme left worth speaking of. She was some sixty-feet long, and was tied up to the bollards of Crosshaven's quay with a row of old car tyres slung along her side as protection from impact with the concrete. Despite this, she resembled a prize fighter who has just lost a bout, being dotted with dents and scores right down to the bare metal.

Liam Hanlon, her owner, master and skipper, stood to one side of her wheelhouse and waved an oily woollen cap at the team as they unloaded their truck onto the quay next to his boat. It was after midnight, a filthy winter's night with the wind roaring above their heads and the harbour utterly deserted. Every sensible man and his dog were in their beds or at the pub, and so far as it was possible to surmise, Cutter thought they were relatively unobserved.

The soldiers unloaded a series of stoutly built crates whilst Willoby looked on. The Special Forces officer seemed to have grown taller with the approach of something approximating action, and he murmured "Ammo, longarms, sidearms, radios, batteries," as the crates were bumped onto the quayside one by one in front of him.

Hanlon was gesticulating and bellowing at the soldiers, telling them to mind the paintwork or he'd be claiming for it. "You think this character can keep a secret like this for more than fifteen minutes?" Cutter asked Jenny as they stood watching.

"I've scared him a little," Jenny said with a wicked smile. "He thinks that if he opens his mouth for so much as a peep, he'll have masked men on his doorstep soon after. It helps that in this country not so long ago that was actually what happened some of the time. Plus, we're paying him a rather exorbitant fee."

"John Bull still has a bit of life in him, then?" Cutter said.

"And a fat chequebook," Jenny told him. She looked at her watch.

"We need to hurry this up a little."

"Where'd you find him?" Cutter asked, still staring fascinated at Hanlon. The fisherman was dressed in a greasy, darkened woollen sweater and waterproof dungarees. He had a thick grey beard and black eyebrows which met above his nose. He looked like Captain Birdseye's evil twin.

"In a pub, where else?" Jenny said with a grin.

Finally the last of the equipment was on board. Stephen, Connor and Abby leapt over the side of the quay onto the pitching deck of the trawler. Connor slipped on the slimy deck and went head first into the tangle of a seine net which was roughly rolled up in the scuppers. He straightened at once with a look of startled disgust on his face. Hanlon laughed and helped him to his feet.

"Don't worry son. We'll all smell like that in a few hours."

Only Cutter and Jenny were waiting on the quay. Hanlon disappeared into the wheelhouse and a moment later the big diesels of the boat began to cough, grunt, then snarl angrily into life. The reek of exhaust and diesel rose up along with the stench of rotting fish. From inside the wheelhouse, Hanlon shouted.

"Get on board, will ye, if you're coming. And cast off fore and aft, some one of yous!"

"The magical mystery tour begins," Cutter said, and went to jump from the quay. Jenny's hand on his arm stayed him a moment. She leaned close, so as to be heard above the roar of the engines. Her breath tickled his ear.

"Be careful, Professor."

"I feel a hundred years old when people call me that."

"Be careful, Nick," she said, and squeezed his arm.

He jumped onto the deck of the trawler. Stephen caught him as he slipped, and steadied him. Cutter thanked him and exchanged a rueful grin with Connor. Two of the soldiers cast off the thick mooring ropes from bollards fore and aft, and the *Polar Star* began moving away from the quay.

Her hull became a live thing under their feet, a creature with movement, force and will. In a matter of moments they were sixty yards from the quay, and Jenny was a mere shape in the darkness.

Behind her the lights of Crosshaven receded as the trawler picked a way out into the estuary, beyond the sheltering mole of the harbour, towards the open sea.

SEVEN

"I'm dying," Connor gasped. "I can't take any more. Shoot me with something Abby, please. Oh, God —"

He bent over the bucket again.

In the tiny cubbyhole which was the *Polar Star's* midships cabin, most of the team were sprawled across their mounded equipment with their hands and feet braced against the metal bulkheads. The boat was rising up and down under them, rolling from side to side for good measure, and the bare bulbs in the deckhead above them flickered weakly as the diesels struggled with the sea outside.

"How long did he say it would take?" Private Doody asked. The medic's dark face held a tinge of green.

"Fifteen hours," replied Watts, the signaller. She was trying to read a paperback, but had to keep one hand free to brace herself when the boat made a particularly vicious roll. She had tied her black hair up in a tight bun and wore a woollen cap over it. Her military issue combat boots made her feet seem outlandishly large.

They were all in black now, dressed for the occasion. Getting changed had been a minor ordeal in itself, and all of them were fielding bruises from the unforgiving steel of the *Polar Star's* innards. The soldiers had donned their webbing; that complex series of straps and pouches that held their basic equipment close to their bodies. The weapons had been broken out also, but even the sight of Bristow's US-made Minimi light machine gun couldn't raise Connor out of his torpor. Abby held back his hair as he retched into his bucket again.

"I didn't volunteer for this," he groaned. "I'd rather be eaten by something prehistoric than spend another fifteen hours of —" His intestines took over the conversation once more. Abby turned her head away.

"I've got some more Dramamine," Doody offered.

"He threw up the first lot as fast as he got it down," Abby said. "Best to let him suffer."

"Oh, that's nice; let him suffer," Connor complained, coming up for air.

"Just think how nice the island will seem after this," Abby said. "It'll be a doddle."

In the wheelhouse, Cutter, Stephen and Willoby stood at the stern bulkhead as Liam Hanlon wrestled with the ship's wheel, humming to himself and periodically breaking out into unmelodic snatches of song. He talked to his boat as he steered her, cajoling the *Star* up the back of each wave, and praising her as the seas ran aft and the bluff bow of the trawler came out of each white foaming trough of broken water.

The ship's forward lights pierced the gloom fitfully, and the radar flickered like a blue TV showing nothing but static, but somehow Hanlon knew where they were. He steered by the compass set in the binnacle before him, glancing occasionally at the dog-eared chart he had unrolled and pinned to the wood of the console. It was fly-blown and wrinkled, but he seemed perfectly happy to rely on the creased and mug-ringed square of paper.

Willoby was less sanguine. He was standing behind the Captain with a hand-held GPS, studying the changing co-ordinates on its LCD screen and sometimes shaking his head in something approaching bafflement.

"I don't know how he does it," he said to Cutter.

"I'm bred to the sea, is how I do it," Hanlon shouted back at them. "Yous can keep your newfangled electronics. A good fisherman can smell what's ahead of him, and feel out the sea like it was the road outside his house." He grunted as the boat was tossed by a particularly brutal wave. The wheelhouse door shuddered as a great mass of water broke hammering against it and then flooded aft along the deck outside.

Cutter wiped cold sweat from his face. Even Stephen looked pale as chalk. But Hanlon remained unfazed.

"'Course, some nights it's easier than others. But I done this trip a thousand times, out for the shrimping grounds west of Bantry. I'm a midwater man — none of that deep ocean scraping for me. Shrimp and mackerel is what I hunt, except there's not so much shrimp left in this part of the world now. Bloody French and Spanish have gone and hoovered it all up with their bloody factory ships."

He wrestled with the wheel for a while, humming to himself and muttering the occasional profanity as his boat slugged it out with the waves.

"That's an eighteen-foot swell, by God. There's not many would be chancing their arm in a sea like this, at this time of year. You're a funny bunch of people." Almost to himself, he added, "Them girls is far too pretty to be soldiers."

Cutter lurched forward to the binnacle and peered out at the arc-lit fury of the waves ahead. He raised his voice so Willoby would hear him. "You think our inflatables will make it in water like this?"

"We'll land in the lee of the island," Willoby told him. "It'll be sheltered there; we'll be out of the wind."

"I hope you folk have brought long ladders," Hanlon said dubiously. "There's thousand-foot cliffs all round Guns Island. A goat couldn't so much as scratch a way up."

"The cliffs are lower on the southeastern side," Stephen told him. "There's a path there up to the plateau above."

"A path?" Hanlon laughed. "I never heard it called that before. The monks made it, a thousand years ago. They had stone cells on the island, sat there praying and hacked out that path from the living rock itself, God love 'em. But a thousand years of wind and sea has been at work on it since. It may look like a nice dotted line on an OS map, but boyo, I'm telling you, I hope you packed a pair of wings."

"We packed rope," Willoby said. "It'll have to do."

A shattering boom sounded as the trawler smashed its bow into a great black and white wave, a foaming monster that roared right up to the wheelhouse windows and their ineffectually whirring circle-wiper. Cutter felt his stomach lift and bounce within his torso, and for the tenth time that night, regretted the whisky he had drunk onshore.

Or else regretted that he had not drunk more; he wasn't sure.

"You were briefed on the Coast Guard report?" he said to Willoby.

"About the *Cormorant*? Yes, of course."

"I knew Jim Mackey well," Hanlon called back at them. He had the hearing of a bat, even amid the bellowed rush of the storm and the struggling diesels. "The *Cormorant* was an old boat, wooden built. He'd been having a hard time making ends meet, had Jim. He should never have taken that old boat out so far, God rest his soul, and the four boys who went with him. They were talking in Cronin's, wondering if you were some kind of salvage team heading out there, but I told them, what can you salvage without a ship to sit in?"

"Very clever of you," Willoby said, raising his eyebrows at Cutter.

"And what do you think we're up to, Captain?" Stephen asked Hanlon.

"Me? Yonder pretty lady said that if I so much as wondered about that she'd have me taken care of the old-fashioned way. You want to watch that girl, lads. She's got ice water in her veins."

"You're right there," Cutter muttered.

"'Course, you're no faint flowers yourselves. I never seen so many guns since the old days, when they brought them in from Libya by the shipload. Still, your business is your own. There's nothing but birds on Guns Island, and you can shoot as many of them as you want, for all I care. I just know to keep my mouth shut."

Once again, Cutter and Willoby exchanged a glance. "Fifteen hours to landfall?" Cutter said.

"It's going to be a long night," Willoby admitted.

The hours drew by. Down in the cramped midships cabin, most of the team slept by fits and starts, jerking awake only when some almighty crash of water sounded against the hull.

Slack jawed and green-faced, Connor was snoring gently with his noisome bucket propped between his knees. Abby was squashed next to him, her head nodding. The rest of the soldiers were dozing, their heads lolling in time with the pitch and roll of the trawler. Only Joe Bristow was wide awake. He was humming quietly to himself as he brushed the working parts of the Minimi with an old shaving brush, and sprayed them with a small tin of WD-40. He looked supremely content.

***

It wasn't Cutter's imagination; the wind was dropping, though the waves were still steep as cliffs in the trawler's arc-lights. There was less broken foam about them now though; these were slab-sided, smooth-rolling hills, and the trawler was riding up and down them as deftly as a toy duck in a bathtub.

Hanlon cocked a lever, and a steady thudding noise started up to underline the throb of the engines.

"Pumps," he said to the three others in the wheelhouse. "We'll have taken on a lot of water. Now the worst of it is past, they'll not strain the engines so much. I put new pumps in just last May. If the boat sank, they'd still be pumping all the way to the bottom."

"Well, that's nice to know," Stephen said.

"It's getting light," Cutter said, rasping a hand over his stubbled chin and yawning. "What time is it?"

"Just gone seven," Willoby said. "Skipper, can't you make this thing go any faster?"

Hanlon laughed.

"What do you think, son? I'm just happy we're still this side of the sea. She's pounding along nicely; don't you be fretting now."

Willoby studied his watch, frowning.

"What's the problem?" Stephen asked him.

"At this rate, it'll be dark again by the time we're getting ashore on the island. It'll make things a lot more awkward."

"Then we'll anchor and wait for daylight," Stephen said with a shrug. He was the same height as the army officer, and of a similar build. Cutter, looking at them both, wondered when the inevitable pissing contest would begin.

"We don't have the time for that," Willoby said. "My orders —"

"Your orders?" Stephen said, cutting him off. "The man who gives those is standing behind you."

"Willoby is right," Cutter said, halting the argument in its tracks before it started to take off. "We make the best of it, get ashore in the dark as well as we can. There's been enough time wasted with this boat trip already."

Stephen backed down, simmering.

The *Polar Star* battled on. They were all dog-tired now, having been on their feet in the pitching wheelhouse for some six hours. Hanlon had a big thermos flask jammed in beside the radar, but it was empty. He seemed to live on tea, and had knocked back cup after cup during the night, hardly spilling a drop despite the bucking of the boat under his feet. Even his eyes were sunken, and periodically he wiped them with a dirty handkerchief.

"Is it a submarine you boys are out looking for?" he asked quietly. Beyond the wheelhouse windows the morning was arriving, grey and chill, the sky and the sea the same colour.

"I can't really say," Cutter told him. Realising then that an opportunity had presented itself, he added, "It might be... and it might not."

Hanlon flipped the switch on the sonar, and a pinging noise began. He alternated his gaze between the sea to his front and the glowing arm of the sonar sweep.

"Take a look at that then," he said, pointing one filthy finger at the sonar.

Cutter leant over the screen and followed the circular line of the sweep. A large flowing dot appeared before them.

"What is it?" he asked Hanlon.

The fisherman didn't reply for a moment. He seemed puzzled.

"It's no boat, that's for sure. And it's not a lost container. It's moving under its own power — you watch it."

Hanlon was right. Cutter saw the shape zigzag slowly back and forth in the seas ahead of the boat. His head snapped up, and he moved to the window, peering out intently.

"Can you see anything?" he asked Hanlon.

"Not in this swell. I've binos in the locker behind you; get 'em out and someone go take a look from the masthead." When they all hesitated, he sneered, "What, a bunch of big tough soldiers scared of heights?"

Willoby retrieved the binoculars from the locker.

"I'll go," he said.

Stephen had them out of his hand before the soldier could react. "My job, I think." He was out the wheelhouse door a second later, the freezing cold spray of the morning entering with his departure.

"Brave lad," Hanlon said approvingly. "I wouldn't climb that masthead in a swell like this for all the tea in China."

***

Stephen paused a second on the deck outside the wheelhouse. The cold air took his breath away, and the spindrift was being hurtled down the length of the boat in packets of white water. He zipped up his parka, checked the tubed collar that was his life jacket, and clenched his teeth as the cold water trickled down his neck and soaked his hair. Then he made his way aft along the slippery deck, moving as slowly as an old man, both hands gripping the guide rail that ran along the superstructure of the trawler.

It was full-on morning now, and looking up Stephen saw gulls battling with the wind overhead. The cloud was so low he felt as if he could almost reach up and touch it. He twisted his body into the safety hoops of the mast and began climbing up, his boots ringing on the metal rungs. As the trawler pitched and rolled under him, he was flung out and in, and he grasped the rungs so hard his hands began to cramp up.

I had to do it, of course; I had to volunteer. He did not even know why.

Soon he was at the top, and the movement of the boat was more pronounced at the tip of the pendulum that was the masthead. He stood in the tiny rusting platform and braced himself against the rails that surrounded him, fumbling and cursing to get the long-barrelled binoculars out of the breast of his coat.

It was a wild and fearsome world up there. Standing twenty feet above the deck, he was able to see the great waves that the trawler was fighting her way through more clearly. An entire landscape was on the move around him, a saw-toothed, white-fringed awesome wilderness of water. He had never seen anything like it before; it was both exhilarating and terrifying to watch.

Remembering something, he delved into a pocket and reached for a black plastic walkie-talkie. *Good old Motorola.* He pressed the *send* button, but of course, no one else on the boat had his switched on.

Brilliant.

A second later however, his own comms crackled, and Connor's voice said thickly, "Hello, who's that?"

"It's me, you twit," Stephen commed back, grinning. "Get up to the wheelhouse and tell Cutter to switch on his radio."

"Stephen! Where are you? I thought —"

"Just do it, Connor. Out."

Lifting the binoculars, he battered his eye socket with the lens, struggling to see through them in the crazy dance of the swaying mast. Finally he gave up, and decided to use his Mark I eyeball instead.

A gull sailed across his vision, so close he could have reached out and slapped it on the arse. He stared out into the greyness, eyes watering under the assault of the wind. It wasn't as bad as it had been, nothing like, but before last night he would still have called this a storm. He marvelled at the courage of men like Hanlon, who took rustbuckets out into this fearsome wilderness and tried to make a living out of it. No wonder it was considered the most dangerous job in the world.

For some reason his thoughts turned to Helen at that moment, and he wondered where she was now; exploring some unknown prehistoric region perhaps, in a world even more dangerous than this storm-tossed ocean. Part of him wished, even now, that he could be with her, but the other half hated himself for even thinking it. Bad enough he had slept with his best friend's wife. What was worse was that it was highly likely she was only using him to get at Cutter — and he had fallen for it. He had let her do it. He missed Cutter's friendship, the easygoing camaraderie of the old days. Between betraying him with Helen, and then this whole Claudia-Jenny thing, Cutter was no longer the man he had been. No longer the friend he had been. That was something that pained Stephen, and angered him at the same time. He wondered sometimes if he and Cutter could go on working together like this, whether things might one day get easier. He hoped so. He —

Something there, in the seas ahead. A glimpse of black, flipping over into the water.

His radio hissed static.

"Stephen, how's it going? Over." It was Cutter.

"Wait one," he commed back.

His eyes streamed and stung as the salt air scratched at them, and he blinked away the spray, tasting it on his lips, feeling it sting his corneas.

There it was again; a snatched glimpse of something disappearing, rolling over into the flank of a wave some half mile ahead.

"My God," he whispered aloud. It had to be huge, the size of a whale. Perhaps it *was* a whale, he told himself, but he wasn't convinced.

"Cutter," he said into the little radio, "do you see anything on the sonar just ahead of us? Over."

"Yes. Less than a mile to the west, almost dead ahead. It's moving back and forth. Can you ID it? Over."

At that moment, he saw its snout break the surface and open up as though it were going to snap at a passing seagull. A great black beast with a mottled, relatively pale underbelly. It flopped down again and disappeared into the canyon of a towering wave.

"Did you see that — did you see that?" Stephen shouted into his radio.

"Negative. The swells are too high. What did you see? Over."

Stephen remained stock still, as though frozen to the mast. He stared out at the blank majesty of the sea and felt a sharp thrill of fear flood his veins. It was one thing to face these creatures on dry land, where there was backup — where there was a place to run. It was quite another to encounter them at sea, in a rusting cockleshell hundreds of miles from anywhere.

He thumbed the comms button.

"We're going to need a bigger boat," he said with a mirthless smile on his face.

EIGHT

Uncomplaining, the soldiers lined the sides of the *Polar Star*, their weapons cocked and ready.

Private Watts was at the masthead, keeping a lookout and sending down periodic reports through chattering teeth. Willoby, Connor and Stephen were sorting through the mass of gear on the deck, lashing rucksacks to stanchions. The two inflatables sat in their white containers, ready to be blown open at a moment's notice. Periodically, Connor went to the ship's rail and heaved bile into the sea, his empty stomach convulsing time and again now that he was able to see the waves rising and falling around him.

In the wheelhouse, Cutter stood studying the sonar, whilst Liam Hanlon remained at the wheel, seemingly welded to it, a part of his boat. He had gone silent; he had seen the fear on their faces and did not know what to make of it.

"It's gone," Cutter said, exhaling relief. "I can't see it anywhere." He paused. "You're sure there are no whales in this section of the Atlantic?" he asked yet again.

"I've never seen one," Hanlon replied. "Are you sure your boy wasn't seeing things?"

"Do you think the sonar was seeing things?" Cutter snapped back.

"Oh, there's something out there, right enough, and it's no submarine. It's too small, and changes course too quickly. I reckon you've found the thing you came out here for, is that so?"

"One of them," Cutter said. He felt almost sorry for Hanlon. The man might be a greedy motormouth, but he didn't lack courage, and he had been brought out here at the risk of his own life, under false pretences. It was the way things worked in this world.

"You think the *Cormorant* met up with our mystery creature, don't you?" Hanlon said.

"It's possible."

The fisherman drew himself up and wiped his forehead with his handkerchief. The lines of his face tightened.

"Aye well, this is no wooden inshore boat. If anything tries messing about with the *Star*, it's going to meet with raw steel."

"That's the spirit," Cutter said, and he clapped the old fisherman on the shoulder. Then, before turning to leave, he glanced down at the sonar.

And a look of horror dawned on his face.

"What the *hell* is that?"

Hanlon turned sharply.

He stared at the screen. "Holy Mother of God; it's right on top of us!"

Automatic gunfire rang out along the ship, cracking sharply over the sound of the wind and the waves, the pulse of the diesels.

"Jesus Christ!" Hanlon exclaimed.

"Mind your course, Skipper," Cutter shouted. He left the wheelhouse and ducked out into the roaring, storm-driven spray of the morning.

"What's going on?" he cried as he lurched aft. Even in the middle of the gale, he could smell the cordite stink of the gunfire.

"Stand fast!" Captain Willoby bellowed. And Cutter saw a sight which would remain seared into his memory for the rest of his life.

The *Polar Star* was in the trough of a great, smooth-crested wave. A mountain of water, they were climbing up its side, the struggling diesel engines ploughing the steel prow of the ship up the flank of the wave as though the trawler were trying to cut it in half. The crest of the wave was higher than the masthead; it was a thirty footer, a monstrous juggernaut of water.

And Cutter could see *into* the depths of the wave, as though he were looking into a vast aquarium that reared high above his head. In that moving titan of water a dark shape loomed, streamlined and huge, longer than the boat under their feet, and sleek-nosed as a missile. The edge of one great flipper broke the surface of the water, a flipper twice as long as a man, and then the wave had moved on under the hull of the boat, and the monster within it had been taken back into the depths once more.

So shocked were the soldiers that after Watts, up in the masthead, had fired a terrified burst, they hadn't even thought to bring their weapons to bear. They stood rooted to the steel deck, machine-pistols forgotten in their hands, safeties still on. In their midst, Connor, Abby and Stephen crouched thunderstruck while seawater sloshed knee-deep around them, pouring out of the scuppers as the trawler began its rocking-horse motion again.

Stephen collected his wits first.

"Pliosaur!" he shouted at Cutter. "I didn't know they could get that big. It must be fifty-feet long!"

"Stand to!" Willoby yelled into the wind. "Safeties off. Get a grip you stupid bastards! Sergeant Fox — if we see that thing again, you open up on it with everything you've got! Fox — are you listening to me?"

"Aye — I mean yes, sir." He turned. "You heard him, you muppets. Get your fingers out and stand to. Bristow, get that bloody Minimi up on the rail. Pete, break out some frags."

"Now we know what got the *Cormorant*," Cutter said. He helped Stephen stand in the middle of the mound of soaking, rope-lashed gear that covered the deck.

"Yeah — now don't you wish we'd flown?"

"It ignored us, Stephen. I don't know why, but it just floated by. Did you see its eye?"

"I did. I thought it was looking straight at me."

Cutter's white, unshaven face broke into an incredulous smile. His own eyes were bright as those of a schoolboy let out for the summer.

"My God, Stephen, did you ever see anything so magnificent in your life? It hasn't swum these seas for 160 million years, and it just drifted by us."

"Incredible," Stephen agreed, smiling at Cutter's excitement.

"It's an air-breather Stephen, not a fish. It'll surface periodically; this thing is not about to dive down deep."

"In other words, it's not going to go away."

"How are the cold waters of the Atlantic affecting it though — that's the question. It seemed sluggish to me. Even something that big might be dying at these temperatures."

"Hence our luck in passing it by," Stephen suggested.

"Yes, could be. If I'd only had a camera."

The boat lurched under them, and the wind shrieked through the guy-wires of the mast. It was picking up again.

"Let's leave the holiday snaps for another time, eh?" Stephen said. He grinned at Cutter, who looked happier than he had in weeks.

Willoby joined the two men, his M-4 slung across his chest. His face was dripping water and he looked as grey as the sea around them.

"All right, you got me; I'm officially impressed. What the hell was that?"

"Liopleurodon," Cutter told him. "The greatest marine predator of all time; one of the Plesiosaur family, from the Jurassic."

"It's actually true then," Willoby said, shaking his head. "I kind of half thought it was a joke, or a front for something else."

"It's all true," Cutter said. "Somewhere in the waters around us there is an anomaly, a gate if you will, between our time and an era that existed in the far past. And things can come through that gate."

"Spielberg would wet himself if he knew the half of this," Willoby said. He seemed to regain some of his martial poise. "How do we kill it, Professor?"

Cutter frowned.

"Kill it — why bother? The temperature of the water is killing it minute by minute. You don't need to shoot it, Captain — it's on its way out already."

"Thank God for that then. By the looks of it, that thing could soak up a thousand rounds without blinking." Then Willoby's face changed. "If stuff like that is slipping through into our seas, then what in the world is running about this island we're headed for?" He asked the question as though it had just dawned on him.

"That's the interesting part," Stephen told him. "Welcome to our world, Captain. You won't have a dull moment, I assure you."

Willoby blinked slowly, deep in thought. He looked at Cutter.

"Professor, I —"

"There it is — breaking surface to starboard!" Watts yelled from her post at the masthead.

The black, mottled snout of the Liopleurodon rose out of the water less than twenty metres away. Its head was the length of a family car.

At the starboard rail, Joe Bristow opened up with the Minimi, spraying automatic fire with the weapon held at his hip, the barrel resting on the rail. Spent casings flew through the air with a tinkling of brass. Around the Liopleurodon's head the water was stitched white. The other soldiers joined in, their carbines on full automatic. The dead man's click sounded in several weapons before Willoby shouted, "Cease fire — cease fire!"

The creature had submerged, though before the waves broke it up, they were all sure they had seen a dark cloud muddy the water in its wake.

Connor staggered over, wriggling his little finger in his ear.

"Do you think we're doing much more than just pissing it off, Professor?"

Cutter said nothing. He stared over the rail of the boat at the blank waves, breathing in the acrid reek of the cordite. His own ears were still ringing. The soldiers were reloading. Bristow's Minimi was steaming in the cold air, the sea spray hissing off the hot barrel.

He turned to Willoby.

"Connor may have a point. A thing that size can soak up a lot of punishment. Captain, unless it's directly threatening the boat, I would suggest that your men conserve their ammunition." He was calm, but there was something akin to fury in his eyes.

"Very well, Professor. I agree," Willoby said. Their stares locked, and the tension between them seemed almost to fizzle for a second, until Cutter turned away.

In the wheelhouse, Liam Hanlon was standing where Cutter had left him. He was chewing on the corner of his handkerchief.

"I should turn this boat around," he said, his voice furious, face livid with fear. "You people got me out here under false pretences."

"I know," Cutter said, and he genuinely felt remorse. "I know. But we've none of us any choice in this. You'll take us to Guns Island now, and you won't say a word about it."

Hanlon was scowling.

"I thought you were soldiers. Now I know you're just lunatics."

"That we are, Skipper. That we are."

***

The day drew on, and the Liopleurodon did not return. The soldiers cleaned their weapons in shifts, fighting to keep the rust off them.

Stephen joined Abby and Connor amidships. They were going through their gear methodically, for the third or fourth time. Connor swore softly.

"What's up?" Abby asked him.

"Forgot my iPod. Knew I'd forgotten something."

"You've forgotten something else, as well," Stephen told him.

"What's that?"

"Your seasickness."

"You're right! I feel fine now. My stomach is still on a trapeze, but it doesn't bother me — how about that?"

"Fear is a wonderful healer," Abby said.

"Fear — oh, come on Abs!"

"I was watching you, Connor. You stopped vomiting the moment you laid eyes on that sea monster, and you haven't had a heave since."

"That's adrenaline that is — it's my primordial survival instincts kicking in."

"Who was it said, 'If you push a civilized man into a corner, you'll eventually find the hot, red eyes of the caveman staring back at you?'" Stephen said with a smile.

"That's right — that's me that is," Connor said, beaming. "Caveman — man of action." He paused. "Can I have a gun now?"

"No!" Abby and Stephen said together.

"According to the GPS, we are now thirty-two nautical miles south-southeast of Guns Island," Willoby said, studying the device in his hand.

"It'll be dark again soon," Cutter said, staring out of the salt-streaked windows of the wheelhouse. "Hanlon, you know the island. We need to find a spot where we can land the equipment on the shore, something with a sheltered approach."

"No such thing as a sheltered approach to Guns Island," Hanlon said. "I can take you to leeward, and edge in close, hold her there while you disembark. On your map, that dotted line you're relying on to get you to the top, it ends at the shore in a wee cove maybe fifty yards wide. It's where the bird-watcher scientists park their boats in the summer, when they come to count the gannets. If you can make it in there, you should have calmer water, even at this time of year." He sucked his teeth moodily for a second. "You don't have survival suits, do you?"

"Just these," Cutter said, tapping the collar of his life jacket.

"Then don't for Christ's sake fall in the water. The cold will knock you out in a matter of minutes, and that'll be that."

Soon it grew dark, and Hanlon switched the arc-lights of the trawler back on. The wind had fallen again, and the swells had shrunk somewhat. Instead of the fifteen- and twenty-foot waves they had become accustomed to, ten footers ran under the boat in smooth succession, like a series of huge speedbumps.

Cutter was at the wheel, the skipper having gone below to catch an hour's sleep. He was standing with the sweat cold on his back despite his warm clothing, peering out at the arc-lit darkness, then at the compass, then at the endless sweep of the sonar. Below his feet the deck throbbed with the steady beat of the engines.

"Four miles," Willoby said, studying his GPS. "I'd better wake Hanlon."

"Give him another ten minutes," Cutter said. "The poor bastard has to drive this thing all the way back to Crosshaven on his own."

"He's a brave man — or a stupid one," Willoby said.

"Brave and greedy, like the conquistadors."

"And you, Professor — does that describe you, too?"

Cutter turned his head to look at him for a moment.

"I'm not in it for the money."

"No, but I saw your face when that thing turned up at the side of the boat. I've seen squaddies look at strippers the same way. You're in it for the thrill."

Cutter snorted, a half laugh.

"Lusting after dinosaurs — what does that make me then?"

"A dangerous man, Professor."

"This, from the big bad SAS officer."

"I'm just following orders."

"Don't give me that shite. You volunteered, Willoby. I've seen your file, remember — you'd volunteer for anything. If any of us is a thrill seeker, it's you."

Willoby smiled.

"I'm a professional soldier — I go where the action is."

"And I'm a professional zoologist. I go where the monsters are."

Willoby leaned forward and switched off the arc-lights of the trawler. At once, the world beyond the windows went dark.

"Hey!" Cutter exclaimed.

"One moment, Professor, let your eyes adjust. Keep staring out there."

They stood side by side at the wheel, the engines churning endlessly beneath their feet, the boat rising and falling.

"There," Willoby said. "You see it?"

Cutter's eyes had adjusted. The sea was a lighter colour now, a pale livid slate in front of him. Above it the sky was darker, and speckled with stars — the clouds had blown clear at last. But something was bulking up out of the sea to blot out those stars, looming closer and taller every moment that the trawler powered westwards. A blank blackness on the edge of the world.

"Land ho," Willoby said quietly. "Professor, we have Guns Island, dead ahead."

"There be monsters," Cutter said grimly. He throttled back on the engines so that their incessant thudding slowed, and the boat lost speed.

"Best wake up the skipper," he added. "In a few minutes we'll be right up against those cliffs."

It was silent on the boat. The team stood on the after deck amid their mounds of gear and weaponry whilst Bristow and Fox stood by with the two inflatables. Cutter was by the open wheelhouse door relaying information back and forth between Hanlon and the others. He was soaked through, freezing cold, and he had not slept in twenty-four hours. The adrenaline rush of the Liopleurodon was only a memory. All he wanted now was to be warm and dry, and to lay his head somewhere dark for eight hours.

Instead, he thought grimly, *I have to climb a thousand-foot cliff and mix it up with a crowd of unknown prehistoric animals. Who'd have thought getting a Phd could land me in stuff like this?*

The seas had eased, and the wind had dropped off to no more than a fitful breeze, the bulk of the island cutting off the malice of the storm, which was still hammering off to the northeast. Looking up, Cutter could see a magnitude of stars, the trailing glimmer that was the Milky Way, and a sliver of moon that came and went through rags of streaming eldritch cloud. It was bitterly cold. He stood in a perpetually renewed cloud of his own breath.

Ahead of the boat, the towering cliffs of Guns Island loomed, a thousand feet of Atlantic-hammered basalt that had once been the lava plug in a great volcano. The seas had risen and worn away the sides of the mountain eons ago, leaving only the igneous central pillar standing. This vast chunk of fire-forged stone had remained here as the world had changed around it, the continents shifting underfoot, the seas deepening, growing colder. Ice ages coming and going, millennia passing as quickly as the pages in a book.

What in the hell was waiting for them up there?

"I see white water ahead, three or four hundred metres!" Doody called from up on the masthead. And then, "Breakers! I see breakers. There're rocks in front of us, boss!"

Cutter poked his head into the wheelhouse. "You get that?" he asked Hanlon.

"I got it," the skipper said. His mouth was a tight line in his beard, his eyes bloodshot and staring wide. He nosed the boat forward metre by metre, one hand on the wheel, the other on the throttles. "There's a current here, works round the island to the east. We'll be in it soon. When we get into it, you get your people off as quickly as you can, because I'll be fighting that water to keep off the rocks. You hear me?"

"I hear you," Cutter said quietly. "Thank you, Captain, for sticking this out."

"I don't want your thanks. I just want to get home in one piece, and I want my money. Start sorting out your dinghies. I'll flick the lights when it's time to launch them."

They stood on the deck, ten waterlogged, shivering people. Willoby and Cutter knelt by the two inflatables, still cocooned in their white plastic cylinders. They flipped open the catches and tossed aside the top halves of the containers, revealing tightly wrapped bundles of day-glo rubber within. When the lights of the trawler went off for a second, they both pulled on the ripcords and booted the bundles into the sea.

Still attached by nylon guidelines, the two inflatables exploded outwards, blossoming and uncurling like living creatures, cellular growth magnified a billion times and speeded up into a few seconds.

"I'd give a lot right now for a decent Zodiac," Willoby said.

"This is all we could fit in the shipment," Cutter told him. "Break out the outboards, Captain."

The team had two small Seagull outboard motors. Bristow and Fox leapt down into the two dinghies and these were handed down to them, no easy task in the rolling sea. The two soldiers clipped the little engines to the sterns of the dinghies, and then sat bobbing there, the rubber boats bouncing against the side of the trawler. Connor looked down at the little vessels as they bobbed, toy-like against the bulk of the ship.

"I never thought I'd say this," he groaned, "but I think I prefer the big boat."

"Come on Connor." Abby nudged him. "Another couple of hundred metres and we're home and dry. I'll heat you up a nice mug of hot chocolate."

"Oh, don't, Abby," Connor rasped. His hand went to his mouth.

"Gear first," Willoby ordered. "Come on lads, we haven't all sodding night." He turned and looked up at the masthead, where the signaller Watts stood, sweeping the horizon with an infrared scope.

"Watts! All clear?"

"All clear boss — not so much as a sardine in sight."

"All right, get down here. Cutter, I want your people split between both dinghies."

Teeth clenched to stop them chattering, Cutter nodded.

"Stephen, you and Connor in the left one; Abby, you're with me."

The dinghies were dangerously overloaded. As the team settled into them they found they had only inches of freeboard, and the swell, which seemed reasonable when experienced from the deck of the trawler, became a roller-coaster motion under them.

Hanlon appeared at the trawler's rail. He cast off first one line, and then the other. As the dinghies drifted away from the *Polar Star* they saw him raise a hand, a mere black silhouette against the garish lights of the boat.

"May God go with you!" they heard him shout, and then he disappeared back into the wheelhouse. The trawler's engines took on power and noise, and the big steel boat began to move away, back out to the southeast, her bow pointed towards Ireland.

There was a moment of silence in the two dinghies. The wind was roaring high overhead, a sound not unlike a train passing by, and both Bristow and Fox were pulling viciously on the starter-cords of the outboards. Finally, the little engines caught, sputtering and coughing like excited lawnmowers. The dinghies began to move.

Cutter looked back and saw the lights of the trawler recede into the black night. Watching it go, despite the close-packed nearness of his companions, he somehow felt incredibly alone.

NINE

Jenny Lewis had seen the interior of a police cell only once before, when as a university student she had been part of a crowd of drunken, gilded youth at Oxford who thought it would be a fine idea to race wheeled refuse containers down the middle of the High Street at 3 a.m. Back then, her incarceration had lasted for only a few hours. A caution had followed, and no more.

This, she thought, *might be decidedly more tricky.*

For some reason, she craved a cigarette, a habit she had not thought of in years. It just seemed the thing to do, a kind of adjunct to the bare-walled room, the heavy formica-topped table with the slot in it where a handcuff could be locked, and the paper cup of vile instant coffee that sat cooling in front of her.

She fiddled with her mobile phone as it sat warm in one pocket. There was a camera lens in one corner of the room, and she had been told not to make calls without permission. Absently, she wondered if they would rush in here, truncheons raised, if she raised it to her ear.

It didn't matter, the battery was dead. Of all the times for that to happen, it had happened now. She hadn't been able to call Lester to warn him. That was a major error. She was paying for it already.

But he must know of the situation by now, she assumed. A British Home Office official had been detained by a foreign government. He must be working on it already.

Had to be.

Jenny looked at her watch. It was 5 a.m. *I'll bet he's still in bed*, she thought wearily. *God, I'm tired.*

The door opened and a man stepped in, dressed in a rumpled suit. He looked as though he had dressed in the dark, and his tie was askew. He sat down opposite Jenny and set two more paper cups on the table from which steam rose, along with a delightful smell.

"Cappuccinos," he said with a smile. "There's a wee Italian café down the road that opens early. You look as though you could do with one."

She sipped at it gratefully, saying nothing.

"My name is Kieran Madden. I'm just here to ask you a few questions," he said. He had a kindly face, square, framed with greying hair. His eyes were pale blue, and tired though he seemed, they were clear and piercing. *This man is no fool*, Jenny thought, and she drank her coffee to gain herself a moment or two of thought.

Madden watched her closely.

"At approximately one-thirty this morning a trawler by the name of *Polar Star* left the harbour at Crosshaven. The skipper's name was —" Here he drew a notebook out of his suit pocket and flipped it open. "— Liam Hanlon. A local man. On board the boat were ten passengers, who took with them a large amount of equipment. That equipment came through Shannon Airport this afternoon, on a chartered airfreight Shorts 360. It was then loaded onto a truck and driven to Crosshaven for the rendezvous. You, Ms Lewis, were also at that rendezvous."

Jenny raised an eyebrow over the rim of her cup.

"Perhaps, perhaps not. I believe the right to remain silent exists here in Ireland also, Mr Madden."

"Inspector Madden," he said, correcting her somewhat curtly.

"Forgive me. I wasn't aware of your rank. Inspector, I have given your people my name, and a number to call. Once that contact has been made, this will all be cleared up very quickly."

"Where was that trawler heading, Ms Lewis?"

"I have no idea."

"Those men on board were soldiers, were they not?"

"I have no idea."

Madden took out a packet of cigarettes, lit one with a plastic lighter, and blew out blue smoke with an obvious air of satisfaction.

"All right," he said patiently, leaning forward. "We'll start at the beginning, shall we?"

Lester did not like being summoned to Whitehall in the middle of the night, yet it seemed as if it was happening all too often these days.

It reminded him of his early days in the service, when he had burned away much of his twenties in endless midnight meetings amid sheaves of documents and interminable committees. He was supposed to be above that now. But when Lord Brooke telephoned in the early hours, one jumped.

Lord David Brooke CMG, or "Call-me-God", as civil servants knew the title. He headed a committee in the Lords that oversaw a great deal of internal spending within Whitehall. If one were coarse about it, one could say that he was the man who paid Lester's wages.

The meeting was at his private residence, too. From experience, Lester knew this couldn't be good. There hadn't even been time to summon his own car. He paid off the taxi and rang the bell, standing in a little portico supported by white pillars. Brooke still lived in Kensington, near some of his clubs. He was a man of the old school. Which meant there would be no fobbing him off with Home Office legalese.

A butler — an honest to goodness butler, in a dark suit — showed Lester upstairs. It was 5 a.m., and he wagered enviously that Jenny was sleeping comfortably in a warm bed, somewhere in Ireland.

Brooke was waiting in his study, and it appeared as if he had been awake for some time already. The look on his face wasn't pleasant.

"You know why you're here," he said. He did not shake hands, or offer Lester a seat. He stood in his dressing gown with his back to a flickering fire. The flame-light danced off cut-glass decanters, leather wing-backed chairs, the gilt spines of books, mahogany, silver. The room breathed of an older, more privileged world. A world that still remembered the past glories, when London had been the hub of international affairs.

It's a different ball game now, but still these old dinosaurs keep their hands in, Lester thought to himself, but he kept his silence.

Instead, he said, "I'm afraid you have me at a disadvantage my Lord."

"Don't you keep track of what's going on in your own department, James? My God, man, my telephone has been ringing off the hook for the last hour." His face reddened, and he looked at a ticking tallboy in the corner. "In a few hours, the Minister will be informed."

A chill crept up Lester's spine.

"The Irish Ambassador will be requesting a meeting with the Foreign Minister this afternoon, an interview without coffee, by all accounts. Perhaps you will have the courtesy to fill me in on your side of the story. If the episode is to go public, then we must be prepared." He fell silent, and waited for Lester to respond. "Well?" he said impatiently.

Lester breathed out quietly.

"I take it this has to do with my department's presence in the Republic of Ireland."

"You're damn right it does! One of your officials is banged up in a police cell at this very moment, and the Irish Navy is fitting out a mine-sweeper with a team to go and chase your Flying Dutchman of a fishing boat. What the hell is going on, Lester?"

How on earth did Cutter get himself tossed in a cell? Lester wondered, hoping the anger didn't show on his face.

"This is the first I've heard of it," he said. Despite himself, he sat down on a nearby stool. His legs had turned to water. His life, his career, all of it flashed before his eyes. What the hell had happened — and why hadn't Jenny contacted him?

Oh my God, it's not Cutter...

Brooke watched him closely, and his eyes narrowed.

"You really are out of the loop on this one, aren't you?"

"My people on the ground should have informed me, but I've heard nothing," Lester admitted. One didn't try to cover up a mistake of this magnitude. One took it on the chin, and hoped for clemency.

"Damned careless of them," Brooke barked. He looked at Lester a moment as if sizing him up, then crossed to the decanters. He poured two large brandies and handed one of the heavy crystal glasses to Lester. "Drink up, my boy. You look as though you could do with it."

Lester smiled wryly.

"How much *can* you tell me?" Brooke asked, sipping his brandy with narrowed eyes. "The more I know, the more effectively I can sit on this."

"I have a team bound for an island in the North Atlantic where we had a base during the war," Lester said. His mind turned furiously. "Experiments were carried out at that time on the island, in the late forties and early fifties. Biological experiments."

Brooke took a seat, mouth pursed.

Lester took the plunge.

"There may be some materials left behind which are now at risk of contaminating the environment. My team has been sent out to neutralise them." There — he had told the lie, or at least bent the truth. His career was now balanced on a razor's edge.

He continued.

"It is a matter of some urgency, and there is a storm over the entire region at the moment. Helicopter flights are impossible, so my team hired a fishing boat to make their way out to the island with as little loss of time as possible. Their equipment was flown out to Ireland in a diplomatic bag —"

Here Brooks covered his eyes with his hand. Lester ploughed on doggedly.

"I believe that must have kicked off the Irish Government's suspicions. The island itself is a contested territory. We've given up our claims on it, and the final decision on its sovereignty is now in the hands of the international courts. Both Ireland and France have laid claim to it." He cleared his throat. His mouth was dry, despite the brandy. "My Lord, we must not let anyone except my team set foot on the island. It is imperative."

Brooke rose again.

"What a bloody awful little mess you have concocted for us," he said mildly. He faced the fire and stared into his glass.

"It can't be done," he said at last. "The Irish are already at sea. And once this lands on the Minister's desk, the French will have to be informed, as well. We cannot keep this an in-house affair, Lester. It's too late for that."

It was over then. The anomalies, the creatures, the ARC — all of it would finally come out in the open. And sitting on top of it all would be the head of James Peregrine Lester, scapegoat-in-chief.

He was finished.

"This must not become an international incident," he said, his mind still turning despite the black despair that was flooding it.

"It's too late."

"My Lord, if we can bring the Irish and French on board somehow, and make them part of the operation, then perhaps the whole thing could still be kept out of the public eye. It's not ideal, but it *is* better than having it splashed across the world's newspapers."

"I'll agree with you there," Brooke said coldly. He stood thinking, staring into the fire, while Lester perched on the edge of his seat with an empty glass in his hand, waiting.

"All right," Brooke said, "we'll give it a try. For Christ's sake, James, get in touch with your people on the ground and apprise them of the situation. If they can get a lid on it before anyone else joins them on this island of yours, then we shall have a chance. I know Jacques Santerre at their foreign ministry — we go back a long way. I'll talk to him this morning and see what I can do.

"The thing about the French is that you can't double-cross them. They find it unforgivable when they have the wool pulled over their eyes. We shall have to lay our cards on the table for them to see, and hope what they see is sense."

"I am very grateful, my Lord," Lester said. A tiny flicker of hope lit up in him.

"The Irish are your problem. I want you on a plane this morning. Phone for a car from here and book something at Brize Norton. Get out there and clean up your mess at that end. I'll handle Whitehall. Is that clear?"

"Very clear, my Lord," Lester said. He stood up. Brooke looked closely at him.

"You're not holding anything back on me are you, James? Now would be the time to say."

"My Lord, I have told you everything I can."

Brooke caught the tiny qualification. He smiled unpleasantly.

"I'll just bet you have."

It was after dawn that Jenny felt the attitude in the room change. Madden had been called out, and one of his subordinates had continued the questioning in a mechanical, listless way. She picked up the alteration in tone immediately, and tried to cudgel her tired brain into some kind of alertness. The caffeine on an empty stomach had made her both queasy and hyped without contributing to her powers of concentration.

Without being asked, she took one of Madden's cigarettes from the pack on the table and lit it, drawing the smoke gratefully into her lungs and enjoying the momentary light headedness it gave her.

"You can't smoke in here," the policeman sitting opposite said to her.

"Tell that to your boss," she said, with the sweetest smile she could muster at that hour.

Before he could retort, Madden came back in. With him were two anonymous, black-suited men with closed faces. They had a soldierly air about them.

"You have interesting friends, Ms Lewis," Madden said. He looked as if he was trying to control his temper. "I'm releasing you into the custody of these gentlemen here from the department of the Taoiseach. You are free to go."

"Free to go... in their custody," she corrected him, standing up. "My thanks for the coffee, Inspector — and for the cigarette."

"It's a filthy habit," he said, watching her.

"Yes — you should try and quit." She smiled again. She liked him, and knew that he was burning with curiosity and resentment.

She walked round the table, knowing the eyes of every man in the room were on her as she moved, and shook Madden's hand. "Perhaps we'll meet under better circumstances, another time," she said as brightly as she could manage.

"I regret to say that I doubt that. We move in different circles."

"*Au revoir*, Inspector."

"*Slan go foill*," he said, the Gaelic words unknown to her. She looked him in the eye.

"Goodbye for now," he added.

It was full daylight now, a dreary windswept day in Cork. Looking at her watch, Jenny realised she had been sitting in the interrogation room for the better part of nine hours. More than anything else, she wanted to find herself a bed and crawl into it.

When she saw Lester waiting for her on the steps of the Garda Station, she knew that it was a vain hope. His face seemed carved out of stone.

"Thank you gentlemen," he said politely to Jenny's companions. They nodded to him wordlessly and then strode away to a large dark car across the street.

"I think we have time for breakfast," Lester said, offering her his arm. She took it, but she had never seen him so closed off and contained.

"I would rather catch some sleep," she said.

"I'm afraid that won't be possible. First, you're going to tell me how you managed to engineer this immense cock-up, and then you're going to be put on a boat," he said.

"A boat?"

"A ship, perhaps. Yes, I think it's big enough to be called a ship. Named the *Aoife*, I believe. You're about to join the Irish Navy."

They proceeded along the street, walking together like lovers sharing confidences. Lester unfurled an umbrella against the rain.

"Guns Island is about to go international. The Irish have insisted on sending a team out to it to solidify their claims upon the damned place, and by later this afternoon, the French will also have been apprised of their actions, and will no doubt be contemplating a similar stunt of their own."

"Have you heard from Cutter?" Jenny asked.

"No. No word. Satellite phones can be unreliable, of course."

"This is a disaster," Jenny said.

"Yes — my thoughts exactly. Our jobs are, to use a cliché, well and truly on the line. Not to mention the threat of criminal prosecution. The Irish Special Branch have smelled your blood; they have not given up the trail yet."

"Why am I going out there?"

"To stymie the Irish, if possible. You will contact Cutter as soon as you can, by any means possible. I have a satellite phone here for you to take on board with you. Damage limitation is the name of the game now. We must keep outsiders away from the anomalies, and keep the creatures away from the outsiders. It's bad enough when our own citizens get eaten — imagine the mess if a bunch of foreign nationals end up as a prehistoric smorgasbord."

"Perhaps it's time it was opened up, made international," Jenny offered. "We've been sitting on this for quite a while now."

"And we will continue to do so," Lester said crisply. "Because that is our job. Ours not to reason why, and all that."

"Very well. You're right."

Lester sighed. "Why didn't you contact me? I had to hear it from Lord Brooke, for God's sake."

"Flat battery."

"Ah," Lester looked almost amused. "for want of a nail, the kingdom was lost. Never mind. What do you fancy for breakfast? Myself, I want a good old English fry-up.

"Do you suffer from seasickness?"

TEN

As they closed in on the breakers ahead, the current took the dinghies and began to sweep them round to the northeast, following the line of the island. All about them in the darkness, white water flashed upon the black fangs of the rocks. The dinghies were sluggish and leaden, overloaded and taking water over their sides.

On both, the team broke out the paddles and began working furiously to help the sputtering little Seagull outboards.

"Go left, go left!" Cutter shouted across to Willoby's dinghy. "There's rocks here, ten metres to our right. Steer left, for God's sake!"

In his boat, Sergeant Fox and the medic, Doody, were paddling like men possessed while Abby and Corporal Farnsworth were baling out the frigid water with cupped hands and anything else they could use. A swell took them and lifted the little craft high in the air, tilting it to one side as it went under them. For a second, the outboard was whirring clear of the water, grinding angrily. Then the swell rolled past them and they were in a trough again.

All was black about them, until Farnsworth and Doody paused to click on their head-torches. In the other dinghy the soldiers did the same, so that there were two little groups of flickering light-wands, wallowing crazily on the gigantic surface of the sea, whilst above them the cliffs of Guns Island reared up into infinity, like the walls of a giant's castle.

Willoby had a large million-candle-power torch in his free hand while he steered his dinghy with the other. He waved the beam around until it chanced across a paleness amid all that black.

"I see the cove!" he yelled over to Cutter. "Thirty degrees to your left. I see sand. Cutter, follow me in!"

He gunned the Seagull and the dinghy punched forward through the waves, spray lashing up white in lace fountains along its bow. Stephen and Connor sat to the front of the little craft with their backs to the waves, trying to keep the water out. Stephen put his arm about Connor's shoulders and held him tightly, but the younger man's eyes were tight shut. He was shuddering with cold and seemed not to care if the boat sank under him.

Slowly, painfully, the two dinghies fought against the current and the slow, massive impact of the deep swells, and began to make headway towards the cove Willoby had pointed out. Jutting away from the tiny beach were two long arms of naked rock, and about them the waves broke in furious explosions of spray.

The dinghies bumped together, and in each their occupants reached across and grabbed the safety lines of the other craft. As these tightened in their fists, so the little boats headed for the beach locked together, bumping and bucking against each other, the outboards struggling noisily.

"Ten metres," Cutter called out. In the bow of his boat, Doody broke open a flare and threw it as hard as he could. It landed above the low water mark and burned orange on the sand, a beacon that drew all their eyes in the roaring darkness.

Something thumped the bottom of Cutter's boat and it shuddered. Then it snagged, and there was a tearing noise, horrible to hear. The dinghy slewed round, tearing the safety lines out of the hands of Abby and Sergeant Fox. They both yelled out as the nylon ropes scorched their palms and were whipped free. The dinghy sagged in the middle.

"Christ, we're holed," Cutter said. He twisted the throttle of the outboard fully open, but the dinghy seemed to be melting under him, growing soft. Water was flooding aboard. He looked forward, to where Willoby had drawn ahead. "We're sinking!" he yelled.

Willoby looked back, but shook his head, the beam from his head-torch waving back and forth. He couldn't turn back. The sea was powering them up towards the beach now. If he tried to turn, the boat would be swamped.

"Oh God," Abby said, shocked as the freezing water came up over her legs, then her waist. The outboard died as the seawater drowned it. The dinghy sank under them, and they were in the icy cold sea, their life jackets popping open around their collarbones, their equipment sunk into the blackness beneath them.

Cutter reached out and grabbed Abby's life jacket.

"S-swim for it," he mouthed to her. The cold was making him hyperventilate. He was whooping for air, the breath sawing into his lungs. He tried to fight the panic, to fix his eyes on the orange light of the flare.

Thirty feet away.

"Come on Abby, come on lass — start swimming or the current'll carry us out again."

They laboured there in the rise and fall of the waves, the five of them splashing and thrashing with clumsy determination. But they couldn't make any headway. The current was taking them away from the beach, and the cold was numbing their minds and limbs. Cutter fought the drowsiness that seemed to be creeping up on him, the fog that clogged his thinking. He was swallowing salt water, his mouth foul with it, and his struggles were growing weaker.

Abby drifted away from him, her head-torch pointed at the sky, a lonely, tiny beacon.

This is it, Cutter thought. *This is what it's like to die.*

Then there was the high-pitched whine of an outboard close by, and a bright light shining in his face. A hand grasped him by the scruff of the neck. Another took his fist and banged it hard against the side of the dinghy. "Grab this rope — get a hold of it and hang on!"

His numb hands managed to curl into fists around the safety line that surrounded the side of the dinghy. He held on there and was pulled through the water, legs trailing. Someone else's legs tangled with his own for a moment, and a skull smashed into his mouth, drawing blood but causing very little pain. He was too far gone to feel pain.

His feet touched bottom. He tried to move his legs and stand, but couldn't get a grip. He fell free of the dinghy, his lifeless hands releasing the rope. Someone grabbed him — there were two pairs of hands on him. He was manhandled by others who were standing in the water, tugging him into the shallows, then dropped in eight inches of seawater and he crawled the rest of the way, sinking to his wrists in the soft, grainy sand, until he was on land again, finally, and the waves were at his feet.

He lay breathing harshly, trying to make himself think again.

A torch was shone in his face.

"Nick — wake up Nick!" It was Stephen's voice. "He's in hypothermia — so's Abby. Get out the sleeping bags. Help me get this stuff off him. We have to try and get them dry."

When Cutter woke, it was daylight.

He lay blinking, utterly confused, not knowing where he was. He could hear the breakers roaring on the shore, the ever-present battling sea, but that wasn't it. He was lying with Abby in his arms, and as far as he could tell neither of them was wearing much of anything. Her skin was warm against him, and he could smell her hair: salt water and diesel, and a last vestige of whatever shampoo she used.

The two of them were cocooned in a single sleeping bag, their flesh pressed close and gaining heat from each other. Abby murmured in his embrace, and nuzzled his chest.

Cutter was entirely bewildered.

A shadow fell across him. It was Stephen, and he was smiling. He turned and spoke to someone, amusement in his voice.

"The sleeping beauties are opening their eyes, Captain."

With that, Abby woke up. She looked up at Cutter's face, six inches from her own, and mumbled sleepily. Then Cutter felt her body go taut as wire against him, and her eyes opened wide.

"Cutter!"

"Don't look at me," he said. "I had nothing to do with it."

Another shadow. It was Willoby.

"You're lucky to be alive, the pair of you. Another five minutes in that water and you'd have been a couple of little bobbing icebergs."

Abby was trying to struggle free of the sleeping bag. Her knee caught Cutter in a tender spot and he winced.

"Sorry, Professor."

"Take it easy, will you. It's not like I bought you dinner or anything."
Her face flushed pink.

"Where are my clothes?" she demanded.

The sleeping bag was unzipped with a tearing whine, and the cold air
rushed in across Cutter's skin, raising instant goosebumps. Stephen
handed him a sodden mass of black clothing. Abby was already on her
feet and pulling on her soaking wet trousers, shuddering as the material
met her flesh, and shaking a bandaged hand in just-recognised pain.

Cutter stared at his own gear with distaste.

"No dry stuff, eh?"

"Afraid not, went down with the dinghy. Besides, all the stuff that
survived is wet, too."

"Well, that's nice."

"Nick, another thing —"

"Don't try to cheer me up, Stephen, whatever you do."

"We've only got one hand-held anomaly detector left and it got pretty
waterlogged. It may well be unusable."

"Brilliant," Cutter muttered grimly. He shook his head and sat up.
"Now that the bad news is out of the way, what's the cheery half of the
story?" he asked, glancing from Willoby to Stephen and back again.

"Take a look," Stephen said, and he moved out of the way.

They were on a long, narrow shelf of stone above the beach. There was
a deep overhang, not quite a cave, but offering some shelter against the
wind and rain. Along it, the team had laid out their gear and karrimats,
and most were still in their sleeping bags. Cutter recognised Connor's
unkempt head of black tangled hair. He was snoring loudly. Stephen and
Willoby seemed to be the only people awake.

"Is everyone all right — did we all make it?" Cutter demanded, shivering in his wet clothes and struggling to pull on his boots.

"We're all here," Willoby said. He had a nasty gash above one eye,
the blood clotted and black. "As soon as I made it to shore we emptied
out my boat and Stephen and I went back for you. It was a close-run
thing. But we lost half our equipment when your dinghy went down,
including the sat-phone. All we have now are short-wave radios. And
we're three sleeping bags short, not to mention water, food, ammunition and weapons. We look — as my old sergeant major used to say —

like three pounds of shit stuffed in a two-pound bag. But we're alive, for now anyway."

"The sat-phone. Damn it all," Cutter said, sitting down again.

"Here," Stephen said, offering him a water bottle. Gratefully, Cutter sloshed some of the salt out of his mouth.

"The mission has become more difficult, but in war the plan is always the first thing out of the window," Willoby said. "We still have the climbing gear, the Minimi, half a dozen of the personal weapons, and enough rations to tide us over for three, possibly four days."

"I'm still waiting for the good news," Cutter said.

"The weather's turning again," Stephen told him. "This is a tidal shelf; when the waves kick up again, where we sit will be hammered by the breakers. We have to get up the cliff as soon as possible."

Cutter looked at the heavily breathing bundles which were the other members of the team. Some of the soldiers were sharing sleeping bags, as he and Abby had done.

"Best way to fight hypothermia," Willoby said, following his eyes. He winked at Abby, and once again she blushed down to the roots of her hair.

"I suppose you saved my life," she said.

"I suppose I did," Willoby told her.

Cutter staggered to his feet, his wet clothes stealing warmth from his body. "Have you found this path we're going to climb?"

Stephen spoke up.

"Hanlon was right. It's been a long time since the monks made it, and there have been several rock-falls since. Come take a look."

There wasn't far to walk. The tide was coming in now, and the little beach had disappeared. The Atlantic breakers were thundering barely twenty metres away from the people in the sleeping bags. Cutter felt the spray on his face.

"We really didn't think this one out properly," he muttered.

"Unfortunately, yes," Stephen agreed. "We've been flying by the seats of our pants for too long. We may have come a cropper this time." They both turned and stared up at the cliff soaring above them.

"Reminds me of Hoy, on Orkney," Stephen continued, craning his neck to look straight up. "I tried climbing the Old Man once, but bottled it a third of the way up."

"I see no path," Cutter said.

"This scree here to our left. Look up it about thirty-five metres. You can just make out a ledge. That's where the path starts, I think. The bottom part of it has been worn away."

"The ornithologists make it up there every summer," Cutter said, following Stephen's pointing finger.

"In summer, yes. And I'll bet they aren't carrying rifles and ammunition."

"There is that," Cutter admitted.

"Nick, we may have bitten off more than we can chew on this one. I'm not even talking about what we might face when — or if — we get to the top. I'm thinking about basic survival on this bare piece of rock. To all intents and purposes, we're marooned."

Cutter was silent as he allowed the words to sink in. The plan had been to use the sat-phone to contact Lester once the team had set up a base of operations on the plateau above. But they were out of comms now, and likely to remain so.

"Lester's a cold shark, but he's efficient, I'll give him that, and he's not stupid," Cutter said. "When he doesn't hear from us, he'll find some way to get in contact. A chopper, I'm thinking, once the weather clears."

"The weather," Stephen said sombrely. Cutter clapped him on the arm.

"Come on man — it's not like you to be down in the mouth. Buck up!"

"You sound like a Scottish nanny," Stephen said wryly, and they both laughed. It was the first time they had laughed together in a long while.

They went up in single file. Sergeant Fox led the way, having been climbing from childhood. Next came Captain Willoby, then Farnsworth, Bristow, Watts, Connor, Cutter, Abby, Doody and Stephen bringing up the rear.

The scree shifted and clicked under their feet, and the equipment they bore made them all clumsy and top-heavy, so their progress was slow. Up at the front, Fox was the only one of them who carried no extra gear. Wielding an ice axe and a nylon rope, he was breaking trail, finding a way forward. He would pause frequently and watch the movement of the scree, gauge the size of the stones upon it. Their ascent was like walking up a sand dune, where the sand grains had been magnified into rocks, some the size of tennis balls, others the size of sheep. And all of them were insecurely anchored to the slope, awaiting the signal that would indicate the start of another avalanche.

Rain blasted into their faces. Though the bulk of the island kept the worst of the wind from them, there were still errant, vicious gusts which came careering down the cliffs to stagger them and make them clutch at inadequate handholds. Soon the rain was turning to sleet. It hammered them without let up, stealing away whatever warmth they had found in their sleeping bags, soaking their clothing. Were it not for the fact that they were labouring hard, thus keeping up their body heat, they would quickly have been on the way to hypothermia again.

Up at the front of the group, Fox paused. The scree slope had been steepening, becoming ever more treacherous. As they ascended further from the reach of the waves, so ice began to form on the rocks. Some of the larger ones had a translucent caul of blue ice on their undersides, and icicles dripping down.

"End of the scree," Fox called down to them. "It's good rock now, no choss or crumbly stuff. Boss, we should think about roping up."

Willoby nodded. "Dig out the harnesses, lads."

They fumbled with the big black Bergens, searching through them for the climbing harnesses. Six had survived the sinking of the dinghy.

"Civvies each get one," Willoby said, holding a harness out to Cutter, who was shivering violently. All of them were, now that they had stopped moving.

"Not me," Stephen said. "I've climbed a bit. I'll be all right."

There was no argument. Before long, Cutter, Abby, Connor, Watts, Fox and Bristow were roped up.

"So," Connor said, fingering the slim, scarlet rope, "if one of us slips, the rest will hold on."

"No," Abby said tartly, "the rest jump off after you. What do you think Connor — come on, switch on!"

"You're beginning to sound like one of these soldiers," Connor grated through chattering teeth.

"I just want to get up this thing, and into a tent. I've never been so cold."

"What, didn't sharing a sleeping bag with the Professor warm the cockles of your little heart?" Connor said, grinning in spite of the discomfort. She shot him a dirty look.

"Cut it out," Cutter said, embarrassed despite himself.

"Sort out your gear," Stephen told them. He gestured to the soldiers, who were securing their weapons and webbing, tightening every strap, checking their bootlaces. "Don't have stuff dangling off you — keep it close to your body." He sighed, and reached over. "Here, Connor," he said, and he yanked tight the buckles holding the Bergen to the younger man's back.

"Ow!"

"If you slip, try and grab hold of something on the way down," Stephen told him with a wicked smile.

"What, like Abby?"

She ignored him this time.

"Move out," Willoby said. He was looking upwards at Sergeant Fox, who was already twenty metres above them, pointing out the way. The sergeant was wearing their only surviving pair of crampons, and had belayed the rope around a large outcrop. He braced himself now with both feet, paying out the rope as the rest began to climb after him.

He gave the thumbs up, and the team began slowly to make their way up the cliff.

The pitch wasn't sheer, but angled at some sixty degrees. The most unnerving thing was the exposure. Even though they had only started off, the distance back down to the sea and the white breakers already seemed a terrifying height.

It was a different kind of fear, Cutter found. When his feet slipped, and his hands latched onto the icy, unforgiving rock, he felt that he was carrying his entire life in the grasp of his fingers. He had a rope running through the carabiner at his waist, but it seemed so frail and thin that the notion of it supporting his weight seemed laughable.

The only *good* thing was that the fear and the concentration kept his mind off the cold, the sleet that was blowing into his left ear and numbing that side of his face, the chafing of his salt-streaked clothes.

The team made three pitches, pausing at the end of each so the rope could be run up again and Fox could climb ahead to scout out the route.

Bristow scanned the rock face above them and spat out a curse. The burliest of all the team, he had the Minimi strapped to his back and seemed not to feel the cold. The melting sleet ran down his face unheeded.

"Path?" he said scornfully. "Path, my big fat hairy behind. There's never been any path here, boss, made by monks or anyone else."

"It's here in places," Willoby told him calmly. "Some of these rocks bear chisel marks. A thousand years is apt to change the geography a little, that's all. In summer, with a light day-sack on your back, you'd be racing up here, Joe, hardly breaking a sweat."

"If you say so, boss," Bristow replied, yet he seemed unconvinced. Digging into a pocket, he pulled out a Kendal mint cake and wolfed it down without offering anyone else a bite.

Connor was staring down at the drop below them, and he seemed transfixed.

"I don't think I've ever been so high in my life," he said.

"Well, you'll be higher before the end," Cutter said. "Hang in there, Connor. Think of all the lovely creatures awaiting you at the top."

"Actually, Professor, I've been trying not to dwell too much on that," Connor replied. "One step at a time, if you know what I mean."

"I know exactly what you mean," Cutter said, with feeling.

The climb continued.

The soldiers seemed to take it in their stride, and Stephen was almost as well conditioned as they were, but Cutter, Connor and Abby weren't quite in the same league, fitness-wise, and soon it became clear that they were slowing up the ascent. The team had to pause more often to let them catch their breath and ease the cramping muscles in their arms and legs.

Willoby ordered Farnsworth, Doody and Bristow to take their rucksacks, and, though Cutter protested somewhat feebly, once the weight had been lifted off his back, he felt more human, less of a labouring animal. They made better time after that, yet as they went higher, so they found that they weren't following a perpendicular pitch, but rather a path of least resistance around to the west. It made their progress easier, but lengthened the climb.

Before long the short winter daylight began to dim, and a great gloomy wrack of sodden cloud drifted over them. Eventually it lowered itself around them like fog, until they could see nothing but the back of the next person in line and the icy rock in front of their faces. Inside the cloud, the temperature plummeted, until even the exertions of the climb couldn't keep them from feeling the cold that ate at their marrow.

"This is no good," Willoby said during a brief rest break. "We need to make better time. If we're still on this cliff-face after dark, we won't make it, and that's flat."

The rest of them stared at him dully. Even the super-fit soldiers seemed exhausted.

"Head-torches on," Willoby said in his clipped, no-nonsense tone. "No more rest breaks unless someone collapses. We keep going now, right to the top. Sergeant Fox, lead on."

Cutter wanted to protest, but his mind was too fogged with fatigue and the penetrating cold. He had been eating chocolate bar after chocolate bar until his stomach rebelled, and now he felt the slack emptiness of the post-sugar rush. He knew Willoby was right, but still hated him a little for being so damned correct all the time.

The bastard really is perfect officer material.

They made it up another three pitches when snow began to fall round them. It didn't fall, really; it was thrown at their faces, and felt hard as gravel against their exposed skin. The wind picked up again, as well, adding insult to injury. They had moved too far west in their meandering climb, and were coming out of the shelter of the island's bulk. The northeast gale was still hammering in from the open Atlantic, and it felt as though the black rock beneath their hands and feet was a path leading into the heart of it.

Doggedly, stubbornly, they climbed on.

Ice collected on their faces and in their ears. They had to rub it off with their gloved hands every few minutes. Underfoot, the rock was treacherous and slick with ever-accumulating ice upon which the snow settled in clogged lines and folds, hiding the worst places.

Darkness fell, but Willoby wouldn't let them pause or even slow down. They worked by the lights of the head-torches, and their world contracted further, into that little beam of yellow light with the snow wheeling thickly through it.

Suddenly there was a cry — Abby's voice, shrill and terrified. Then a massive tug at Cutter's waist, jerking him off his feet. He went head over heels, struck his shoulder agonisingly on rock, followed by another concussive impact on the side of his face, hardly felt, then he was tumbling, falling free through the air, astonished, too astonished even to make a sound.

The harness caught his weight. He slammed to a halt in mid-air, the breath smashed out of his lungs, the nylon at his waist feeling as though it were about to cut him in two.

Warm liquid trickled down one cheekbone, and that side of his face felt numb. He moved his head and the beam of the head-torch caught Abby's white face. She was dangling below him, six feet away.

The pair of them were hanging free only for a split second; then they swung in and hit the rock with a jarring thump that set the lights reeling in Cutter's head again.

"Abby," he called, and he reached out his hand. He could hear the others shouting, but they were invisible beyond the curtain of the whirling snow.

She was unconscious, a small slug of blood oozing from one nostril. Cutter cursed madly, and swung on the rope, trying to reach her with a gloved fist.

"Stay bloody still!" Willoby's voice came out of the snow. "Cutter, Abby, try and get a foothold on the rocks."

"She's unconscious!" Cutter yelled back, his dry mouth cracking the words.

"Don't move then — we'll try and haul you back up."

Hanging as limply as a sack, Cutter felt a momentary pang of gratitude that he couldn't see the drop below him.

"Abby," he said quietly. "Abby, lass, wake up."

She stirred, groaning in pain as the climbing harness bit into her. She was hanging almost upside-down, and the blood oozing from her nose had begun to slide in a thick line up her face, into the socket of one eye.

"Jesus, Abby," Cutter whispered.

He could hear the rest of the team grunting, like slaves hauling on an oar. He rose one foot, two, then a yard. Below him, Abby swung, limp as a drowned kitten.

"We've got you, Nick. Give me your hand." It was Stephen. He took Cutter's arm at the wrist and hauled him inwards to the rocks. Other hands grabbed him.

"Thank you," he murmured shakily in Stephen's ear.

Abby's eyelids were flickering as they pulled her back up. Connor crouched beside her and wiped the blood from her face. His eyes were glittering with tears.

"Make room there, son," Willoby said with unusual gentleness. He grasped Connor by the shoulders and set him to one side. "Bristow, keep an eye on him. Doody, get over here and bring your kit."

Doody, the medic, scrambled towards them.

The soldiers were belaying slack lengths of rope about the nearest rocks, securing the team to the cliff-face. The snow blew steadily in their eyes, and the wind had picked up into a roar, as bad as it had been back on the trawler — perhaps worse, for now they were unbelievably exposed to it, clinging to ice and rock hundreds of feet above the Atlantic.

Doody peeled back one of Abby's eyelids and shone a pen light at her pupil. She screwed her eyes shut and tried to bat his hand away. He grinned.

"She's coming round. Might have a slight concussion." He was feeling her head, his black fingers pressing in on Abby's platinum blonde bob.

"No fractures I think — a bit of a bump, that's all."

"I'm all right," Abby said. She sounded drunk.

"How many fingers am I holding up?" Doody asked her.

"Three — ow! My head hurts."

"Doody, when you're done with her, check Cutter," Willoby said. "Sergeant Fox!"

A head-torch bobbed in the darkness above. "Yes, boss?"

"How far is there to go?"

A pause.

"I think we've about cracked it, boss. Can't be any more than four or five more pitches."

Willoby bent over Abby. He fished a thick bar of chocolate out of his pocket.

"Eat this," he said.

"No, I couldn't, not right now."

"Eat it; you need the energy. And if you throw it up again, you'll know you've got concussion." As she bit into the chocolate he grinned, and touched her arm. "Good girl."

"Good girl," Abby parroted angrily as he turned from her to Cutter. "What does he think I am, his pet Retriever?"

"What happened?" Connor asked her. He was wiping his eyes and sniffing mightily.

"I don't know. My foot just went out from under me. God, Connor, I'm so tired."

"Me too," he said. "I'm starting to think this cliff goes on forever."

Once Doody had finished examining Cutter, they started off again. The medic had stuck some butterfly stitches on his head wound, but as they continued to climb, Cutter found it was his shoulder that was troubling him most. He began to favour that arm, and his other grew weaker as it took more of his weight.

I can't keep this up much longer, he thought. He looked up and down the line, at times barely able to make out the figures in the blowing snow. The soldiers were climbing steadily, but the spring had gone out of their movements. In the light of the head-torches they moved now like weary old men, or miners after a long day's toil at the coalface. Cutter felt a pang of guilt as he saw how his team's gear weighed them down, but none of them uttered any complaint.

He clenched his teeth and climbed on.

Time passed with little talk out of any of them. There was only the stone underneath their hands and boots, the rope tugging at their waists, the dimming glow of the torches, and the incessant howling of the wind. *Climbers*, Cutter thought with grim satisfaction, *have it worse even than fishermen. What loon would do this kind of thing for fun?*

There was a cry up above, and it was Fox's voice. Cutter couldn't make out the words, but they were passed down the line.

"He's at the top. We're nearly there."

Strangely, the words did not buck him up or flood him with new energy. If anything, they took away his last reserves of strength. *When we get to the top*, he thought, *this thing is only starting. God knows what we'll find up there.*

"All bad things come to an end," Fox said as Cutter reached him.

The man could still grin. Cutter didn't know what he was made of, but it was pretty stern stuff. "Up you come Professor. We're at the top. Come along now." Then to Abby. "Come on miss — give me your hand. Head over to the boss there. We need to get the tents up ASAP."

Cutter found that he could stand upright, and there were tufts of grass underfoot, feeling somehow strange beneath his boots after the unrelenting stone of the climb. He unclipped his harness from the line, looked back to see Abby and Connor supporting each other over the lip of the cliff, and limped slowly over to Willoby. The SAS officer had thrown off his Bergen, webbing and rifle and was hunting through the big rucksack like a man possessed.

"We need shelter," he said brusquely. The light of his head-torch was now a yellow, fitful beam through which the snow whipped manically before disappearing.

"We don't know what's up here," Cutter said.

"It doesn't matter. If we don't get ourselves out of this blizzard, we're going to start losing people. Wake up, Cutter; we're not out of the woods yet. Doody — is that you? Lend a hand here. Get the bloody tents up. Bristow, Farnsworth, help him. Sergeant Fox, I want a head count and a kit-check."

"Yes, sir," Fox responded.

They fought the tent upright in the bitter wind. Four of them had to sit on the corners to stop it blowing away. Then Willoby slid the aluminium poles through the fly-sheet and the thing rose, forming a black dome. They pegged it down and set large stones on the pegs.

To one side, Stephen, Connor and Watts were fighting to do the same. Cutter gave them a hand, his shoulder now an eye-watering throb of pain which seemed to go all the way down his spine.

"Everybody inside," Willoby said when the two tents were up. "Get as much of the gear in as you can."

"What about stag duty, sir?" Bristow asked.

"The hell with it. Nothing is going to wander about in this storm. I want everyone sheltered, sleeping bags out, and if you can, get a brew on." He hesitated. "Cutter."

Cutter was standing staring out into the darkness of the howling night, in a world of his own it seemed.

"Cutter."

"Look, Willoby," Cutter said. And he pointed.

Willoby followed his gloved finger. Off in the darkness there was a light — no, two lights. Or were there three?

It was hard to tell.

"What in the world?" Willoby asked. "Is someone here ahead of us?"

Cutter shook his head. "Not someone, something. Those are open anomalies, Captain."

They stood side by side as behind them the rest of the team crammed themselves into the bucking, thrashing domes of the two tents, and all around them the storm raged without pity.

"Doors to another era," Cutter said, "lying wide open."

Willoby snicked off the safety of his M-4, and then back on again.

"We'll have to chance to luck tonight," he said. "Whatever is here, whatever is out in that darkness, we'll just have to hope it hates the cold as much as we do. The storm will cover us, sight, sound and smell. We have to wait for daylight."

Cutter nodded.

"All right then." He ground his chattering teeth together, and tried not to let the fear show on his face.

ELEVEN

The *Aoife* had begun life as a large British minesweeper. Built on the Clyde in the late sixties, she was near the end of her useful life. The Irish had refitted her, added a helipad to her fantail, and now used her for fisheries protection and enforcement, a last vestige of what might be called gunboat diplomacy.

Jenny stood on her rather Spartan bridge along with her captain, Robert Harney, and a crowd of anonymous ratings who manned the wheel, the sonar and whatever sundry other bits of equipment a small warship needed people to look after. Jenny had passed through her seasickness in the first few hours, of which she was rather proud, and now she stood looking out at the awesome power of the great Atlantic swells as they came barrelling in from America and Iceland to smash against the bow of the ship and half-bury her in foam and green water.

She was, frankly, terrified, but everyone else seemed to take the majesty of the storm as a matter of course, and so she stood holding onto a railing, pretending to be interested in what was going on, her face a wax mask of calm. *Keeping the British end up and all that*, she mused ruefully.

Harney was a tall, lean man with a face that looked as though it had spent years looking into the wind. He was old enough to be her father, but still possessed a roguish handsomeness. *Something like a thin Sean Connery*, she thought. From what she had overheard, he had been ordered out to sea at a moment's notice, his crew's shore leave cancelled, and yet he didn't seem to mind. Several seamen left on shore, such was their haste to cast off, and then this unknown female passenger foisted upon him, along with a small team of his country's best soldiers.

Perhaps it made a change from chasing Spanish trawlers, or whatever it was he usually did out here in this God-awful place, she pondered silently. Perhaps he was just a philosophical man who took it all in his stride. Sailors often were — Jenny had chanced across a few in her dealings with Whitehall, and always found them to be less touchy and macho than soldiers.

Maybe the sea keeps them humble, she thought, looking out at the chaotic wilderness of water before her.

"There'll be no getting the chopper up, not in this, Ms Lewis," Harney said.

"We have to land, Captain. My department have heard nothing from the people on the island for well over twenty-four hours."

"They actually climbed up those cliffs?"

"That was the plan, yes."

"Fair play to them. But I'll tell you now, miss, if this storm doesn't moderate some in the next few hours, then you'll be doing the same."

The thought chilled Jenny. She could ride a horse, swim and shoot a clay pigeon out of the sky with a fair degree of competence, but mountaineering had never been one of her interests. She clicked her heel on the steel deck of the bridge impatiently.

Harney saw the gesture, and smiled.

"You might also think about getting changed. I've not yet seen a lady climb into a helicopter in stilettos. My QM will be happy to sort you out with appropriate clothing."

Jenny nodded. She disliked uniforms intensely, a legacy of school, but Harney was simply stating the obvious.

There's no way I'm climbing up that bloody cliff, she thought. *Lunatics like Cutter may consider it an option, but I do not.*

She went below to a tiny, grey-walled cupboard that sailors laughingly called a cabin, and found that a neat set of clothing and equipment had been set beside her holdall on the bed. She opened the holdall at once and went through it, but everything seemed in order. Lester had given her a satellite phone, a laptop, a GPS and an automatic pistol — a Glock 9mm. *How thoughtful of him*, she reflected dryly. *He really does know the way to a girl's heart.*

She had been around soldiers long enough to know how to make certain the weapon was made safe, with no round up the spout. She closed the door to her cabin, set a chair against it — none of the doors had locks — and quickly set up the sat-phone. She dialled Lester's mobile and waited, sitting on the edge of the bed and fingering the fabric of the uniform they had left out for her.

"James Lester." The voice came through, crisp and clear.

"James, it's Jenny."

"One moment."

There was a silence; from the sound of it, he had placed his hand over the phone. When he spoke again his voice was lower.

"Well?"

"We're a few hours out from the island. Still no word from Cutter and the team. If the storm doesn't let up, then there's no way to make a landing."

"But a landing must be made, all the same." Lester's voice was calm, controlled, but cold as the winter sea. "It may be that Cutter and his people are incapacitated, or that they got their sat-phone eaten by a Brontosaurus. I don't care. If the Irish set foot on Guns Island, you must be there with them. Is that clear?"

There was a small silence.

"Perfectly," Jenny said, her voice almost as cold as his had been.

"Good. I'm rather glad you called, actually. There have been a few more developments at this end."

"Where are you?" she asked, trying to keep the irritation out of her voice.

"In Brussels, brushing up on my *Français*. The corridors of the EU are not to be navigated lightly. I think that, if you have a moment, you might discreetly inform the Captain of your cockleshell that the French are on their way."

"What?"

"A French frigate, *La Gloire*, is preparing for the journey to Guns Island even as we speak. So far, I've been able to dissuade them from making a landing, but they intend to make their presence felt. Here, they're talking about setting up a maritime exclusion zone."

"But that's awful!" Jenny gasped. The implications were clear. "It'll be splashed all over the newspapers."

"Perhaps, perhaps not. I think it may actually be for the best. If the French are busy strutting the high seas, they may be too pre-occupied to think about what's really going on right under their noses." Lester cleared his throat, and lowered his voice a trifle more. "I've been authorised to use the bioweapons story as a smoke screen for the anomalies."

"But it's not true, is it? That was just a rumour."

To her surprise, there was a moment of silence on the line.

"You could say that's the beauty of it. In fact, it *is* true, completely true. That's why Captain Willoby got the job of accompanying Cutter."

"What do you mean?" Jenny demanded. She stuck her finger in her free ear to cut out the rumblings of the ship around her.

"There's a bunker on the island with biological materials still stored within. It's sealed in concrete, and the materials are probably dust after fifty years, but Willoby's prime mission is to make sure that bunker is secure. And to keep Cutter and the others alive, of course."

Jenny blinked, taking in this information, slotting it into her map of things.

"Who knows this, James?"

"The Irish, the French, the whole kit and caboodle. It is, as of this moment, our official line. Ironically enough, the only person who doesn't know it by now is Cutter."

"I'll have to tell him."

Lester sighed. "Of course you will."

"The whole thing has blown up in our faces," Jenny said with a sigh.

"It has, rather," Lester drawled. "From here on in, we will have to be content with keeping dinosaurs off the front page. That is the mission, Jenny. Do I make myself clear?"

"Once again, James, yes."

"If the balloon goes up on this one, then we'll both be standing outside King's Cross with begging bowls for the rest of our professional lives. Everything rides on your ability to keep this thing under wraps."

"People's lives are also on the line, James."

"Those are the risks that come with the job," he replied; then he paused. "Look, I have to go. I want regular reports. Use this line, and let me know the moment you set foot on the island."

"I can't hope to conceal the creatures from the Irish team," Jenny said quickly. "It's a small island, after all."

"Do your best. And do try not to get yourself killed."

With that last note of compassion, the line clicked off. Jenny frowned, checked the battery indicator, and then slowly began changing into the camouflaged uniform that had been set out for her. She lurched from one side of the tiny cabin to the other as the *Aoife* continued its battle with the Atlantic.

"There's a window," Captain Harney said. He straightened from his perusal of the meteorological data. "We've almost passed through one arm of the storm, and there's going to be a lull of sorts — no telling how long it will last, but it should be enough to get the heli out to the island and back. It'll take two trips to get the entire team out there."

Jenny stood in her ill-fitting, uncomfortable new wardrobe and cast her eyes over the rest of the "team". They were all crowded on the bridge: four soldiers, two pilots, and one older man with the longer hair and pastier features of a civilian. There had been no introductions. She was being tolerated here, but certainly not welcomed.

The older man looked her up and down. He had the same closed set to his face that she knew well from Lester, a kind of cold arrogance. *Bureaucrats the world over*, she thought, *they're all the same*.

"Very well, Captain," the bureaucrat said. "Make it so. My team will be ready to fly out within ten minutes." Signalling to the soldiers, he left the bridge without another word, and they trooped after him like so many robots.

"What a lovely, warm chap," Jenny said. The Captain laughed.

"Civil servants," he responded, "they think the world begins and ends with them." At Jenny's wry look, he coughed and added, "Well, most of them, at any rate."

Two young men in flying suits had remained on the bridge, and Jenny approached them.

"I don't believe we've met," she said sweetly, extending a hand.

"Lieutenant Sean Brice," said the first, who appeared to be somewhat dazzled by Jenny's smile. "Irish Army Air Corps. I'm your pilot for today. This is Sergeant Les Mullan, my copilot." Brice was a young, blond-haired slight fellow, and Mullan a stocky, no-nonsense NCO type with a black crew cut and shrewd eyes.

"You're happy about going up in this weather, Lieutenant?" she asked.

"If the Captain says it's okay to fly, then it's okay to fly."

"Excellent. Could I ask you both a tiny favour perhaps?" She flashed another smile.

The two pilots looked at her, noncommittal, though she was certain Brice had reddened perceptibly, and she thought he looked worried. Mullan remained stoic.

"Do you think I could be on the first flight? I have friends on the ground out there, you know, and I've been so worried..."

Brice grinned, relieved.

"I don't see a problem with that," he said. "None at all."

The helicopter was an elderly Westland Scout. Jenny clambered into the back with a knot of cold fear tightening in her stomach. The ship was still pitching up and down under them, and the airframe of the tiny craft seemed to bend and rattle with every gust of wind. It seemed frail beyond belief, and when a burly soldier clambered in beside her, she felt a sense of claustrophobic panic.

The soldier rested the muzzle of his rifle, an Austrian Steyr, on the floor, and nodded at her.

"John McCann," he said, in a low West-Cork brogue. He had two red zig-zags on his bicep, the mark of a corporal. He looked more like a farmer, with a big, red face and massive hands. Jenny's throat had closed up, so she just smiled at him.

The turbine above their head started up, quickly building to a deafening whine. Mullan, the copilot, leaned back and pointed at Jenny's head. She understood, and unclipped a spare set of headphones that was hanging on the bulkhead, setting them over her ears. At once, some of the noise was cut off, and she could hear the quiet, professional murmurs of the pilots in front of her. Their calm and competence was reassuring.

She looked out of the square Perspex window and saw fifteen feet away the bureaucrat and the rest of his team staring at her from the side of the helipad. The man looked furious. She had beaten him to the punch. Jenny smiled at him, and chanced a small wave, which he did not return.

Sore loser.

Of course, she would have to work on him once they were all on the island. It was a task she didn't much look forward to. He looked like an uphill struggle.

"Tango two zero, you are cleared for take off." The voice crackled in her ears.

"Zero, roger that, lifting off now."

The Scout rose into the air, and was immediately shunted sideways by a great gale of sodden air. Jenny yelped despite herself, and gripped the thigh of the soldier who sat next to her. He began to smile like a red-faced Cheshire Cat.

"Haven't flown before?" he asked kindly.

"Not in one of these." She closed her eyes for a moment as the helicopter rose and was shaken by the wind as though it were a rat in the jaws of a terrier.

"Good God! I thought we were supposed to be in a lull of the storm," she said with alarm.

"This *is* a lull," McCann said. "If it weren't, we'd be halfway to France five minutes after take-off." He grinned, and seemed to be enjoying her discomfiture.

They rose above the ship, the Scout shaking and shuddering every foot of the way. Even McCann's face lost some of its florid colour as they were bludgeoned up and down in the sky.

"1200 feet," Brice's voice said up front. "Cloud ceiling 1500. Course one-two-five, speed eighty-five knots."

"Roger that," Mullan said beside him. Even seated in the rear of the little aircraft, Jenny could see the strain in both their shoulders, and noted their constant adjustments of the controls.

A short time later, they spoke again.

"Guns Island, dead ahead. Dropping down."

"Roger that. 800 feet. Two miles out. Airspeed ninety-two knots."

The helicopter descended, until the monstrous waves below seemed almost close enough to touch. But it was calmer down here, she noticed gratefully, in the lee of the island.

I'll never enjoy a fairground ride again, Jenny thought. She lifted her hand from McCann's leg. It felt cramped and sore. He rubbed his thigh.

"That's some grip you have on you!" he commented wryly.

She said nothing, her full attention taken up now with the spectacle of the black mountain. It seemed as if they were hurtling directly toward it. For a moment, she thought of Cutter and the others with real pity — they had climbed those cliffs, or had tried to.

My God, it must have been horrendous. She wouldn't let herself dwell on the other possibility; that they had not made it to the top at all.

"Two minutes." Brice's voice sounded in her ear. "Bringing her up now."

"1200, 1300, 1400," Mullan intoned.

"Coming up on the south side," the pilot told them.

They cleared the cliffs, and at once the wind hammered into them again. The pilot swore, and lifted the collective, his feet see-sawing on the pedals. "Jesus, that's some updraft. Help me hold her, Les." The airframe shook and rattled and the turbine roar above their heads intensified as the rotors fought the wind.

"Bring her up, *bring her up!*" the copilot yelled.

"I've got her, I've got her. Damn, no."

The helicopter tilted almost on its side, throwing Jenny against her seat belt, leaving her hanging in the air. McCann's rifle slipped out of his hand and clattered to the floor of the aircraft, then banged against the port-side door.

"Christ, Sean, get her nose up!" the copilot yelled, raw fear in his voice now.

The Scout wheeled across the sky like a swatted fly. Jenny saw the sere, snow-scattered ground below come zooming at her window.

She screamed.

TWELVE

Connor lay and looked up at the ceiling of the tent. All about him, the sound of the wind was a relentless roar, and the tent was thrashed by it, beaten back and forth until the poles that supported it creaked and groaned.

There was a grey light in the air, an almost-dawn. He was wet through, but warm. On one side of him the army medic, Doody, snored softly, and on the other Abby lay frowning in sleep, a tiny crust of dried blood flaking off her cheek. There were five of them in the tent, all told, and they lay on their karrimats in a few millimetres of water, with the sleeping bags unzipped and piled over them. Like a litter of puppies, curled up together.

Puppies! Yeah, right. Connor found himself smiling at the image. Then he looked at Abby again, and swallowed. For a few seconds last night, he had thought her gone, and the pain of those moments was still with him.

Unwilling to revisit the memory, he eased himself out from under the sleeping bags, and immediately felt colder. He still had his boots on, and within them his feet felt like wrinkled prunes. He found it hard to remember the last time they had been dry.

He clambered over his companions as gently and quietly as he could and unzipped the front of the tent. At once, the wind caught the tent flap and set it rippling and snapping. He poked his head out into wrist-deep snow, amid a cloud of the powdery stuff. It was colder, much colder than it had been the night before, and the snow was blowing like smoke across the ground, collecting in hummocks and mounds where the grass grew in tufts. But he preferred the snow to the rain.

God, he hated getting wet.

He peered back into the semi-darkness of the tent. Everyone was still asleep, even the soldiers. Their faces looked blue-grey in the early light of the predawn. One of them, Farnsworth, had slept with his pistol to hand — a Browning 9mm. Connor looked at it, then, stifling a shiver, he gently took the weapon, and crawled all the way out of the tent. He zipped closed the flap after him, and straightened, groaning as his damp limbs eased out their kinks. *This is what it'll be like to be old*, he thought.

He hobbled away from the tents with the pistol in one hand, rather proud of himself for his acquisition. Then he put his back to the wind and whistled soundlessly as he answered nature's call. When he was finished, he hopped up and down on the spot, trying to generate some warmth.

The cloud was so low he felt as if he could stand up on his toes and touch it. It had stopped snowing, he realised, but snow was tumbling across the top of the island in white powdery sheets. Looking north, he could see a couple of hundred metres before the cloud and snow blotted out the further horizon. The plateau which was the top of the island was broken up in furrowed stone gullies and crags. Where there was shelter, yellow grass grew in clumps, but nothing taller than that.

The place felt like a hostile, alien planet. *Like Mars*, he thought. *Mars is cold. But it's red, too.* This place felt like a wilderness at the end of the world.

He walked forward, away from the tents. Looking back at them he saw that the snow had piled up on their windward sides. Their dark colouring stood out against the colourless landscape. A shiver ran through him.

I could really go for a hot cup of coffee, he thought.

He stumbled, not looking where he was going, and tripped headlong into a small gully, a mere gash in the skin of the island. Braced to impact against hard rock, he landed instead on something yielding, something so utterly unexpected that it took his breath away. He stumbled to his feet as fast as he could, pointing the pistol.

A low groan filled the air, a great bass noise that Connor felt vibrate in his own flesh. There was a cloud of steam, and a stale, sickening smell, like mouldy grass. Connor backed away slowly, eyes wide. He opened his mouth, but nothing came out, and it closed again, as though he were a fish gasping for air.

"Iguanodon," Cutter's voice said behind him, and Connor spun in panicked surprise, still waving the pistol in front of him. "Put that thing down before you hurt yourself, or me," Cutter said, then he turned his attention back to their discovery.

"God in heaven, an Iguanodon. See the thumb-spike? It's a young one, hardly five, six metres long. Quite a find, Connor."

Cutter was standing with an M-4 held loosely by the stock, staring down. The animal had fallen into the sheer-sided gully and broken at least one of its legs. It was dark brown, with white stripes along its spine. Its eye flicked back at them sluggishly, and it raised its head a fraction, then fell back again. There was ice glistening upon its lower limbs, and one hind leg was bent at a horrible angle.

The animal moaned again, a deep mournful sound.

"It's been here a while; it's just about had it," Cutter said, his voice changed now. "Must have stumbled there in the dark." He walked around the beast, examining the ground. He bent and wiped snow away from the grass with his hand. "There was more than one; this is all torn up over here."

"It's in pain," Connor said, staring in awed fascination at the great, broken beast.

"I know," Cutter said. He brought the carbine up to his shoulder, clicked off the safety, and fired.

The crack was obscenely loud, but the wind seemed to bear it away almost at once. A glistening black hole appeared behind the creature's eye, and the head quivered, then flopped down. The massive ribs moved in and out for a few moments more, and then were still.

"Professor," Connor said, "was there no other way —"

"This is what we're here for," Cutter said, his eyes dark and unreachable. "This is what we're here to do." He turned around and began walking back to the tents. Already, people were piling out of them, the gunshot having roused them, the soldiers scrambling to their feet.

"God forgive us," Cutter said, "it's what we've always been good at."

Willoby charged up, his voice angry.

"I'll thank you to give me my weapon back," he said bluntly. "What the hell's going on, Cutter?"

"Iguanodon with a broken leg," Connor said breathlessly. "Cutter killed it."

"Sergeant Fox," Willoby said loudly, "take Bristow and check it out."

"Right boss." The two soldiers ran past Cutter, their eyes wide.

"The Iguanodon is Early Cretaceous," Cutter was saying as Connor trotted alongside him, but the Liopleurodon is Jurassic —"

"Late Jurassic," Connor said. "Could be there's an overlap. It's not impossible."

"So you think they could both be from the same period."

"It's possible, isn't it?" Connor had forgotten about the cold, the wind, the snow and his wet clothes.

"I suppose, though I think it's much more likely that we're talking two different eras here." Cutter halted in his tracks and looked back at the snow-swept blankness of the northern horizon. "I saw three anomalies last night, in the distance, before we turned in. They're probably gone by now. But were they all linked to the same epoch or are we talking two or three different eras? That's the question."

"Cretaceous," Connor said, eyes shining in his pinched face as he imagined the legions of other creatures he might encounter. The very thought thrilled him in ways he couldn't express.

Cutter stared at him.

"Be careful what you wish for, Connor," he said quietly.

The team reassembled at the tents. They were a sorry looking bunch, wearing wet clothes that were now freezing on their backs, and most sporting some kind of gash or bruise. Connor handed Farnsworth back his pistol with a sheepish grin.

"Had to pee — thought I'd take some, you know, protection." The soldier's expression was hard.

"Wake me up next time; I'll make sure nature's wonders don't get a look at your tender spot," he snapped.

Beside him, Doody smothered a laugh.

***

"Set up camp," Willoby said, addressing the group. "Fox, I want this place squared away within the hour, all three surviving tents up and secured against this bloody wind. I want everyone to change their socks and put on whatever we have in the way of dry clothing. Look after your feet, people, and don't stand around in the cold while you're wet. Bristow, make a brew for us all. Watts, check out the comms situation. I want a sitrep on range and batteries.

"Doody, check everyone over for frostnip, trench foot, aches and pains. You know the drill. I want to know the ammo and food situation down to the last round and biscuit. Come on people, you're not on your own time any more; we're at work now. Cutter, a word in private, if you please."

Willoby led Cutter away from the campsite. They stood looking down on the Iguanodon carcass.

"We stick together, from here on in," Willoby said with quiet savagery. "No more bloody bimbling off. We've no idea what's wandering around this island, or what's going to pop out next from those anomalies of yours. Is that clear, Cutter?"

Cutter raised his hood against the wind.

"Captain, you almost sound as though you're giving me orders."

"Your people have to utilise a bit of common sense," Willoby said. "We don't let each other leave the camp alone from now on. I say again, *is that clear?*"

They peered at each other for a moment, then Cutter nodded.

"Fair enough. I have one order of my own though."

"What's that?"

"These creatures have nervous systems quite unlike our own. Some of them, you shoot them in the head and they'll not know they're dead for another ten minutes, and by that time you're just jam in the grass. No one opens fire until I okay it, Willoby. Are we agreed?"

Willoby nodded.

"All right. That's your field, and so it's your call."

With remarkable swiftness, the campsite was transformed from the squalid mess of the night before into a well-regulated and seemingly shipshape establishment.

The three tents were set up properly, their edges weighed down with lichen-covered stones to prevent the vicious wind from carrying them away. The gear was unpacked and a line of wet socks was soon knotted to a length of paracord and suspended from a nearby crag. Some of the soldiers preferred to wear their wet footgear around their necks to dry them.

The team hunted out what remained of their rations, and behind a stone-built windbreak they prepared the first hot food they had tasted in days, holding their hands up to the guttering blue flames of the little gas burners to feel the warmth. Snow was gathered up and melted for drinking water, though according to Cutter's map there was an old well on the island, built into the abandoned military post on the north side.

Cutter's first instinct had been to pack up the tents and make for it at once, but, on reflection, he found himself agreeing with Willoby's more cautious approach. The anomalies Cutter had seen gleaming in the dark the night before had all been in that direction, and it was better to recce the area out before going charging up there with all their gear packed on their backs and who knew what awaiting them.

"This will be our base of operations for now," Cutter said as the team gathered around him behind their stone windbreak. "As soon as we've organised ourselves, Captain Willoby, Bristow and I will head north, to check out the lie of the land and see what other creatures are roaming around. Stephen, you're in charge while we're gone."

Stephen nodded.

"Connor, you and Abby do your level best to get the hand-held detector working again. This is a relatively small area we're working with, but it would still be useful to know when the anomalies are up and running."

Cutter paused. "Abby, are you listening to me?"

She stood with her head cocked to one side, her blonde hair plastered over her bruised forehead, and her hood around her shoulders.

"Cutter, do you hear that?"

"What, the wind?"

"No, something else. I'm sure I —" Then she shouted, "Quiet! Quiet everybody!"

The entire team froze at the tone of her voice.

"I hear it," Watts, the signaller said. "Boss, it sounds like a heli."

All their senses straining, they rose to their feet, listening intently, trying to filter out the ever-present roar of the wind.

"It's coming from the south," Willoby said at last. "A helicopter, by God."

"It's a brave man flies in this," Stephen murmured. "Or a stupid one." He whipped out his binoculars and stepped away from the group to scan the leaden sky. "Can't see a thing." But the noise was becoming louder minute by minute.

Then it erupted into view over the edge of the cliff, a small, grey-painted aircraft with an Irish tricolour on its tail boom. It swung round in the sky above them and soared past, the wind turning it around in the air so that one moment they were facing the cockpit, and the next the tail rotor.

"He's too low!" Doody shouted.

The pilot must have been fighting for control, but the aircraft simply wasn't powerful enough to fight the massive blast of the northeasterly that was racing across the plateau.

"Come on, come on man." Cutter found himself muttering through clenched teeth. "Get her down — just set her down."

"Oh, no," Abby mouthed.

The helicopter reared up one final time, was slammed sideways by the storm and came down again tail first. It disappeared over a ridge. They heard the crash, sharp and loud, and then there was only the sound of the wind again.

The team stood frozen, disbelieving.

Willoby collected himself first.

"Doody, get the medkit. Bristow, Minimi. Farnsworth, you're with us. Fox, you and Watts stay here. Try the comms; that heli was Navy, it must be from a ship nearby. They may be able to read our signal. Let's get to it, people."

Cutter and Stephen joined the group that set out for the north, and the six of them set a fearsome pace as they made a beeline for the crash-site. Stephen had brought his sniper rifle, but Cutter was armed only with a pistol. None of them wanted to think too hard about what they might find in the downed helicopter.

***

Jenny's eyes were gummed shut. She tried to raise her hands to rub them, but only one would move. She prised open her eyelids, wincing as whatever had glued them shut took a few eyelashes out at the roots.

She could hear metal ticking, and the wind rattling something loose, a metallic banging sound. The quiet was eerie after the roar of the turbine. She couldn't quite recall what had happened. Part of her wanted to close her eyes again.

"Hello?" she said.

A moan answered her. There was a body lying limp across her legs, warm and heavy. She could not move.

Memory flooded back, and with it came panic. It was blood on her face; her palm was red with it. So much blood — how bad was it? She touched her matted hair. Blood was oozing out of it.

McCann was unconscious in her lap, and the entire helicopter was lying on its side. They were at an awkward angle, but at least she wasn't hanging in mid-air, as she had been when she lost consciousness. One door had been smashed off above her, and with a turn of her head she was looking up at the snarling, blank curtain of the sky.

So much for the lull in the storm.

"Hello?" she said again. "Lieutenant Brice?"

No answer. She could see the two men in front, hanging limp in their seats with their helmets lolling to one side. They looked like discarded dolls.

Don't panic — think about this. How to get out. She could smell aviation fuel all around her, and it was the terrified thought of it catching fire that finally galvanised her into movement.

She shoved McCann's body away from her legs, gasping as the seat belt cut into her side. Some ribs cracked there. As a child, her pony had thrown her, and the pain had been the same.

Not serious, she told herself. *Concentrate.*

She freed the belt buckle that anchored her in place and at once slid down to what was now the bottom of the aircraft. It had once been the starboard door. The pain forced a cry out of her, and brought tears to her eyes.

Angry now, she twisted in the shattered confines of the aircraft and then had to stop, as her brain was fogging up again. Blood was dripping in coin-sized drops onto her hands. When she shook her head to clear it the drops spattered over the interior of the helicopter, as if she had shaken a scarlet-dipped paintbrush.

The sight of it made her stomach twist.

She stood up. From the front seats there came a moan, a stirring.

"Brice?" she said. No answer. But at least someone else was alive. She had to get out — she was going to be sick. She started to climb up toward the doorless side of the aircraft above her.

Something struck the side of the broken helicopter with a metallic bang. She froze.

Again, a crash on her left, towards the tail-boom, and then a scoring sound, as though something sharp were being trailed down the skin of the aircraft.

Jenny froze.

"Cutter?" she whispered.

There was a low grunting noise outside, a snuffling, and then a series of sharp, loud barks, like those of a seal. Jenny shrank down into the well of the helicopter, trying to make herself small. Her hands went out by themselves, searching over McCann's body. He had a pistol strapped to his thigh, but was lying on top of it. She tried to lift up his limp body. The pain in her ribs exploded, as though fireworks had gone off in her head.

An exclamation escaped her lips, a sharp cry. Covering her mouth, she listened silently.

A moment later the carcass of the aircraft shuddered as something heavy climbed up it. The whole airframe tilted, and there was the unmistakable sound of claws scrabbling on aluminium. McCann shifted, allowing Jenny to find the grip of his pistol, and she began to tug frantically on it.

The light was cut off above her. She raised her head slowly, and looked up.

A head was framed in the opening above, a long snout with yellow, gleaming eyes and lines of teeth. The snout alone was big, a yard long perhaps. She felt the exhalation of the creature's breath, a carrion stench. The breath curled around her in a foul, steaming fog.

Her fingers slipped off the pistol grip.

The thing barked at her, a dry, piercing series of sounds which were caught inside the aircraft and hurt her ears. She could smell the blood on herself, all around her. But she could not move.

The creature opened its maw and tensed. It seemed as though it was about to launch itself right into the wrecked aircraft. She could see its claws now, braced on the doorframe. Her hands fluttered wildly, and she couldn't even scream, for the terror had turned all of her muscles to water.

Just before it leapt, something dark spat out of its head, and the great snout was jerked to one side. A fine spray of blood had exploded from near the top of its skull. The creature was unbalanced for an instant, and Jenny was able to see with perfect clarity one of the great luminous yellow eyes as it flooded dark. Then it half jumped and half toppled off the helicopter with a thin screech.

All this happened in half a second, and in that half second, Jenny distinctly heard the crack of a gunshot, catching up with the supersonic bullet that had preceded it. She fell, and lay back on top of McCann's body, feeling cold and sick, the nausea so powerful that she didn't even feel relief at her deliverance.

Minutes passed, and she heard voices outside, then feet in the crunching snow. She cleared her throat.

"In here! Help us!" The reek of blood and aviation fuel became too much for her, and she vomited into her lap.

"The copilot is dead," Willoby told Cutter. "The pilot is coming round, and the other passenger seems in decent shape. They're pretty banged up, but they'll make it."

Cutter was kneeling beside Jenny as Doody stitched shut the gaping scalp wound that ran behind her ear. Her face was white as marble except where the blood streaked it, and her hands were clenched into tight fists. Cutter touched one, his face dark and unreadable.

"Cutter," Willoby said patiently, "what was that?"

It was Stephen who answered. He still had his sniper rifle held up to his shoulder and was scanning the crags which bounded the horizon with the patient intent of a born hunter.

"A Theropod," he said. "I saw its forearms as it took off."

Cutter rose, collecting himself.

"A big one, with long forearms. An Eotyrannus maybe, they were a known predator of Iguanodon." He smiled bleakly. "Connor will be mad as hell to have missed it."

"That bloody thing was twenty-feet long if it was an inch," Doody said, still stitching.

"I'm fairly sure it's a pack hunter," Cutter explained. "Where there's one, it's likely there's others. We have to get back to the camp as quickly as possible. All this blood will draw them, if they're out there."

Willoby swore. He looked the wreckage of the helicopter up and down. They had dragged the occupants some fifty metres away, wary of anything that might set off the fuel that saturated the area around the wreck.

"Six of us, and three wounded to carry, plus one body. Can't be done in one trip. We take the living and leave the dead."

Joe Bristow, his shaven head bristling, said, "You can't do that boss. That big ugly bastard will come back and eat him." He was looking at Les Mullan's corpse. The copilot's neck had been broken, his lower limbs shattered, but his face was almost untouched. It stared peacefully up at the sky, a waxen mask.

"No choice, Joe," Willoby said quietly. "Break out your ponchos lads. We'll carry them —"

"No," Jenny said clearly. Her eyes had opened.

"Jenny!" Cutter exclaimed, and he knelt down beside her again. She smiled at him.

"Glad to see you made it, Cutter," she said. Then in a more determined voice, "I can walk back myself. How far do we have to go? We're not leaving anyone behind for these things to feed on."

Willoby looked at her with a new respect.

"The lady has spoken. Very well then. Pack up lads, and let's be on our way. There's not much daylight left."

They made slow progress until Corporal McCann woke up unexpected-ly, and with Doody under one arm and Bristow under the other, was able to limp along instead of being hauled in a poncho. Stephen brought up the rear, turning every few yards to eyeball the windswept crags behind them with his rifle sights. After they had limped and hobbled some 200 metres, he called up to Willoby at the front of the little straggling column.

"They're behind us! I see two of those creatures. They're quartering the ground. Looks like they're trying for our scent." He went on one knee, sighted, and fired a single shot, startling them all. Then he jerked back the bolt to eject the casing and seat another round.

"Missed, damn."

"Move it!" Cutter hissed loudly. "Those things could be as fast as bloody racehorses."

They stumbled on. At last they saw ahead in the gathering darkness the glimmer of a torch, and were met by Sergeant Fox. He had his M-4 cocked and ready.

"I heard shooting," he said, eyes wide at the new additions to the team, the body of Sergeant Mullan with one arm dangling limply out of the poncho.

"Cover our rear," Willoby told him. "Don't fire unless you have a clear shot."

"Yes, boss," he replied. "So, what am I firing at?"

"Big bloody monsters, Calum — now get to it."

They made it to the tents at last, a quiet, tired crew with a sombre load. Jenny, McCann and Brice were wrapped up warm in the tents with Doody to attend to them while the rest of the party took up firing positions around the camp.

Darkness had fallen just before they reached the tents, and sleet was pouring in on the back of the wind, the beginning of a bitter night. The cold and wet bored into them, soaking them all over again. Whatever warmth had been generated by the journey back to camp was quickly lost.

"The weather's in our favour," Cutter told Willoby. "Might just throw them off the scent."

"I hope so," the soldier told him. "We can't stand-to all night in this."

They lay on the hard ice-strewn rocks, shivering and staring out into the flailing storm-torn dark, as wary and afraid as cavemen peering into the blackness of an ice-age winter. But nothing came.

Finally they called it a night, and set one-hour sentry slots for all the soldiers... and Stephen, Willoby having been reluctantly impressed by the shot which had almost taken the Eotyrannus's head off at 400 metres in bad visibility and a high wind. Cutter, Connor and Abby also wanted to go on 'stag', as the soldiers called it, but the Captain refused.

"You're the brains of this operation," he told them. "We need you alert and alive and keeping the information flowing."

Jenny lay in an arctic sleeping bag, a field dressing bound behind her left ear. Cutter sat beside her in the tent while behind him Abby and Connor were huddled with another sodden sleeping bag wrapped around their shoulders. Connor's hair hung in lank rat's tails down his forehead and he was shivering convulsively. News of the Eotyrannus had sparked up a return to his old self, but now he was staring at the prospect of another wet, freezing night, this time with large predators roaming the crags and wastes beyond the campsite. His taste for adventure seemed to be at its lowest ebb.

He sat with the electronic guts of the portable anomaly detector spread on a handkerchief in front of him and mechanically dried the components, one by one, but his heart didn't seem to be truly in it.

Abby's head was nodding. Once, when it came to rest on his shoulder, he closed his eyes and buried his nose in her hair.

"That poor man," Jenny was saying. "Dying in a place like this."

"At least it was quick," Cutter said.

"Cutter, what the hell are we doing here?"

Cutter smiled down at her. She had taken his hand, and her fingers were warm against his own chilled skin. "Trying to clear up a mess, I suppose, same as we always do. It's just that this time we're a bit further out on a limb than usual."

"This is going very wrong, Nick."

"We'll muddle through," he told her. He didn't sound convinced, though.

"We have your sat-phone," he continued. "It made it in one piece, and three of you made it out of the chopper with only minor injuries — there's that to be thankful for. As Lester would put it, we're still fit for purpose."

"Lester!" she said, anger flitting across her face. "All James Lester gives a damn about is his ascent of a very greasy pole."

"He shouldn't have sent you out here," Cutter admitted. "This isn't your kind of scenario, Jenny."

"I know. Public relations, eh? It never said anything in my contract about storms at sea, helicopter crashes and marauding prehistoric predators."

He patted her hand.

"In the morning we'll pack up and make for this abandoned army post in the north. We can't spend another night in the open, not in this weather. After that, things will be a little more..." He searched for the word.

"Reasonable."

THIRTEEN

In the night, the wind fell, and Cutter woke up to the strangest sound: silence. The storm had been a part of their world for what seemed like so long now that its absence was a new and amazing thing.

He left the tent with the plastic brick that was the sat-phone in one hand, and with the other he tucked a borrowed pistol in his jacket pocket. Outside, the air was freezing cold and still full of water vapour. He looked about himself in dismay. The island was covered in thick, freezing fog, visibility down to perhaps fifteen metres. It was so thick that he could feel it moving against his face, and tasted salt on his dry, chapped lips. It reminded him that they were getting low on water.

Doody was on stag behind the Minimi, lying on a karrimat with his cheek leaning against the weapon's stock. As Cutter approached his head snapped upright and he cursed.

"Good job it was you," he said. "If it had been the boss, I'd be in for a rocket, snoozing on stag."

"If it was an Eotyrannus, you'd get more than a rocket," Cutter retorted. He sat down and he and Doody split a bar of chocolate, savouring the sugar and the boost in energy it spread through their systems at this enervating hour of the morning. "No sign?" Cutter asked.

"No sign. Though there could be half a dozen of the bastards a hundred yards off in this fog, and you'd not know."

"All right, Doody. When's your relief?"

"Your mate Hart takes over in ten minutes."

"How are our patients?"

Doody rubbed his hand over his face.

"The squaddie, McCann, will be fine. He just got a bump on the head and a lot of general bashing around — no worse than a good night out in Colchester. The pilot, Brice, has the same, but his right arm is broken, too. He won't be flying any helis for a while."

"And Jenny?" Cutter asked, affecting what he hoped sounded like clinical detachment.

"You mean the brunette beauty you're soft on?"

Cutter glared at him. "What did you say?"

Doody chuckled. "It's all right, sir, it's just a bit obvious, that's all. She's fine, too. Mild concussion, five stitches, two cracked ribs. She's got bottle, that girl. She'll be up and about today, I'll bet you anything."

Cutter nodded. "Thanks Doody."

"Don't wander off!" Doody said quickly as Cutter walked away. "SOP is now to pee in pairs."

"I'm a civilian. I don't have Standard Operating Procedures," Cutter told him. "But if you hear me being eaten, do come running."

He walked some sixty yards out of camp, pausing every now and then to listen. No noise but the sound of water trickling. The island seemed dead and deserted. He wondered if the anomalies were still open.

Connor has to get the detector working again.

He set up the sat-phone, extending the tiny dish and setting it on a nearby rock. Then he hit redial.

The phone rang twice, and a voice said, "You took your time."

Cutter smiled.

"Good to know you missed me," he said, and listened with relish to the silent astonishment on the other end.

"Cutter! So you're alive."

"And kicking, Lester. But only just. It was a bold move, sending Jenny out here to check up on us."

"It was necessary."

An edge of anger crept into Cutter's voice.

"You bastard. She was almost killed."

"What happened?"

"Her helicopter went down. She's marooned here now, the same as the rest of us. One of the crew was killed in the crash, and another was seriously injured."

"I see." Then silence.

"Don't you want to know his name? His next of kin will need to be informed."

"All in good time, Cutter. After all, it wasn't my decision to get the Irish military involved in all of this. And at this moment, none of you exist, Guns Island is deserted, and the media are going to keep believing that for as long as possible."

"Well, so long as everything is neat and tidy in the corridors of power," Cutter replied, without bothering to disguise his disgust.

"What communications do you have?" Lester asked, with a patience that was quite unlike him. Perhaps he felt a measure of guilt after all.

"Two-way radios with a limited range, and this sat-phone. That's it. The long-range UHF was lost in the sea, along with half our other gear. Lester, we have injured people here. We need a resupply and a casevac as soon as possible. We're short on food, water, medical supplies and —"

"Are you giving up on me, Professor?"

Cutter bit back his fury.

"I'm merely stating the facts."

"What about the anomalies? Are they still open — have you seen any creatures?"

"We've seen three distinct species so far, one at sea and two on land. Our anomaly detector got scrambled. We're working on it."

"My, you have had an unfortunate time of it."

Cutter thought of the sea crossing, the climb up the cliffs, hauling back the dead body from the crash site.

"You could say that," he said, closing his eyes for a second.

"There's an Irish Naval vessel in the vicinity, and a French one will be on the way. I'll see what I can do to get another aircraft out to you. But it all depends on the weather, Cutter."

"You won't get anything in today," Cutter told him. "We're in the eye of the storm, and socked in with fog."

"Do you actually have a plan?" Lester asked him.

"The anomalies seem to be at the north end of the island, and that's where the old outpost is, too. We'll make for there. We need protection from the elements, and from the wildlife, and concrete beats the hell out of a nylon flysheet for that sort of thing. Once we've made the move, I'll contact you again." He paused. "We'll have to conserve the batteries on this thing. It's the only link we have with the outside world."

"Very well." This time it was Lester who paused. "Jenny — I take it she's fine."

"She's banged about, but she'll live."

"Good. I wish you good luck, Cutter. And I will see what I can do about another helicopter."

Cutter clicked off the connection and set the phone back in its cradle before packing up the dish and wiring. Then he rose and walked wearily back to the campsite, whilst around him the fog gripped the island in a silent shroud.

Connor stood, clicking a switch on the portable anomaly detector back and forth.

"It's fixed," he muttered, "I know it is. Professor, it should be in perfect working order."

"Then why isn't it picking up anything?" Cutter demanded irritably.

"Perhaps there's nothing to pick up," Stephen said over his shoulder. He was busy cramming his gear into his rucksack, like the rest of the team. Jenny and Brice sat to one side. The Irish pilot had his splinted arm set in a sling, and his face was drawn with pain and grief.

"You mean there are no anomalies within range," Cutter said, his eyes widening slightly as it dawned on him.

"It's possible, isn't it?" Stephen said. "We know they have a fairly short shelf life. The latest lot may have simply run out of time."

"Perhaps it's the storm," Connor surmised, "or rather, the lack of it."

"The weather?" Jenny said. "You think the weather has something to do with it?"

"We've never encountered this many anomalies in a single place before," Connor said defensively. "Suddenly we have this storm, this island, and a whole shed-full of the things. Maybe it's a combination of meteorology and geology that has drawn them to this spot." They were all watching him now. He ducked his head. "It's just a theory," he mumbled.

"And not a half bad one," Cutter said, clapping him on the shoulder. "The main thing is, there's a better than average chance that there are no anomalies open at present on the island. If that's the case, then it's time we were on the move."

"There could still be creatures out there," Stephen protested. "They don't all pop out of existence when the anomalies disappear."

"No, but we know there's a finite number of them, at least for the moment," Cutter replied. "And they aren't just going to pop up out of nowhere. My map says there's a well up at the outpost, and the place is built like a bunker, easily defended. It will be our base of operations on the island."

There was a silence as they all looked at him. Even Abby had a kind of reproach in her eyes.

"You still think we can do this?" she asked.

"I spoke with Lester this morning. He's going to try and get another helicopter out here to take out Lieutenant Brice and bring us a resupply. When that happens, we'll be as good as new."

Jenny delicately touched the dressing at the base of her ear.

"Perhaps not quite as good as new," she said.

They packed up the camp in less than an hour, and once again shouldered their sodden rucksacks. Far from looking like a crack semi-military operation, they resembled a band of vagabonds. They were filthy, shivering, soaked through, grey-faced and tired. Willoby, looking them over, grinned broadly.

"The last time I saw an outfit that looked this shit, it was a bunch of Argentinians coming in to surrender to us," he said. "Cheer up, people, it's just a few hundred metres, and then you'll have a real roof over your heads."

Connor looked out at the blank wall of the fog that surrounded them.

"Let's hope dinosaurs don't like a roof over their heads, as well," he said moodily.

Sergeant Fox and Stephen took point, setting out some ten metres ahead of the rest. They were just visible through the fog, and whenever they lost sight of the main party they would wait for it to catch up. Next came Willoby and Cutter, then Jenny, Connor and Abby, then Brice, helped along by the Irish soldier, McCann. Doody walked close behind them, then the signaller, Watts, and Farnsworth and Bristow at the rear.

The dead copilot's body they wrapped in a poncho, as before, and took turns to carry it, even Jenny insisting on lending a hand. Brice looked at the body of his friend and said nothing, but shuffled along with a pistol in his free hand, looking as though he longed to use it on something.

Their progress was slow and halting. Though Guns Island wasn't large, the plateau across which they were trekking was a broken landscape of deep gullies, steep crags, and broken boulder fields that were slick with ice and snow, and all the more menacing in the silent, dripping caul of fog which enfolded them.

At the front, Fox waved Stephen over. He was crouching and holding a prismatic compass in his free hand.

"Hey, look at this."

Stephen knelt beside him. The needle wasn't pointing north, but oscillated continuously through all the points of the compass.

"I've seen something similar in the Cuillin Mountains," Fox told him, "but never this bad. There must be some weird geology under our feet."

"Are you happy with where we're going?" Stephen asked him. He was scanning the fog around them with the sniper rifle snug in his shoulder.

"Aye, it's no great problem, over a half kay or so. I'd hate to try and navigate this place in the dark, though."

Back down the little column, Connor came up beside Cutter, holding out the portable anomaly detector.

"Not a twitch," he said. "Professor, how long do you think this eye of the storm thing will last?"

"Not long," Cutter said. "A few hours maybe."

"I almost think I preferred the wind," Connor told him. "This silence is creeping me out. I thought there were huge colonies of birds here."

"The gannets head for the South Atlantic in the winter. They only come here to breed in the summer months. Bloody good job, too. This island houses perhaps a fifth of the world's breeding population — can you imagine the havoc if the anomalies had opened when there were half a million gannets hatching out their eggs underfoot? It would be an ecological catastrophe."

"The RSPB wouldn't be too chuffed," Connor agreed.

Up front, both Stephen and Fox went to one knee in the same moment, and Fox raised a clenched fist into the air.

"Go firm," Willoby said.

"Eh?" said Connor.

"Stand still. Keep your eyes open and your mouth shut." He loped ahead to join the two men who were only shadows in the clinging mist.

"What is it, Calum?"

"Stones clattering ahead. Could be just a minor rockfall."

"Check it out," Willoby ordered.

Fox and Stephen set off into the fog. In twenty seconds it had swallowed them up and it was as if they had never existed. Cutter joined Willoby, wiping salty moisture off his face. He drew his pistol.

"Problem?"

"Just be still, Professor."

The seconds ticked by. They heard a click of stone ahead, but the fog seemed to dampen down all noise. It was as though they knelt in a vast, stony-floored cathedral whose walls were white and blank all about them.

A clattering of rocks ahead, just as Fox had described. Willoby brought his M-4 into his shoulder and looked down the iron sights which were fixed atop the telescopic ones. Whatever was out there, it was close.

A large shadow loomed up out of the mist. Cutter raised his pistol and pulled the hammer back to full cock. His mouth was dry as sand and his heart was hammering in his chest.

The shadow became two human figures, Fox and Stephen stumbling back through the fog towards them. Cutter let out a shaky breath and set the hammer to half-cock again.

Willoby lowered his rifle barrel.

"Bloody fog," he said. "We'll have a blue on blue if we're not careful."

"There's something out there," Stephen said. He was panting. He and Fox had the wide-eyed, livid look of frightened men. "It was moving around us in an arc, coming round our left flank. It seemed to back away when we approached."

"It was big," Fox said. "I thought I caught a look at it; it was a shadow as big as a frigging house, boss." The four of them knelt in a little knot of indecision for a minute before Cutter spoke up.

"We have to keep moving. If we're being stalked, then standing here is just issuing an invitation to lunch. But we should stay closer together. Pack animals pick off stragglers from the herd first."

"Pack animals?" Willoby said.

"Could be our friend the Eotyrannus again, and he's unlikely to be alone. Captain, we need to get to this base of ours as quickly as possible."

"Nothing like stating the obvious," Willoby said dryly. "All right; Hart, you and Fox stay close in with the rest of us. And if you have to shoot, for God's sake make sure your arcs are clear. A gaggle of people with automatic weapons can be as dangerous to each other as they are to the enemy.

"Let's move."

They set off again, this time moving as a single group. Abby and Connor were given Mullan's dead body to carry and the rest of the party walked along looking outwards at the surrounding fog, wincing at every clattering rock their feet kicked aside. They made another 150 metres before Bristow and Farnsworth, at the rear, passed forward the order to halt.

"It's behind us," Bristow said. Despite the cold, his crew-cut head was streaming with sweat, and heat rose in wisps of steam from his clothing.

"Is it moving?" Cutter asked.

"I hear the rocks shifting. It's not running or anything; it's moving slow, quartering the ground to our rear."

"Keep going," Willoby said. "We don't stop for anything. Come on people, best foot forward. It's not far now."

They slogged on. Time seemed to pass interminably, and the ground they were traversing seemed all the same; a grim, icebound landscape of stone and lichen and scattered clumps of frozen yellow grass. There was no horizon, only the island beneath their boots and the all-enveloping shroud of the fog.

"I think I hear something," Farnsworth said at the rear. "Joe, I'm sure."

"Come on Pete — you heard the boss. Keep bloody tabbing."

Farnsworth turned round. "But I tell you —"

It exploded out of the fog, launching itself through the air. Twenty feet of massive, sinewed muscle, it came down on Farnsworth and smashed him onto the stones, ripping him open like a paper bag, spreading his entrails far and wide, a scarlet explosion.

Bristow got off a long burst of automatic fire, the tracers streaking wildly above the animal's head. Then he turned and ran.

"Stand fast!" Willoby shouted. They were all pelting past him into the fog. The creature raised its snout from Farnsworth's bloody carcass and barked sharply.

From off in the fog, an answering series of barks sounded.

A second Eotyrannus burst into view, careering out of the fog like some demon out of a child's nightmare. It missed Jenny by less than a yard, skidded on the icy stones, and fell to its side with a crash. Teeth bared, Cutter turned around and emptied a clip into it, pulling the trigger of his pistol as fast as his finger could move. The creature screamed furiously, a shrill shriek that lanced into their ears. It pulled itself up on its side just as Cutter's pistol gave the dead man's click, and the slide jammed rearwards.

He had emptied the magazine.

Cutter threw the pistol at the wounded beast, grabbed Jenny's hand and ran, trailing her after him.

The party was scattered, amid a panicked shouting of orders and a flurry of gunshots. The wounded creature found its feet and let out a high-pitched screech, blood pouring down its side. Watts turned and fired a streak of tracer into its head. The animal jerked and staggered, bellowing in pain and anger. The other one was darting from side to side, snapping out at the people running past, confused perhaps by the wealth of prey it had discovered.

The team was splintered, losing one another in the fog.

Connor, Abby and Doody sprinted stumbling up a rocky slope and found themselves staring down into nothingness; they had reached the cliff's edge. They turned back to face the way they had come. More shots were being fired below them, and the Eotyrannus was shrieking like a thing possessed, then barking as if to signal to its fellows.

"I'm open to ideas," Doody said, hefting his carbine.

"We have to go back," Abby said, cocking her MP5.

"It's all right for you two — you have guns," Connor wailed.

Doody pulled a pistol from his thigh holster and handed it to him.

"It's not cocked. There's seventeen rounds in the clip. Shoot the dinosaurs, not us."

"Got it," Connor said, cocking the weapon with a satisfying metallic clack.

"Let's go," Abby said. "We left that guy's body back there."

"Stuff the body," Doody told her. "We find the others, we stay alive. That's all there is to it."

They went back the way they had come.

Cutter and Jenny tucked themselves in a narrow rocky cleft and leaned on each other, gasping for air. Neither was armed. They could hear the other members of the party shouting — Willoby's voice in particular, off to their left — and staccato bursts of gunfire.

"They got the drop on us," Cutter panted. "Are you all right?"

"Fine. My God, Nick, did you see that poor man —"

"Don't think about that now. We have to get back to the others. We're unarmed, and at least one of those creatures is up and around and looking for a fight. We won't last five minutes on our own."

Jenny was shaking her head.

"I just panicked. I'm sorry."

"We all did — it's nothing to be ashamed of. It may have saved a life or two." He caught his breath. "Can you run?"

"Yes — yes I can."

"No point charging wildly around the island. We're liable to get shot ourselves. We'll make for the base. Sooner or later, the rest of them will all have to go there."

Jenny was still holding his hand, clenching it so tight he thought he could feel the knuckles grate together.

"Hey," he smiled, "it's all right. This is my job, remember?"

"I'm going to take this up with my union," she fired back, and he was heartened to see the feistiness come back into her eyes.

"Good lass. Now let's go before I change my mind."

Stephen and Sergeant Fox stood together, back to back. Fox slid another magazine into his carbine and let the working parts go forward, pushing a round up the spout.

They had shouted their heads off, once they'd stopped running, but no one had replied. Stephen had lost all sense of direction. It was as though the fog and the panic had blunted the finer workings of his brain. He drew a deep breath, content for now to rely on Fox's interior compass.

"All set?" he asked him.

"Aye. What now? I heard the Captain shout out a minute ago from our right, but there's not a sign of the rest. They took off like a bunch of rabbits. We're all over the bloody place now and the radios won't work in this weather."

"We keep heading north," Stephen said, "as we were before. If we just blunder about aimlessly in the fog, we won't achieve a thing."

Fox shook his head.

"I think we should try and rejoin the boss."

"Calum, we haven't a hope. We —"

They heard a woman's scream, sounding far off to the south. Then it was cut off by an animal bellow, and a long, savage burst of automatic fire.

"Jesus Christ," Fox said

The Eotyrannus had disappeared, leaping out from among them as though it had made a sudden decision. Its mate was still stirring feebly, until the Irish pilot, Brice, walked over to it and with an eerily calm face shot it in the head.

Willoby looked around.

"Stay close people. Who do we have here? Brice, Watts, McCann, Bristow —"

The animal was back upon them while their minds were still numbed by the shock of the first attack. Out of the fog it jumped, a taloned phantom that landed square on the back of Anita Watts, the signaller. The impact smashed her to the ground, her rifle flying off to be lost in the fog. She twisted under it, screaming, and then the creature bit down on her head with terrifying force. There was a sharp crack as the bones of her skull gave way, and her agonised shriek was stifled.

The creature raised its head in triumph.

Willoby and the Irish trooper, McCann, stood side by side and emptied their magazines into the monster. Both were shouting as they fired, nameless noises their ancestors might have uttered as they took on some primeval creature with flint and fire-hardened wood. The bullets ripped through the creature's belly and ribs, stitching an explosive series of red holes in its skin, blowing apart muscle and bone. Sixty rounds cannoned into it, and it reared up on its hind legs, staggering, the claws on the hind feet clicking against the rock.

Then it toppled over, and began thrashing madly, uttering a frenzied, high-pitched squealing and sending fist-sized stones flying through the air. Willoby and McCann changed mags, and emptied two more clips into it as it struggled. At last it lay still, its claws buried in agony in the ground, Private Watts a broken, limp corpse beside it.

As they ran something large loomed up out of the fog, and Jenny shrank to Cutter's side. They had heard the gunfire, the screams, and had no way of knowing if any of the others had made it.

It was a building, slab-walled and ugly, reinforced concrete that was topped with a frosting of ice and disfigured with circling fans of lichen. In the fog it looked almost like a lost temple waiting to be discovered. Deeply inset to one side of the wall, a green-painted steel door stood, massively padlocked.

Cutter eased off his rucksack. In all the excitement, he had never thought to abandon it, but now his shoulder was complaining again, and his head throbbed with pain. He checked the sat-phone in its side pocket, and breathed a silent prayer of thanks that it was still undamaged.

"Looks like we're here," he said to Jenny, and handed her his water-bottle. She drank from it, and gave the container a shake. "Is this all you have left?"

"We're running low on most things, it seems. Including people."

They both stood there and listened. The shooting and screaming had stopped, and the fog-bound island was as quiet as the grave. Jenny shuddered as the comparison occurred to her, and she wondered if they would ever see Abby, Connor or Stephen again.

"Let's see about getting inside this place," Cutter said.

"Nick —" She set a hand on his arm. "I have to tell you. That cover story about the biological agents —"

"Yes?"

"Well... it's true. The whole thing is true. There really *were* experiments conducted here in the fifties, and there may well be active agents still inside this place."

Cutter mulled that over for a minute, then smiled.

"Lester," he said, half-admiringly. "He really does cover all the angles, doesn't he?"

"It's Willoby's job to secure the bioweapons. It's why Lester was given so much cooperation from the military. The Captain's mission is twofold."

"Well, for all we know, Willoby may be dead."

"No such luck, Cutter."

The voice spun them round. He was standing there, not fifteen feet away. There was blood spattered over his face, and his eyes were set and hard as glass. Behind him stood several of the others. Cutter saw the Irishmen, McCann and Brice, and the shaven-headed Joe Bristow.

Something in his heart lurched.

"Is this all?" he asked hoarsely. "Is this all that made it?"

"I don't know," Willoby said. He wiped the blood from his face absently. "Farnsworth and Watts are dead; those I saw. The rest could still be scattered anywhere. Both dinosaurs have been killed; we finished off the one you wounded and took out the other one as — as it — anyway, they're both dead."

Cutter looked him in the eye. "I'm sorry about your people, Captain."

He nodded.

"We have to go back. If at all possible, we have to bring them home." He cleared his throat. "For now, we've at least made it to the base. We have to find a way in and then take stock. Once we've done that, I'll head out again to look for the rest of our team. Dead or alive, I mean to find every one of them."

They stood there a moment as the fog filled the air around them. It was as though they couldn't quite bring themselves to soldier on. It occurred to Cutter that the silence which now enveloped the island again meant that their friends were either safe, or they were dead. No one was shooting any more.

He walked over to the great, steel, padlocked door set in the side of the wall.

"Let's get on with this," he said.

***

A quarter of a mile away, Doody raised his rifle.

"There's something moving ahead."

Connor and Abby both froze. The three of them stood in a kind of half-crouch, weapons pointing out into the fog in all directions. As Connor scanned the blankness in front of him, he found himself wondering if any of the others had survived. And he tried to forget the burning panic that had made him take off like a scalded rat. It was sheer luck that he had run in the same direction as Abby and Doody.

Perhaps it was the fog; it seemed to sap his courage somehow. He hated not being able to see what was out there. It made the whole thing into some second-rate horror movie he couldn't switch off. It made everything somehow dreamlike.

At least I'm with Abby, he thought. *That's something.*

A light blinked on in the fog, then off again. Doody began to grin.

"Hoy, who's that then?"

"The big bad wolf," the reply came back. Stephen Hart and Calum Fox walked out of the fog, smiling grimly. Abby ran forward and embraced them one after the other.

"We thought you were a creature."

"Yeah, and I was about to open up on you!" Connor exclaimed, thumping Stephen on the arm. Stephen gently pushed aside the barrel of the 9mm that Connor was waving around in his relief.

"Glad you didn't. God knows who would have ended up getting shot."

"Are you alone?" Abby said. When they nodded, she added, "What now?"

"We find the others. Those things didn't get everybody, I'm sure of it. We move north and look for this base that we were heading for. It's all we can do."

"I'll lead," Fox said, and he set off at a brisk stride. The rest followed on. Connor trailed after them.

"Guys, wait up." He trotted hurriedly after Abby.

"Come on Connor!"

"Can you feel it, Abs? Can't you feel it?"

"What — what am I feeling?"

Connor stopped as a beeping noise came from his pocket. He fished out the hand-held anomaly detector. A light was blinking red and the LED screen was lit up in one corner.

"Oh, no," he said.

"Connor — I swear to God, if you get left behind, I'm not going back for you." Abby tugged at his arm.

He stood planted in one spot, his normally cheerful face drawn and sombre. He showed her the detector.

"I was going to ask you," he told her, "if you could feel the wind." He raised his head and the sound of it rose around them, sweeping over the crags and sere grass of the island, shredding the fog moment by moment, broadening out their world.

"The eye of the storm is past, Abby," he said. "The anomalies are back."

FOURTEEN

Even in the concrete-roofed shelter of the northern base, they could hear it. Joe Bristow, standing guard at the doorway, came halfway down the steps.

"Boss, it's starting to blow up a storm outside again," he called, raising his voice to be heard over the strengthening wind.

Willoby grimaced.

"It'll clear the fog, at least." He coughed. "There's a well in here somewhere. Hard to believe this island actually has a water table. From the schematics we were shown, the bunker has several levels to it. This is admin. Level two is living, and below that the labs, I think."

"Nice to be well informed," Cutter said. He massaged his sore shoulder. "All right, we're in. Now let's get back out there and find our people."

"We left gear behind, too, and the dead have weapons and ammo we badly need," Willoby told him. "We have to —"

"Boss!" Bristow shouted, but this time his voice was filled with sheer delight. "Boss, them hairy-arsed bastards is walking right up to the bloody front door!"

The occupants of the room piled over to the doorway to find Stephen, Fox, Abby, Connor and Doody standing there with big grins on their faces. There was a flurry of back-slapping and the odd hug or two. Cutter stood before Stephen as the latter lowered the heavy sniper rifle from his shoulder with a groan.

"Glad you made it," he said.

"You know me, never one to leave a party early," Stephen told him. They shook hands. "Shall we —?" Stephen asked, opening his arms.

"Nah, leave that for the girls," Cutter told him. "You're too ugly to hug."

The wind was back to roaring like a freight train overhead, and brought with it a torrent of sleet and snow.

The team rolled out their karrimats and sleeping bags and laid them on the floor of the concrete cube that was the base's hallway. There they took stock of their fragile economy while the redoubtable Joe Bristow manned the Minimi at the doorway, peering out through slitted eyes at the blizzard which had replaced the fog. It was uncanny how the island had gone from one extreme to another in the space of an hour, Jenny noted.

"This really is a weird place," she said, shaking her head as she retied the sling on Sean Brice's broken arm.

"From what I hear, our government is arguing with the French over it," Brice said. "As far as I'm concerned, the bloody French are welcome to it. Thanks, miss."

"It's Jenny," she told him. "I think the time for formalities is long gone, Lieutenant."

"My apologies for the landing. The updraft took us by surprise. I've never encountered one that strong before. Les, now, he was more experienced. He would have —"

Brice stopped. He blinked furiously.

"He has a fine wife, and a daughter. They should know what happened to him."

Jenny sat down on the dusty concrete beside him.

"Yes they should. He died doing his job well and bravely." She hesitated, searching for the words. "You've seen incredible things on this island, Lieutenant, impossible things. I hope you do realise that your government is unaware of them, that all this is top secret — in the most serious and non-James Bond way possible. You must never speak to anyone of the things you have seen and will see on Guns Island."

Brice studied her carefully, and she wondered what might be going through his mind. *His life — the way he sees the world around him — it's all changed*, she mused, and the thought was tinged with a familiar regret.

"You're way too pretty to be doing such a dirty job," he said. After a moment he added, "Well, I'd best see what I can do to help." Then he rose and joined John McCann, his countryman, who was seated on the other side of the room cleaning his rifle.

There was a series of clangs as Willoby beat the padlock off another door with the butt of his rifle.

"The old SLR was better for this sort of crap," he said, grunting as he struck home. Finally the rusting padlock fell free, and he yanked open the steel-plate door, grinding it back on its hinges. He coughed and stepped back from the darkness he had uncovered, setting a hand over his mouth.

"Old air," he said, and clicked on his head-torch. "At least I hope that's all it is."

Cutter stared for a moment, then followed him into the darkness. It was musty-smelling, but as dry as a pharaoh's tomb.

"They built this place well," he said to Willoby. "Fifty years, and there's not a drop of damp. This facility was sealed up tight as a balloon."

"Bio bullshit," Willoby said. "They didn't have any other option, did they? Unless they wanted to see three-legged gannets breeding on the island."

"It was real, all of it. I know that now," Cutter said. "Jenny told me, Willoby."

"I had a feeling she might. You get to this stage in an op, and all the secrets crawl out of their holes. But it doesn't matter. We have the here and now in front of us, life and death. *That's* what's important."

"And the mission," Cutter said.

"And the mission," Willoby agreed. He scanned the room, his torch-light flicking from wall to wall as he turned his head.

"You and I are much alike, Cutter. From what I've been told —"

"From your brief, you mean," Cutter interrupted.

"All right then. From the file I was given on you, it seems you're your own man, who keeps chasing what he wants until he gets it. I can relate to that."

"What are we doing now, Captain? Bonding?"

Willoby shrugged. "At least we're both at the sharp end, not like the people who sent us out here. We're both expendable, Cutter — in their eyes, at least."

"Well, I won't argue with you on that one," Cutter admitted.

They peered into the dimly lit darkness, but all they saw was empty shelves and barren countertops, the occasional bit of refuse interrupting an otherwise deserted space. Whatever had been here, it had been taken away long ago.

A beam of light illuminated them both.

"Professor?" Connor's voice asked. Cutter shaded his eyes.

"Over here. What's up, Connor?"

The younger man walked across to them, his feet stirring up a thin patina of dust from the concrete of the floor.

"Take a look at this," he said.

His hand-held anomaly detector was blinking.

"They're back," Cutter said. "Along with the storm."

"It's more than that, Professor. The detector isn't picking up the anomalies outside — it's found one very close by. Look at the signal — we're practically standing on top of it."

"That's impossible," Cutter said. But he knew it wasn't. If anomalies could appear in the London Tube, then there was nothing to stop them from materialising here.

"Take a look at the readings, Professor. The detector is working perfectly, and the bearings it gives are on this location."

Cutter and Willoby looked first at each other, and then at the locked doors that led out of the black room they were standing in.

One of those doors had letters painted on it, proclaiming 'Security Clearance Required', and the paint was flaking away. Another said 'Admin', and a third was entitled 'Systems'.

"There are two levels below us, you said?" Cutter asked Willoby.

"And those are the ones whose existence they admit to," the SAS officer replied. "Who knows what's really down there."

They stood for a second, the implications working in their heads.

"No, it's got to be a coincidence," Willoby said at last.

"But bioweapons," Cutter said. "That term covers a lot of ground."

"If it *were* true, they'd never have abandoned this place, or they'd at least have kept it quarantined, kept the birdwatchers away."

"What?" Connor asked, shivering. "Professor, what are you two talking about?"

"If there's an anomaly in the base — actually inside of it, then it might indicate something we'd never before considered," Cutter said. "If the construction of the base is somehow linked to the existence of anomalies on this island, then it might mean these things aren't a recent phenomenon. This place hasn't been operational for fifty years, for God's sake."

"Like I said, it's probably a coincidence," Willoby told him. "Got to be."

"I want to see those lower levels," Cutter said firmly.

"I'm afraid that's impossible."

"You're lying, Willoby. Your job was to come here and secure the site. You can't do that effectively if you don't have some means of accessing every level."

"So long as the seals are in place, my job is done," Willoby snapped. "You said it yourself, they built this place well; it's still bloody airtight. That means my mission is over. The biological agents remain contained. Whatever is below us can stay there and rot. We're not going to delve any further into these black rooms.

"Case closed, Cutter."

Cutter shrugged.

"All right — fair enough. You can't blame me for being curious. It's my line of work after all."

"My secondary mission," Willoby continued with a humourless smile, "was to keep your team members alive. To do that, we need to find water, and make this place secure against attack."

"Then I guess I vote for the door marked 'Admin'," Cutter said softly.

"My third objective," Willoby ground on, "is to retrieve the bodies of the dead and the equipment they were carrying."

"You go out there now, and you're a dead man," Cutter warned him.

The soldier turned away, but not before Cutter had seen the deep bone-weariness in his face.

"I'm not that easy to kill," he said.

As the bad air cleared out of the anteroom, so the team moved into it.

The outer hall, which they now called the first room, was already acquiring a widening pool of rainwater and melted sleet that the storm was flinging in through the open doorway. No one suggested that the door should be closed. It seemed unlikely that the Eotyrannus would be able to find it in the storm, and apart from the airtight seal around it, shutting it would have left them in utter blackness. The base had been built to withstand air bombardment and had no windows. The roof was several feet thick, and though there were ventilation grilles set along the walls, their louvered coverings were all shut.

"They made this place proof against pretty much everything," Calum Fox said, darting his torch here and there about the walls. "Not just explosives — it's set up to survive nerve agents and all sorts of weapons. Thank God the Cold War's over, I say."

"Tell that to Watts and Pete Farnsworth," Bristow grunted. Doody had relieved him of the Minimi, and now he was towelling the melted ice off his face and neck. "When you're dead you're dead, whether it's in a nuclear winter or —" He looked out at the angry weather beyond the far doorway, where Doody lay shivering under a poncho, the butt of the Minimi in his shoulder. "Or torn to pieces by something that shouldn't exist. Maybe something that was created here, for all we know, bioweapons! Who knows what they were at in this godforsaken place, or what they cooked up in their test tubes."

Stephen re-entered the base, dripping wet, snow in his hair. He was carrying half a dozen hard plastic water bottles.

"Not much use; the wind blows the snow across them. There's maybe a half litre in each — better than nothing."

He handed out the water and the team clustered around him to drink greedily. The salt air had left them all parched.

"You see anything out there?" Cutter asked him.

"I was only ten feet from the front door but, yes, I saw an anomaly off in the distance, maybe a quarter of a mile away. Hard to tell — it came and went in the storm."

"Any creatures?" Abby asked him.

"Not a one. Maybe they peek out through the anomalies, get a load of the weather, say 'Sod this for a game of toy soldiers', and piss off back to the Cretaceous."

They all laughed.

"I wouldn't mind a few hours in the Cretaceous," Connor said with feeling. "At least it would be warm."

"Take away the rampaging wildlife, and it would be like a stay in the Bahamas," Cutter told him.

"Oh, don't Professor," Abby said, shivering. "I can't remember the last time I was warm or had dry feet."

There was a cacophony of bangs from the inner room. Willoby was still trying to smash the locks off the doors, and these were proving more difficult to master than the rust-eaten exterior ones. Finally they heard him shout. "Stay out of this room — stand clear!" And there was a shot that stung their ears in the confined space.

"*Ow*!" Connor exclaimed. "Instant tinnitus!"

The whiz and crack of the bullet whined about the walls of the other room just as Willoby dived out of it head first. They stood looking at him, and he grinned sheepishly.

"Never shoot off a rifle in a confined space with lots of concrete about," he said. "Still, it did the trick. Bristow, come with me, and bring your torch."

In the end, Cutter, Connor and Abby joined them, and the three civilians coughed and retched as Bristow and Willoby levered open the massive rubber-edged door that led to 'Admin'.

"Let it clear," Willoby said, waving his hand in front of his face.

"It's like opening Tutankhamun's tomb," Abby said.

"I tell you what it's like. It's like entering Moria," Connor said darkly.

"I knew you'd bring *The Lord of the Rings* into it at some point," Abby said, trying her best to sound disgusted.

"Cut it out," Cutter snapped. Their torch beams played upon the half-century of blackness that lay before them. They saw stairs going down and a door at their bottom. This door was wood, and it was open.

"Once more into the breach," Willoby intoned. He set off down the stairs into the darkness.

Outside Doody sipped at his water bottle, crunching the ice within and stifling his shivers. His eyes were smarting from lack of sleep, and everything he ate or drank seemed to taste of salt.

He stared out at the storm-wracked whiteness of the winter day and thought of his girlfriend back in Hereford. A bed, with her in it — and beside the bed a tall pitcher of clear, cold water. His tongue ran around the inside of his mouth as he thought about it.

Something moved out there, a shadow that came and went between shifts in the snow.

"Crap," Doody whispered. He sighted down the barrel of the Minimi, tugging the butt of the weapon into his shoulder.

There it was again.

From out of the storm there came a strange, hooting bellow, a noise like nothing he had ever heard before. It was answered faintly, from further away. The shadow moved in the whipping snow. Doody's eyes watered as they fought to stay open in the wind. The island went blank again, and there was just the unending howl of the gale, the battering of the tempest as it lashed the patient stone. Doody breathed out.

"It's enough to make you old," he muttered.

In the dormitory there were still iron-framed beds with their mattresses rolled up and lashed upon them. They were all in perfect condition, sealed off from the world for decades, left behind as they had been abandoned by the personnel of the base back in the 1950s.

Abby twisted a tap, more in hope than in any realistic expectation. It creaked dryly in her hand.

"Damn," she said aloud.

Cutter opened a heavier door. There was still grease on the hinges. Within was what looked to be some kind of pumping mechanism, and a forlorn steel bucket.

"Is this your well, Willoby?"

He pumped the lever at the side of the machinery. It cranked easily in his hand, and from far below them there were a series of clicks and clanking sounds, but no water came gurgling out of the spigot to fill the bucket.

Willoby bent over the cistern and lifted off the heavy metal lid.

"You need water to make water," he said. "We have to fill this before we start pumping, to get the thing going." He rubbed a hand over his face. "Joe, come with me. You too, Fox — with those creatures running around, there's strength in numbers. We'll head outside and fill some more water bottles while it's still light. Cutter —"

"I'll mooch around a bit. Maybe we'll haul some of these mattresses upstairs," Cutter said.

"Suit yourself. Come on Joe." The soldiers left, tramping back into the darkness with the beams from their head-torches playing like light-sabres across the walls.

"These will be better than sleeping on concrete, at any rate," Abby said, poking a mattress with a dubious finger.

Connor had already unrolled one and launched himself upon it with a squeal of metal bed-springs and an eruption of dust. He sneezed three times in rapid succession.

"Aw, Abby, it's great," he said, sniffling loudly. "Besides, we're not too clean ourselves."

She shot him an angry look. "Speak for yourself."

"Quiet, both of you," Cutter said, exasperated. He was wandering up and down the long dormitory, flashing his torch about him. Another door. He opened it. "Kitchen here. The canteen is just beyond. This place is much bigger than I thought. They must have had several dozen people working here at one time."

He walked back smiling, and tossed a tin can onto Connor's stomach. "Hungry?"

"Not for baked beans circa 1951," Connor said. He threw the can across the room with a clunk.

The soldiers stood exposed to the wind and sleet, a cluster of water bottles standing tilted towards the storm at their feet, held in place by a small piled wall of stones. Doody had told them about the shadowy figures in the snow.

"Boss," Fox said, "it's just a thought, but Pete was carrying all the demo gear on him. It's still out there, in his Bergen: C-4, det-cord, detonators, flash initiators — the whole heap. I'm just thinking, if we had it we could set a few booby traps for these bastard monsters, instead of trying to take them down with 5.56mm rounds..."

"They should have issued us bloody bazookas for this one," Joe Bristow said moodily. "It took four full mags to bring down the one that got Anita. If three or four of them take it into their heads to try and get into the base all at once, we'd run out of ammo before we stopped them."

"Point taken," Willoby said. "One thing at a time though."

"What are these bloody scientists doing here anyway?" Bristow went on. "All they're managing to do is put themselves in harm's way, and for nothing, so far as I see."

"They're experts," Willoby said patiently. He scanned the black crags of the plateau through his telescopic sight. "They have to monitor these things, these anomalies, and check out what comes through them. Imagine if a pair of something came through from the past and managed to survive here, and breed somehow. What a cock-up that would be."

"Let them at it, I say," Bristow retorted. "No offence, boss, but me and the lads, we can't help feeling there's something you're not telling us."

Willoby lowered his rifle and looked at him gravely.

"All in good time, Joe," he said. "All in good time."

FIFTEEN

Cutter played his torch over the door. It was massive, rubber-sealed, with not a speck of rust upon it. The padlock that secured it was the size of his fist.

"Connor," he said, "I'm counting on you."

"I only know the theory," Connor said quickly. "I've seen it done, and I have some of the tools, but..."

"Just do it, Connor," Stephen said. He looked back at the open doorway two rooms away, where Doody still lay behind the Minimi. Brice and McCann were asleep. All the other soldiers were still outside.

"All right, all right." Connor slipped a small leather pouch out of his inside pocket and unzipped it.

"Looks like a manicure set," Jenny said with a mischievous smile.

"Yeah, your nails could do with a polish, Connor," Abby teased.

"Oh, thanks." Connor slid out a couple of slim steel tools from the pouch and inserted them into the keyhole of the padlock. There were a series of minute clicks as he began working them back and forth.

They stood clustered around him, hiding him from the doorway. It was getting dark outside, and the light from their torches grew brighter as the gloom deepened around them. Connor was breathing heavily through his mouth, easing the two thin tools back and forth, in and out in the guts of the padlock.

"I think I — yes!" The padlock sprang open. "What do you know? I could make a living as a burglar, I could."

"Stick with the day job," Cutter said, patting his shoulder. "Right, if the others come back before I do, tell them I'm out answering the call of nature," he said.

"I'm coming with you," Jenny insisted.

"Listen, I —"

"I told you the truth about Willoby's mission. Now I want to see the reality of it for myself, Cutter. No arguments."

"Okay, okay, you guys close the door after us, but not all the way. We need air, remember. Whatever you do, don't let this thing slam shut on us."

"Go for it Professor," Abby said.

Cutter and Jenny slipped into the blackness on the other side of the door, and hid their coughing in their palms. There was air inside, but it was dead and stale and full of dust particles which the torch beams picked out in bars of drifting gold.

Glancing behind them, Cutter watched as the door swung back to within a centimetre of fully shut, and the noise of the storm outside was almost wholly cut off. They were in a lightless silence — it might have been halfway to the centre of the Earth.

"This place gives me the creeps," Jenny said softly, in little more than a whisper. Cutter could feel her warmth beside him; they were standing with their shoulders touching.

"We don't have much time," he told her, and he cautiously walked forward, looking to left and right. They were in a small anteroom, with desks and chairs and filing cabinets. A Bakelite phone, and on the wall a complex set of controls and instruments, dials and knobs that seemed like something out of a former age.

"They controlled the air flow and temperature from in here," he said.

"It was like a spaceship," Jenny marvelled.

"Yes, it was — and here's the airlock."

Another massive door, this one unlocked by turning a large iron wheel. It hadn't been padlocked.

They must never have imagined anyone getting this far.

Nevertheless, Cutter's fingers slipped on it and he cursed in a whisper as he fought it round anticlockwise. There was a clank, and he swung the door open on silent hinges. Once again, he and Jenny almost gagged at the dead stench of the air that rushed past them from beyond.

"It's a lab," Cutter said when he had got his breath back. He flashed the torchlight over workbenches, Bunsen burners, racks of test tubes. In one corner there was a containment cabinet, and in the other a fumehood.

"Now we're getting there," he said. "They must have had some funky stuff going on in here."

"Let's hope it's all dead," Jenny murmured, walking up and down between the tables. "No documentation of any kind left behind, not so much as a clipboard. You can even see where they peeled things off the walls."

"Yes," Cutter agreed. No samples either, no slides, no chemicals in jars. Glass, wood, rubber and steel were all they abandoned. "All the guts of the operation went with them when they left."

"What were you hoping for, Nick?"

"I don't know. Some kind of clue as to why this place was built here. Besides the official explanation."

There was another door at the rear of the lab. Cutter manhandled it open as he had the first, and beyond it stretched a broad passageway angling down, stairs on one side of it, a ramp on the other. The fire-extinguishers still hung on the walls, and there was a large sign at the bottom of the stairs saying 'Bio-Containment Area', while below it stood the most massively constructed door they had yet seen. It was like the entrance to a bank vault.

"This is it," Cutter said. "This is the nub of the thing, right here."

They stepped quickly down the stairs, curiosity overcoming their fatigue. There was another circle-lock on the door, but it wouldn't budge, though Cutter strained at it until his eyes bulged and the sweat popped out along his forehead.

Jenny tapped him on the shoulder.

"Cutter, before you give yourself a hernia, look here."

A small box was affixed to the wall to one side of the door. Jenny clicked open the lid, and within was a numbered set of tumblers, shining brass and thick with grease.

"A combination lock," she said.

"Damn," Cutter said hoarsely. "We fell at the last fence."

Darkness came upon the island, and in the black howling maelstrom of the night outside, they could hear the frenzied roar of great animals fighting and hunting and calling to one another.

Willoby, Fox and Bristow returned with bottles of water, and together they heaved-to the outside door and left it wedged open with a small boulder, as though trying to block out the horrors outside. They filled the cistern and got the hand-pump working again. The first few bucketfuls were cloudy and sour, but after that it came up as sweet and clear as anyone could wish. The team filled their bottles and drank pint after pint of the beautiful stuff, marvelling that something as simple and plain as water could taste so fine in their mouths, better than the choicest champagne.

Applause accompanied the first sound of rushing water, yet it seemed to Willoby that Cutter and Jenny were subdued. He shrugged.

Maybe they've had a tiff, he thought to himself. *This isn't exactly the perfect spot for a romantic getaway.* So he turned his attention to more important matters.

They hauled the mattresses out of the dormitory, and set up their sleeping bags on them, glad to be off the chill concrete of the floor. They all were still wearing wet clothes, but when conversation turned to their first campsite, at the southern headland, they thanked their lucky stars for the sturdy walls around them. The thought of another night in the tents, with the storm still raging and the creatures roaming the island freely, wasn't something any of them wanted to contemplate.

Their only problems were technological. The sat-phone wouldn't work with three feet of concrete above it, and the batteries of their head-torches were running down fast. This was a particular worry until Connor, rooting around in the base kitchen, discovered a small box of candles. These were lit in several corners of their sleeping accommodation, and the place began to look almost homely, in a stark, sombre sort of way.

"It's like a cross between Colditz and a monastery," Abby said as the team lay down on their mattresses and stared at the candlelight, while the storm roared stubbornly outside.

"Beats the heck out of a tent," Connor said. "I'm not the camping type, never have been. Give me four walls and a roof any day of the week."

"What about the caveman we all knew and loved earlier?" Abby asked him.

"Ah, well now, there's a time and a place for everything, Abs."

Willoby came over and crouched down beside Cutter. Quietly, he said, "In the morning I want you to sound out the possibility of a casevac. Brice doesn't look good to me. Doody says he's running a fever, and he's almost out of decent painkillers. In another twenty-four hours, we'll be down to aspirin and sticking-plasters. Plus, we've enough food for another thirty-six hours, tops."

"There's tinned stuff in the kitchen," Cutter said. "It's old, but sometimes that kind of thing can surprise you."

Willoby smiled faintly.

"I've eaten sixties-era tinned rations before now, but the stuff here would be pushing it a bit. We can't afford for anyone to get food poisoning. Professor, tomorrow I'm taking a team out to find my dead and bring them in. After that, we leave this place on your say-so. But frankly, I don't see what good you're doing here from this moment on. You're just putting people's lives at risk."

"So I take it you consider your primary mission to have been accomplished, Captain Willoby?"

There was something about the tone of his voice...

"Everything seems in order here."

"And you're not remotely curious about what's in the sealed vault that lies below us?"

Willoby stared at him. Fury flared up within him for a second; then it was gone, leaving him feeling washed out, tired to the marrow.

"You went down there, of course. I should have known."

"I went down there, but I could only get so far, as you knew I would. One last door remains shut on the secrets."

"With God knows what on the far side of it. Even wearing NBC gear, I wouldn't go down there, Cutter."

"I think the whole bioweapons thing is a front."

"It was a front, which was actually real. A classic double-bluff. Everyone's a winner. The bunker is intact, and your anomalies are still kept off page one. What more do you want?"

"To understand these things!" Cutter hissed fiercely. He lowered his voice as other members of the team looked round, surprised. "Your bioweapons are nothing but a drop of water in a rainstorm compared to what these anomalies might be doing to the very fabric of our world. Space and time, Willoby. They're tearing holes in the very laws that make up our physics."

"Not my problem," Willoby said. He looked away.

"What is it you know that you're not telling us? You said it yourself earlier, man; we're here at the sharp end, and the bastards who sent us here are just pulling the strings."

"There's more to it than that, Cutter."

"Then do me a favour; come down to the vault with me and open it. Because they gave you the code, didn't they, Willoby? You know how to open that last door. I can see it written all over your face. And deep down, you're as curious about it as I am."

"Curiosity! Is that what it comes down to?" Willoby demanded savagely. "People have *died* —"

"And more will die, many more, before we understand these things."

The two men stared at each other.

"My career would be over," Willoby said.

"With the military, certainly. But you never know — I might be able to find an opening for you somewhere else."

Willoby shook his head, smiling.

"You slippery bastard."

"You'll do it then. I'll take as much of the responsibility as I can. They can't sack me; I'm the only loon they have willing to front this stuff."

"Maybe I'll sleep on it. I have letters to write tonight," Willoby told him.

"Letters?"

"To the families. That, also, is part of my job, Cutter." With that, he walked away.

The middle part of the long winter night drew near, and Stephen was on stag with the Minimi trained on the outer door. He drew satisfaction out of the simple demands of the job. Stay awake, watch the door, be ready to open up on anything that tries to come inside.

He could hear them out there, in the storm. He felt almost sorry for them. They had come through from a warm, familiar world, and had found themselves in this subarctic hell in which they wandered around, dying by inches. Such magnificent animals, any one of which would be worthy of a lifetime's scientific study, and he was sitting here ready to kill them without hesitation or remorse. He didn't like the way this job had gone, and he didn't like the things he and Cutter had become involved with. There were too many soldiers, which somehow always seemed to add up to more death.

This is not scientific enquiry, Stephen thought. *It's the law of the jungle. And sitting here, in the midst of this desolation, we're nothing but bait.*

He tried to remember everything he knew about Eotyrannus, but kept coming back to the fact that they were superlative hunters and killers. Perhaps the earliest Tyrannosauroid ever found, pre-dating Tyranno-saurus rex by nearly eighty million years..

But maybe the most fearsome of their characteristics was the fact that they were pack hunters, and where there was one, there were sure to be others.

Two had been killed, and now Stephen was quite certain that the rest of the pack had followed their fallen brethren through the gateways. They were out there now, coursing through the dark like hounds on a scent. They would scavenge the bodies scattered about the island, and then they would start following the blood trail.

Here.

Get it in the head, he thought calmly. *Get the first burst in its head and you may stop it long enough to prevent it tearing you to pieces. Of course, if there's another one right behind it, you're nothing but dog food anyway.*

He almost jumped out of his skin when Abby came up quietly and joined him at his post.

"Jesus, you scared me!" he murmured. "Didn't your mother ever tell you not to sneak up on a man who's holding a machine gun?"

"My mattress smells," Abby complained.

"We all smell. I'm surprised you even noticed."

"I was well brought up, me, not like the rest of you tramps."

"Tramps — well, I like that." In fact, he did. She sat down beside him, and together they listened to the eerie sounds of the night.

"God," Abby said, "I'm so sick of the sound of the wind."

"At least the rain and sleet will help wash our scent away," Stephen told her.

"How long can this storm last, anyway?"

"It's a bit of an event, it seems. I did a little light reading before we left the ARC. Storms like this one only appear once or twice in a generation. The low pressure here is trapped between two high pressure systems, one over the Western Atlantic, and one over the European continent. So it sits here, turning endlessly, until at last it loses energy and the other systems swallow it. Guns Island is an unfortunate place: it happens to be square in the middle of that region of the Atlantic where this phenomenon often happens. It happens all over the planet, but mostly out to sea, so it's not picked up the way it would be if it were circling over Cambridgeshire, say."

"Lucky us, to be here at just the right time."

"Timing — yes, it's everything," Stephen said. And then it struck him. "Abby, the storm... it was already in full flow when Connor discovered the anomalies, wasn't it?"

"As far as we know."

It was on the edge of his thoughts, a kind of realisation, like a forgotten name perched on the tip of his tongue.

Something moved outside. There was a clatter of dislodged stone.

"Stephen —" Abby whispered.

"I know. Get back." He brought up the barrel of the Minimi, the bipod swinging as he lifted it clear of the floor.

In the crack of the doorway there was a sharp snort, like that of a horse blowing down its nose, only shriller. The door moved a centimetre, then two, as something nudged against it. Stephen felt Abby's small hand gripping his shoulder until her fingers seemed almost to be grating bone.

A dark muzzle poked through the doorway, just the tip of it. They saw the slit nostrils opening and closing, snorting out warm breath into the freezing night air. Beside Stephen, the candle flickered as the widening crack let in more wind.

Oh, don't go out, he prayed. *Don't go out and leave us in the dark.*

He swivelled his head minutely. His head-torch was lying on the ground four feet away. It might as well have been a thousand yards. Beside him, Abby was as frozen and immobile as a marble caryatid.

The snout withdrew. They heard it snuffling around outside, the click of rocks turned over by massive claws. Then there was only the howl of the storm, that familiar backdrop to all their experiences here.

"It's gone," Abby whispered. "It went away."

Stephen shook his head. The Minimi was aching his arms with its weight but he could not let the barrel drop. He held it trained on the door as though it were held in place with invisible strings.

"Torch," he said in a low voice. "Get it."

She scrambled for the torch on the ground, and just as she reached for it, the creature's head pushed fully through the doorway, followed by its neck and one shoulder. The head turned towards Abby, sniffing, and pushed the heavy metal door wide open, grinding back the large stone that had secured it. One yellow eye was cocked at them, and the animal uttered a series of harsh, piercing barks. It was so close that even in the guttering candle light they could see the feather-like quills that fringed along the top of its head.

"Get out of the way!" Stephen shouted at Abby. She was in his field of fire. He stood upright just as the maw of the animal opened and it pushed fully into the room, its long hands held out in front of it.

Stephen kicked Abby sprawling, squeezed the trigger, and the Minimi exploded in a furious flash of gunfire.

The candle was blown out, and in the sudden blackness the gunflash seemed almost to make things slow down, with a kind of stroboscopic unreality. Stephen saw Abby's blonde head moving frame by frame in a film of his own mind's nightmare; he saw the Eotyrannus stalk into the room, vast beyond belief in the confined space, and the retort of the gunfire blasted away his hearing, so that he was deaf, aware only of the high hissing sound in his head.

Tracers snapped out of the machine gun in his hands, and he watched in shattered glimpses of light as the creature came hurtling towards him, and was progressively torn up by the fusillade of bullets. Then the beast crashed into him, and he felt the hot breath of the thing as those hundredweights of flesh and bone and muscle and shredding teeth bludgeoned him to the ground and smashed him onto the unforgiving concrete.

***

"Stand-to!" Willoby shouted, and in the adjacent room the rest of the team scrambled out of their sleeping bags and reached for their weapons, clumsy and groggy with sleep. They bumped into one another, slipped, tripped and cursed as the hard angles of their firearms caught each other in the ribs.

"Out of the way!" Willoby yelled, shaking off the effects of fatigue, and he pitched through into the darkness of the outer room, weapon raised, cocking it as he went.

It was pitch-dark in there, a blackness full of an animal screaming. He heard Abby shrieking out Stephen's name. He clicked on the torch attached to the barrel of the M-4 and it lit up the vast, fearsome head of an Eotyrannus, not eight feet away. It was covered in blood.

Willoby fired two rounds into the creature's eye, and the head snapped back. He darted the rifle-torch about the room, stabbing out into the darkness, and caught a glimpse of Abby as she tried to haul Stephen's body away from the creature.

"Fox, Bristow, on me! Fire only at identified targets. We've got friendlies and enemy all mixed the hell up in here!"

A warm spray hit him in the face. He tasted it on his lips; he did not know whose blood it was.

The creature was thrashing and roaring and barking like a thing possessed.

Cutter joined him. He had a big torch, the wide-beamed one they had brought off the dinghy. It lit up the room like the stage in a theatre. Half the floor was swimming in blood. The Eotyrannus was still struggling, but like something that has nothing but pure will left to keep it alive. Willoby put five more rounds in its head, and it gave a high-pitched gargling hoot, then was still, the head hitting the floor with a crack.

They were all half deaf with the gunfire, but even so, Willoby could hear the high-pitched barks of more creatures right outside.

"Christ, it's a whole pack of them," Cutter said. "Abby, are you all right?"

"It's Stephen; it landed on him. I think it hurt him pretty badly."

"Get him out of here, back down the stairs. All of you, out of here," Willoby said. "This is soldier's work."

"We'll be in the labs," Cutter said. "Nothing can get through those doors."

"I'll join you down there. Grab the gear — leave nothing behind! Joe, Calum, help me close this bloody door."

The three soldiers put their shoulders to the door and began to heave it closed, but there was a sudden, massive impact on the far side that jolted them backwards. Willoby was bowled off his feet and an Eotyrannus's head snapped through the widening gap. The soldiers couldn't hold back that massive force.

Joe Bristow whipped a hunting-knife from his belt, still pushing at the door, and stabbed the creature near its eye. The Eotyrannus yowled in pain and as quick as a darting snake, it snapped out and closed its jaws about Bristow's head. He was lifted off his feet, screaming.

"Shoot it! Shoot it!" Willoby yelled, and Doody raised his weapon, but there was nothing to aim at — only the lower half of Bristow's torso disappearing through the gap in the doorway, his muffled voice still shrieking outside. Calum Fox grabbed his boots and tried to pull him back through the door, but there was a savage tug, and he was gone. Faintly, they heard his screams disappear into the howling storm.

"Oh, Christ," Fox said. There were tears streaming down his face. He bent and picked up his carbine, and then made as if to go out the door, his eyes not quite sane.

"No, Calum." Willoby shouted.

"Joe's still alive boss — we have to go out and get him!"

"He's as good as dead Sergeant, and if you're his friend you'll hope he dies quickly." Willoby looked around at what was left of his team. "We have to —"

He was interrupted by a chorus of sharp barks outside.

"God almighty, they're still out there," Doody said.

"Grab your gear and head down the stairs. Follow the civvies. Move it, lads!"

They seized their rucksacks and pelted down the stairs into the darkness, Willoby providing rearguard. When they reached the labs level Cutter was there at the heavy door.

"Come on!"

Willoby turned as he got to the door and raised his carbine. The torch attached to the barrel followed his gaze. At the top of the stairs two Eotyrannus stood, watching. Both were covered in gore. As he stared, they both crouched, and held out their arms before them as though they were about to catch a ball.

"They're going to spring — come on!" Cutter yelled, and tugged at Willoby's arm.

Willoby fired off a full magazine wildly at the stairtop, and then ducked past the heavy steel door. There were people on the other side, their faces lit with a zigzag of head-torches.

The door was slammed shut. Cutter began spinning the lock closed just as a massive weight thundered into it. The steel vibrated under the impact, and even through all that metal and concrete, they could hear the creature on the far side screaming its frustration.

They stood at the door, panting, scraping the stale air into their lungs.

"That's it now," Willoby said. He wiped the cold sweat from his face. "They've got us trapped."

SIXTEEN

"I don't suppose anyone thought to grab the candles," Connor said. He and Doody and Abby were bent over Stephen, and the beams from all three of their head-torches were glowing a sickly yellow.

"This is a sealed environment," Cutter said. "So long as this door remains closed, we're eating up the air in here, which wasn't great to begin with. The candles would only burn it up faster. Use your torches as little as possible everyone — you don't need three there. And try not to move around too much. We have to conserve the oxygen in here."

"So it's stay here and suffocate, or go outside and get eaten," Connor said. "Professor, I have to tell you, those choices both really suck."

"Ammo check," Willoby said. "Come on lads, get a grip. McCann, you too. You're a soldier. We need you now."

The Irish trooper joined Doody and Fox and held out a hand.

"John McCann, Irish Rangers," he said. "I've three full mags, ninety rounds — that's it."

Fox shook his hand. It seemed strange to Cutter, but the soldiers seemed to take comfort in the symbolic gesture.

"Welcome to the team, John. It's a laugh a minute." Fox turned to Willoby. "We left the Minimi upstairs. All we have are the M-4s and the Glocks. Boss, I'm down to forty rounds, tops, and two clips for the pistol."

"Same here," Doody volunteered.

"I've one full magazine left, thirty rounds," Willoby said with a weak smile. "It's not enough, not enough to go back out there." He looked around at the austere concrete walls of the lab. "We need an idea, Cutter, and we need it fast."

Cutter was bent over Stephen, frowning.

"He's broken some ribs and he's bruised purple from chin to crotch," Doody said, "but I don't think there's anything internal. He'll come round in a while, and it'll hurt like hell, but he should be all right. Meanwhile, he just needs to be kept warm."

Cutter patted the medic's shoulder.

"Thanks," he said. Then he straightened, checked the big hand-held torch, and flashed its wide beam about the room, until finally it came to rest on Willoby.

"Captain, I think it's time we had a look beyond that locked door of yours."

Cutter, Willoby, Connor and Jenny stood before the massive entrance labelled 'Bio-Containment Area', and tried to breathe slowly. Already, the air inside the bunker seemed to be thinning, and they were panting slightly, as though they were at high altitude.

"Anyone starts feeling lightheaded, sit down at once," Cutter said. "Captain, would you like to do the honours?"

Willoby stepped up, slung his carbine, and flicked open the lockbox at the side of the door. He began clicking the brass tumblers into place one by one. When they were arranged to his satisfaction he grasped the steel wheel that sat in the centre of the door, and twisted it slightly.

There was an audible click.

"Are you sure you want to do this?" he asked Cutter.

"If we're to die down here, then I'm damn sure we can at least satisfy our curiosity before we pop off," Cutter said.

"Hear hear," Jenny added. Willoby smiled at her.

"You really are a strange sort of civil servant, Miss Lewis." He began spinning the wheel-lock.

A clank, and the door seemed to vibrate for a second. Then with a grunt Willoby began to haul it open. The hinges squealed. It was like trying to push-start a car. They all put their backs into it, and eventually moved the massive structure of steel and rubber three-quarters open.

"My God," Willoby said.

They weren't looking into blackness. In the space beyond the door there was light, a strange, glass-sharp, flickering light. They entered the chamber, and found that they were standing on a broad catwalk. Below them there was a well, the base of which wasn't concrete, not man-made, but the black, granite bedrock of the island itself. And upon that rock, a ten-foot tall pillar of light gleamed and glittered and spun, shards of light spangling out from it and rejoining it again.

"Every time I see them, I wonder at how beautiful they are," Cutter said. He leaned on the railing of the catwalk and smiled.

"Bioweapons," Jenny said with a curl of her lip.

Connor was staring at the little LED screen of his hand-held anomaly detector. It was winking green. "I knew it! I knew there had to be one here somewhere."

Willoby stared at the anomaly like a man entranced.

"So that's it. That's the door to another world." He kept his gun at the ready, though, as if wondering what might appear through this hole in space.

"Another time," Cutter corrected. "The world of the past, or the future, but our world, this world." He looked at his watch.

"What's it doing here?" Willoby asked. "I mean, they must have built this place around it, to study it, but then it was just abandoned. Why?"

"My guess is the anomaly simply disappeared," Cutter said. "It's what they do, Captain. They come and go — we don't know why or how. When the thing first appeared, they built this place to study it, then it up and left. Well, so did they."

"And who do you suppose *they* are?" Jenny asked.

"The same people they always are," Cutter told her. "The puppet masters — the men who pay Lester's salary, who fund the construction of facilities like the ARC. Their faces change, over the years, but their agendas do not. National Security, Defence of the Realm — call it what you will. We're all a part of it, whether we like to believe it or not."

"The military-industrial complex," Connor said. "That's what Eisenhower called it."

Willoby coughed. They turned to face him.

"That's all very well Cutter, but the facts on the ground haven't changed all that much. We're still trapped in here, without any way to replenish our rations, and predators roaming the corridors. And there's no telling what might come at us from this angle."

"But we're not trapped," Cutter said. "Not any more."

"I don't follow you."

Cutter pointed at the anomaly. "There's our way out."

The others stared at him, astonished.

"You've got to be kidding," Jenny said, aghast.

"I'm open to alternative suggestions," Cutter shrugged. "We're standing here waiting to die, and if we open the vault door, the Eotyrannus will be in among us. We have wounded men, and we're low on ammunition. We wouldn't last thirty seconds. If we go through the anomaly, however, we get another chance."

"There could be fifty more creatures waiting on the other side," Connor protested.

"If there were, don't you think they'd come through? People, I have been through anomalies before — I've walked on the far side. Helen has been navigating these things for years. Once there, we need only find a portal that will bring us back, but in another location. It's dangerous, yes, but it's not hopeless, and we're pretty much out of other options."

They stood staring at the bright, glittering Christmas tree that was the anomaly.

"I'll go through it first, alone," Cutter offered. "That way, we'll know if what is on the far side is survivable."

"You could land anywhere — even in the sea," Connor protested.

"That's a chance I'm willing to take."

Cutter began walking down the sloping catwalk, noting abstractly the design of the place was more than a little reminiscent of the interior of the ARC.

"Don't do it!" Jenny sprang forward and seized his arm. "We can't afford to lose you."

Cutter's face brightened.

"Glad to hear it." He glanced around the room again. "But we're running out of alternatives — especially the wounded. Help simply won't arrive in time. I have to go —"

"Well, be careful," Jenny said, with an edge to her voice.

"I'll be back." Cutter squeezed her hand. Then he continued down the ramp to the rocky surface of the central well. He stood before the anomaly and let the turning, wheeling shards of brightness wash over his skin. Then he took a deep breath, and stepped into the light.

"I don't believe it," Willoby said. "He's gone, just like that." The SAS officer leaned on the catwalk railing and hung his head. "This is insane, all of it."

"It does seem that way, at least at first," Connor said. "But you get used to it. Beats going to lectures any day."

Willoby stared at him.

"You people are all one can short of a six-pack."

The three of them stood and peered into the coruscating heart of the anomaly as it flickered and spun, fragments of light splintering across the chamber like the reflections from a disco ball.

"We may never get out again, if we go in there," Willoby said.

"If we stay here, we're likely all dead, anyway," Jenny told him. "At least this way there's a chance."

Connor was looking at his fob watch. "Three-and-a-half minutes. Come on, Professor; how long does it take to have a quick look around?"

Cutter exhaled. His eyes were closed. He took one, two, three steps forward, and all at once the warmth hit him, a solid wave of it, like stepping into a steam bath. It seemed to him as if he had forgotten what true warmth felt like.

He breathed in deeply.

Thick, warm, oxygen-rich air. He drew it into his body in lungful after lungful. It was clean, wholesome, and it smelled of green, growing things, and underneath that a tang of salt, the essence of the sea.

He opened his eyes.

The sunlight was dazzling. He was standing in front of a wide, open expanse of tall ferns which extended off to woodland perhaps a kilometre ahead. There were hills in the distance, all tree-clad, with wide clearings. Further away, between the hills, he could just glimpse the blue glimmer of the sea.

He blinked, trying to identify the plant life he could see all around him, trying to get a handle on the time and place. There weren't any flowering plants here, but he could see pine trees. It was late then, getting on for Late Jurassic, more probably Early Cretaceous. The Jurassic had been drier, hotter, a time of savannahs and deserts. The scene before him reminded him a little of Montana.

Early Cretaceous, the same era that had produced the Eotyrannus and the Iguanodon. That meant at least one of the anomalies outside was from the same time, so there might be one or more around here that would take them back to the twenty-first century.

He knew he should get back. But he stood a moment more, savouring the warmth, the clean air, the bright sunlight.

A herd of animals moved, off in the distance. He couldn't quite make them out, Sauropods of some kind, perhaps. He watched, marvelling at the huge creatures as they trundled across the plain.

Time to go back.

He wiped the sweat from his face, and then stepped back through the glittering portal of the anomaly.

And into chill, gasping darkness. He actually stumbled, the change was so great. A hand steadied him.

"Cutter!" It was Connor.

"We were starting to wonder if you'd been eaten," Willoby said with grim humour.

Cutter was gasping for breath, and the sweat which the Cretaceous had raised on his skin began turning icy.

"It's the Early Cretaceous," he told his companions. "There's good air, warmth, and no predators about that I could see. This is where we go, Captain."

Willoby said nothing for a long moment, only stared at Cutter as though trying to read his mind.

"Very well," he said at last. "We'll go through. I'll go gather up the rest of the team. Connor, come with me; you'll need to help carry your friend Hart."

Off they went, the stuttering beams of their head-torches flickering yellow as they climbed the stairs to the rooms beyond. Cutter sat down on the blank rock at the foot of the anomaly.

"Is this really it?" Jenny asked him. "Is this really all we can do?"

"It's a damn sight nicer on the far side than it is here," Cutter said.

"Maybe so, but what if we get stuck there? These things open and close all the time — suppose we can't find our way back?"

"I have a feeling that as long as this storm lasts the anomalies will keep reappearing on the island. I'm almost certain that's why this place was built — to study them. But whatever brings them here, and keeps them here, has to do with the geology of the place, and the atmospheric conditions prevailing at certain periods in the past. The storm and the stone, if you will. The other anomalies that are out on the surface of the island right now must have their counterparts, some of them in the time I just visited. With Connor's detector, we should be able to find them, and come back through."

"Back onto the plateau of Guns Island, with a pack of Eotyrannus running wild upon it. We'll be back at square one."

"We won't be trapped, for one thing, nor starving or bleeding to death," Cutter said a little sharply. "And if we come back through an anomaly elsewhere on the island, I'll be able to use the sat-phone to call in help. Too many people have died. We need to be reinforced, or to get off the island altogether."

"I vote for the second of those," Jenny said, tapping her foot and folding her arms.

"I might be with you on that one," Cutter said with a smile.

The surviving members of the team came labouring down the stairs, laden with equipment and weapons. As Connor and McCann half-carried Stephen down to the anomaly, he raised his head and said groggily, "I want to go home."

"No such luck, mate," Cutter said. "How do you feel?"

"Like an elephant just used me for toilet paper. Are we really doing this, Nick?"

"We're doing it," Cutter said firmly.

"The creatures are still hurling themselves at the doors," Doody said. "Stubborn bastards, I'll give them that. And it sounds as if there are more of them than before. It's only a matter of time before they break through."

The team stood before the anomaly, waiting for Cutter's signal.

"Once we go through this," Cutter said, "we'll be in a world no human being was ever meant to exist in. So keep your wits about you. Open your eyes, and don't try to blast everything that moves. We'll be small mammals in a world of reptilian giants. Try not to get underfoot." He paused, looking them over. "All right then, let's go."

One by one, they walked or hobbled through the shining gate of the anomaly, leaving behind the world they knew, and entering an alien past.

SEVENTEEN

James Lester had studied French at school, and spoke it moderately well. It was an adornment to one's CV considered advisable in Whitehall, even now. *Never rely on an interpreter unless you really have to*, that was the mantra.

And never run an operation in tandem with a foreign government; that was the other, Lester thought. The old rivalries which had drenched Europe in blood for centuries had all but abated, but every nation state still had secrets it wanted kept. With the entanglements of this operation, Lester's department had been caught with its pants down. No wonder the ship's Captain had seemed so quietly amused as Lester had hurried aboard. Service personnel loved it when their pencil-pushing bosses caught it in the neck.

In a wine-fuelled post-summit haze of *bonhomie*, his own superiors had decided that James Lester would accompany this ship into the wild blue yonder, "to show solidarity with our Gallic friends." And, no doubt, to piss off the Irish for making such a fuss over the whole affair in the first place.

So he had been flown out to the *La Gloire*, and was steaming toward a situation that was already a disaster.

Vive la solidarité!

They were to liaise with the Irish patrol boat *Aoife* south of the island itself. The Irish had already lost a helicopter to the place, and even though they had been informed that the crew had been located, their concerns were ramped up to a level just south of frantic. They had already tried to mount a rescue by boat, but the high seas had rendered this impossible; it was all they could do to keep on station.

So Guns Island was still inaccessible.

Even satellites could make nothing out, the place being perpetually covered in thick cloud. Whatever was happening there, for the moment there was nothing the outside world could do about it.

The frigate breasted the heavy seas with relative ease, a large modern vessel with a 200-man crew and an excellent selection of wines on board. Lester had already dined in the wardroom and the civilised nature of the meal had assuaged his irritations somewhat. Now, dressed impeccably, as ever he stood on the bridge of *La Gloire* and contemplated the endless swells of the North Atlantic whilst the business of the ship went on around him.

We should have sent a ship of our own, he thought, *though with all these defence cuts we'd be lucky if we could scare up a bloody rowing boat.*

Captain Palliere, a dapper, dark, surprisingly young man, stepped over to Lester's side and offered him the use of a pair of binoculars. Lester demurred politely.

"I don't think there's much to see out there at the moment *Monsieur le Capitaine.*"

"Out at sea, there is always something to look at," Palliere said in fluent English. "For instance, only an hour ago my lookout insisted he saw something like a massive crocodile breach the surface astern, he said it looked like a sea serpent."

"Extraordinary," Lester said. "Perhaps he had had too much wine at lunch."

Palliere cocked an eyebrow. "This makes me think of what it must have been like in the old days, the Cold War. I have not seen so much mystery aboard ship in a long time. You British, you trust no one, and those you trust you try to manipulate. It has always been so. Myself, I have always preferred Le Carre to Fleming in any case." He shook his head with a grin. "You have been up to something out here, I think, something you would much rather keep to yourselves."

"There are matters of some delicacy afoot, it's true," Lester said vaguely. He cleared his throat. "But I have already hashed this through with your superiors, Captain. Your course of action has been agreed upon, and your orders have been cleared with both our governments. You are to enforce a maritime exclusion zone of twenty nautical miles around Guns Island, and leave it at that."

Palliere nodded. Something cold came into his grey eyes.

"I am a creature of the service to which I have devoted my life," he said. "I will obey orders, of course. But there are other laws and imperatives when one is out at sea. Be aware, Monsieur Lester, that if I see men in trouble, then it is the age-old tradition of mariners that I should do everything in my power to aid them. That will take precedence over any other orders, in my mind."

Lester found himself almost liking this neat, determined young man, every centimetre the officer, but with an edge of dark humour about him.

But all he said was, "I see your point."

"You have been up to something out here," the Captain repeated, "and now you've been — how do the Americans put it? You've been caught with your hand in the cookie jar. We are here to help your people, but do not mistake our aid for complicity."

Lester smiled. "I'll take that on board, Captain."

Palliere smiled back. "Excellent. I would be honoured, circumstances permitting, if you would join me for dinner this evening."

"I should be glad to." Lester actually bowed a little. For a few moments he had almost imagined himself back in a former age, when France and Britain had been rivals and enemies, whilst maintaining a healthy respect for each other. This shrewd young captain would take some careful handling.

I'm like that little Dutch boy with his finger in the dyke, he thought. *I can't keep it plugged for much longer.*

They set up camp in a small, isolated copse of oaks and willow amongst massive ferns as tall as their heads, and exclaimed at the huge dragonflies that came and went, shimmering through the trees.

There was a narrow stream coursing through the copse, and the water was as clear and clean as anything on Earth. Cutter tried to insist that it be treated with puri-tabs before anyone drank of it, but by then it was too late. The thirsty soldiers had filled their water bottles and glugged it back as though it were beer, wondering at the fine, hard taste of it.

"Great," Cutter said, packing a parka around Stephen to make him more comfortable. "Now we've got untreated Cretaceous water in our bellies, with God knows what kind of parasites in it."

"The water's clean — they gave me some, and it's the best I've ever tasted," Stephen said, wincing at the pain of his broken ribs. "This is still planet Earth, Cutter. The bacteria aren't alien, just a little different perhaps. You're just being difficult."

"The less interaction we have with this world, the better," Cutter insisted. "I don't have to tell you that, Stephen. Who knows what smallest event here might have ramifications for the rest of history?"

"Relax, Nick. Short of introducing a plague, I doubt if there's much we could do that would resonate across a hundred million years."

"I just hope you're right." Cutter was looking across the little campsite at Jenny. She had bound her hair back in a bun and her face was free of makeup. She looked much younger. More like the Claudia he had known, a woman he had perhaps been in love with.

McCann and Fox stood guard as the others went through their equipment and tried to find something to eat in the crushed chaos that was the inside of their rucksacks. So much had been left behind in the mad flight from the Eotyrannus. Ration-packs, ammunition, sleeping bags, torches, spare batteries. Connor had his hand-held anomaly detector, which was something, and Abby had had the presence of mind to bring along the sat-phone, so if they did manage to find an anomaly that could lead them back to the island they would be able to call for help, which was something else.

But apart from that, they were as far out on a limb as any human being had ever been, stranded a hundred million years from home with barely any food to keep them going.

"There's a bloody great herd of something moving across the plain to the north," Fox said. "Any ideas, Professor?"

Cutter joined him at the edge of the copse and stared through the pocket binoculars that Willoby had loaned him.

"Iguanodons," he said, "like that poor, injured creature back on the island. Hopefully that means there's an anomaly back to Guns Island somewhere near by."

Fox nodded. "What kind of creature are they?"

"Herbivores," Cutter replied, "moving in a big family group. There must be nearly a hundred of them. They're keeping the young in the middle, and the adults are on the outside."

"Like bison," Stephen said, lifting himself up on one elbow and clutching his ribs. "What do you think, Nick — is there time for a little scientific enquiry? We could settle the whole warm-blooded dinosaurs debate right now; think of that!"

Cutter lowered the binos.

"Even if we did find that out, how would we prove it? I can see it now: a paper based on examinations of real, live specimens as opposed to deductions from the fossil record. We'd be laughed out of academia, Stephen."

"Well, it's not as if we get to tell the academic community anything about what we do, as it is," Stephen replied. "We're forced to live with the accumulation of knowledge for its own sake — there'll be no Nobel Prizes for us, I'm afraid."

"I wonder if they'd be good to eat," Fox put in. Cutter stared at him. "What? I'm hungry. If we brought down one of those things, we'd feast like kings."

"No eating the dinosaurs," Cutter said, wagging a finger at the Sergeant. "It's bad enough we're here, without hunting the local wildlife to compound the issue."

"Calum has a point, though," Willoby said. "We've almost nothing in the way of food — enough for perhaps one more decent meal. And we have to keep our strength up somehow."

Cutter gestured to the herd of massive animals in the distance.

"You want to just walk up to them and start taking potshots? We've no idea how they'd behave. They might stampede, or they might just stroll over to you and paste you into the ground with one foot."

"Point made," Willoby said. "Something smaller perhaps."

"You show a soldier an entire, untouched new world, and all he can think about is his stomach," Cutter said, shaking his head.

Willoby grinned. "Just think about it, Professor. Nice big juicy Iguanodon steaks, grilling over a fire."

"That's another thing. I'm not sure about lighting a fire either."

"We're low on ammo — we'll need a fire for protection, especially at night. God knows what prowls these plains once the sun goes down."

"True — it's not known for certain if dinosaurs hunt at night or not." Stephen spoke up.

"The thing is, Nick, the fossil record is probably just a glimpse of some of the creatures that inhabit this era. There might be all sorts of species out there, big and small, that we've no idea about. And as for their behaviour, it's all conjecture on our part. I'm with Willoby on this one — we should light a fire tonight."

Cutter subsided, frowning.

"Aye, well, maybe you're right."

The Irish pilot, Sean Brice, joined them in the crackling bracken. "There's something on the far side of the trees I think you boys should take a look at."

They marched to the southern edge of the copse. There were willows there, with drooping limbs dipping in the stream as it curved about the trees. Their foliage made a perfect hiding place from which they could stare out at the tall ferns of the plain beyond.

"Christ," Willoby said.

Connor and Abby joined them, as wide-eyed as children.

"Look at that, Professor, coming down the hillside!" Connor exclaimed in a hoarse whisper.

Three large animals in a group, a kind of v-formation. They were theropods, standing on their hind legs, and they were making a beeline for the Iguanodon herd.

"What are they?" Brice asked under his breath, as if afraid the creatures would hear him.

"Some kind of Allosaurid, I think," Cutter said. As he crouched there behind the screening limbs of the willows, he felt a stab of pure fear, a primitive reaction to the sight of a massive predator. It was followed by a kind of intellectual joy, as he stared closely at the animals and catalogued their appearance and behaviour.

"Looks like Tyrannosaurs," Willoby said. "I've seen them in films."

The three massive predators were loping easily across the plain less than a mile away, eating up the ground at the speed of a galloping horse. Even at this distance it was easy to see that they weren't running flat out.

"No, T-rex was even larger," Cutter murmured. "My God, I think they're Neovenators — one of the largest European predators during the Early Cretaceous. Look at that huge skull."

"Wow," Connor whispered. "They must be nearly thirty-feet long."

"You could loose off a hundred rounds at one of those," Brice said, "and they wouldn't turn a hair. Still feel like heading out on the hunt, Captain?"

Willoby whistled soundlessly.

"They have a marvellous sense of smell," Cutter said. "Thank God we're downwind and in these trees."

"There they go," Abby said. "Look at them run!"

The three creatures suddenly picked up speed and began moving across the plain at an astonishing pace, spreading out as they went. They leaned into the run, and their tails trailed straight out behind them.

The herd of Iguanodons finally realised what was bearing down on them and from their ranks there rose a loud chorus of hooting noises, like bass sirens. The herd moved along the plain, raising a vast cloud of dust, and then seemed to halt, the adult animals facing outwards to meet the threat.

The three predators disappeared into the dust cloud, and from within it there issued a horrific cacophony of bellows and roars. The cloud rose higher, and the herd broke, stampeding off to the north in a great, thundering mass.

The team, lying over a mile away, could feel the earth shake and shudder beneath them under the impact of all those hundreds of tons of rampaging flesh and bone. They lay awestruck, and watched the drama unfold until the dust travelled into the distance, up to the higher ground close to the sea.

Then, as quickly as it had begun, the carnage ended. Around them, the world grew quiet again, and there was just the wind travelling through the trees, and the sound of the stream gurgling to itself.

"We have to move," Cutter said. "We can't stay here."

"What's the problem?" Willoby asked.

"It looks like we're smack dab in the middle of an apex predator's hunting ground. If they kill today, then they'll be lethargic for a while, digesting their meal. We should move out tonight, after dark, head for high ground."

"Damn it, Cutter, is it really necessary?" Willoby asked.

"The Neovenators will investigate anything new that crops up in their hunting territory — if not to eat, then to make sure it doesn't represent a threat, or a rival. Lions do the same. We can't coexist with those animals, and they won't let us. We shift camp tonight."

"Let's hope you're wrong about one thing then," Abby said with a weak grin. "And dinosaurs don't hunt at night."

As the sun went down, they packed up their meagre belongings again and prepared to set out. Before they did, Cutter had Connor check the anomaly detector. The light was red, and the screen was dark.

"Not a sausage, Professor," Connor said, disappointed. "Do you want me to keep it on?"

"No, Connor. Save the battery." By the time they had set up camp, they had trekked out of the range of the anomaly that had brought them into this world, so they wouldn't confuse it with any other, new, phenomena. Now, as they set off again in the cool of the evening, it felt almost as though they were walking further away from home, further from the only sure link they had with their own time.

They left the campsite as they had found it, gathering up every scrap and tin on Cutter's insistence, and set off across the darkening plain. Doody cut Stephen a stout staff, and he used it to lean on as he limped along in the midst of the party, hissing with pain as his cracked ribs opened and closed within his chest. Beside him, Brice walked holding his slung arm to protect it from the bumps and stumbles of the trail. The two had found a kind of fellowship in their injuries, for both were battling severe pain which could not be remedied. Doody's medkit was stripped almost bare, and apart from a few aspirin and some dressings, there was nothing left.

It was as though the party was being stripped back to its essentials, leaving behind the trappings of civilisation.

They trekked in waist-deep ferns, feeling as if they were wading through a pale sea towards land on a far horizon. The sun set in a breathtaking contusion of broken scarlet cloud, like the workings of some immense, dying factory on the edge of the world. Cutter stared at it.

"It's beautiful," Abby said.

"Looks to me like volcanic activity, out in the west. After Mount St Helens exploded in the US there were spectacular sunsets over half the hemisphere for months. All the ash in the air catches the light you see."

"You're a real romantic, Cutter," Abby said.

As the light faded, so the stars came out. And what stars! Cutter stopped in his tracks to stare up at them, open-mouthed, and the rest followed suit. The entire sky was awash with constellations, the Milky Way a huge glittering highway of light. The moon wasn't yet up, but the stars were so bright they made a light of their own.

"I've seen night skies before, in Norway, that would take your breath away," Fox said. "But this is something else altogether."

"I see the Great Bear," Connor said. "At least I think I do, it doesn't look quite right."

"They're not the stars we know," Stephen said. "Some will die; some haven't yet been born. A hundred million years hence, things will have changed. The universe is an evolving entity, still expanding."

"In a few million years, an asteroid will fall to earth, in the Yucatan, and in the aftermath of its impact, this world we see around us will end," Cutter said. "The K/T event. Geologically speaking, it's just around the corner."

"Always look on the bright..." Doody sang, and the rest of the party laughed. Even Cutter smiled.

"All right, children," Willoby said, bringing his carbine into his shoulder. "Time to make some tracks. We've a fair hike ahead of us before dawn."

It felt eerily exposed to be walking openly across that great plain of ferns, and they kept close together, moving at the pace of the slowest among them, which was Stephen. He did his best to maintain a good clip, but it was obvious he was in a lot of pain, and he leaned heavily on Doody's staff, his teeth bared, and sweat gleaming cold on his brow in the starlight.

After half an hour or so, they came to the spot where the Iguanodons had been grazing. Here the ground was battered and torn up, and there were mounds of droppings several feet high, still steaming in the cool night air.

"Smells like horse poo. Not so bad really; I was expecting something really gross," Abby said.

"Imagine the roses you could grow with that stuff," McCann chuckled.

Willoby held up a hand.

"Sssh! Something up ahead." In the quiet of the night they could distinctly hear the metallic click as he flicked off the safety catch of his rifle.

Cutter joined him. Willoby tapped his ear and then pointed ahead of them. There was a snuffling noise ahead in the trampled ferns, the crackle of broken stems.

They moved forward, and when they saw movement ahead, halted again.

There was something small and dark crouched ahead of them, rooting at the ground. It paused, and they saw the gleam of its eyes.

"Looks like a badger," Willoby said, disbelievingly. "Cutter, close one eye." Then he clicked on his rifle-torch for a second.

The animal snarled, caught in the bright, dazzling light. It backed away, and then turned and ran with a slow, lolloping gait into the darkness.

"That wasn't a dinosaur," Willoby whispered.

Cutter looked puzzled. He opened both eyes, his night vision preserved by Willoby's warning. "It looks like an early mammal. I don't think the remains of mammals have been discovered in this area at this time, but that's not to say they didn't exist — unless it's not supposed to be here and has stumbled through another anomaly..."

"Is it dangerous?"

"To us? No. It won't tackle anything our size. Good sign though, as it means there's nothing bigger roaming about."

They walked forward to see what the creature had been feeding on. It was the slimy carcass of a young Iguanodon, only some six-feet long.

"Looks like it was just being born when the Neovenators attacked," Cutter said, bending down to touch the cold, torn up flesh of the creature. "There you are, Willoby; if you want meat to eat, it's lying there."

Willoby screwed up his face, but he pulled out his knife and cut away some of the creature's flesh. He made no move to eat it, though — instead, he emptied one of the rucksacks and packed the meat inside it.

"It'd be like eating roadkill," he explained. "I'm not quite hungry enough yet."

"You're a human being. That means you're a scavenger. It'll be millions of years before we can be considered predators ourselves."

"I guess I'll wait," Willoby said. "At least this way, if the times comes, we'll have something to fall back on. All right, bring up the others. We're wasting time here."

They continued on their way, skirting the site of the dead Iguanodon and making better time in the trampled swathe of earth that the passing of the creatures had left. The night was uncomfortably quiet. Occasionally they could hear hoots and growls off in the distance, but there were no nocturnal birds to be heard, no foxes barking, no owls. The environment seemed somehow more alien at night than it had during the day.

"I smell the sea," Abby said as they trudged along.

The moon was up, three-quarters full, and even its white face was changed, the craters in different places.

"But what sea is it that you smell?" Connor asked. "My Cretaceous geography isn't all it should be."

"It's the Atlantic, or will be," Stephen said, hobbling along behind them. "Pangaea, the great landmass, has come apart and now the continents are becoming recognisable. Greenland and the UK are pretty much next-door neighbours, and there should be plenty of islands, too. The sea should be shallow still, not a proper ocean at all."

"Just think, if you could only control the anomalies," Connor said. "Slip into time or any place you wanted. Think of all the questions you could answer."

"Who knows?" Stephen said. "Maybe we'll figure it out some day. I know that Helen —" He stopped, catching himself.

Connor and Abby said nothing more, but looked at each other in the moonlight.

They reached the end of the plain some time towards dawn, and halted there to rest and take stock in the shadow of the hills. The ground rose before them, ascending in loose outcrops of dark stone and open slopes covered with conifers. They could smell pine resin in the air now, and there were pine needles underfoot. Nameless insects clicked and chirruped in the trees around them, but otherwise the night was silent, and the moon sailed like a silver galleon amid a sea of stars.

"Take away the monsters, and this would be a hell of a beautiful world," Calum Fox said, sitting with his M-4 in his lap.

"The Brecons are about as wild as I like it to get," Doody retorted. "Sarge, what do you think's happening back at home. You reckon there's a rescue team on the island yet?"

Fox nodded. "Bound to be, weather permitting. The Irish will be champing at the bit to get to their downed chopper. That's about a quarter of their air force, right there." Brice and McCann looked up and scowled at this, but said nothing.

Cutter and Connor stood a little apart from the rest. Connor had clicked on the anomaly detector and was sweeping it around in an arc.

"Nothing, Professor. Not a blink."

"What's the range of this thing, Connor?

"Only a few kilometres. Maybe even less. It'll work better on the higher ground."

"Why is that?"

Connor shrugged sheepishly. "I don't know, it just does."

Exasperated, Cutter said, "You built the damn thing!"

"I know Professor, but I tend to just have a feel for things. I put 'em together and they work, but half the time they behave in ways I can't entirely explain."

"Connor, you may be the most maddening genius I've ever known. Give it another sweep when we get to the hilltop. How's the battery?"

"Ah, not so good. I don't think it appreciated being dunked in the sea."

"Terrific. Well, conserve it as much as you can. Without that damned contraption, our chances of stumbling across another anomaly don't look so hot."

They set off again. The sky had begun to pale in the east, turning a delicate eggshell green at the horizon. Dawn wasn't far off.

Cutter estimated that they had covered some fifteen kilometres. They were climbing up a steep, rocky, wooded slope now, and their progress had slowed dramatically in the darkness under the trees. They encountered loose rocks and tree stumps and fallen branches which were hard to navigate in the dark, and Stephen had to be helped along, with Connor on one side of him and Abby on the other. His breath had become a rearing rattle in his throat.

McCann was on point. They saw him raise a hand and make a fist up ahead. At once, they all sank down to the ground, breathing hard.

Cutter and Willoby moved forward and joined him.

"What the hell is that?" the Irishman whispered, pointing.

They were near the top of the ridge now, and the slope had levelled out. The trees were thicker here, and there were waist-high ferns carpeting the floor of the wood. They were wet with dew, and so the entire team were soaked to the waist. But up ahead there was a more open space, and glints of the setting moon were lancing into it. There was a huge mound there, with what looked like broken branches sticking up out of it. But the mound smelled strongly of dung and warm animals of some sort; and it was moving. They could hear the quiet susurration of huge lungs breathing in and out.

"Go left," Cutter murmured. "Go around them."

"What are they?" McCann asked. "Meat-eaters?"

"No, they're a kind of Ankylosaur, I believe. Armoured dinosaurs — see those spikes. It's a family group. If we wake them up, they'll charge us to protect the young. We have to be quiet."

"No shit," Willoby whispered. "Lead on Cutter. McCann, go back down the line and clue everyone in — no noise, no talking."

"Got it." The big Irishman sidled off with surprising stealth.

The party crept past the heap of sleeping animals. The largest were four or five metres long. Some were standing, asleep on their feet, and others had curled up on the ground.

"Polacanthus, I reckon," Connor whispered out of the corner of his mouth, and Stephen nodded. He was white-faced with pain, and sweating heavily despite the cool night air. It was chillier up here on the hilltops than it had been down in the plain, and drier. Thankfully, the pine needles underfoot muffled their progress, and the team was able to sneak past the sleeping dinosaurs without incident.

They reached the highest crest of the ridge just as the sun was coming up, and halted there to catch their breath and watch the silent majesty of the dawn as it broke open over this vast, wild world.

On one side, the plains rolled on for miles, stretching out like a sea of ferns that was lined with watercourses and dotted with woods. On the other, the proto-Atlantic shimmered and caught the light out to the edge of infinity. There were islands out there, wooded and green, and beyond them, the guess of another large landmass at the edge of sight.

At the shore there stretched lines of rock reaching out into the water, and low cliffs. Upon these, the team could see Pterosaurs sunning themselves, stretching out their wings like cormorants to catch the warmth of the rising light. Down on the rocks, creatures which might have been huge crocodiles lay in rows, squabbling and crashing off into the waves. It was a world that the sun brought to life, a theatre of giants.

"It's beautiful," Jenny said, joining Cutter as he stood silent and rapt upon the hilltop. "I had an idea it would be terrible, frightening, and it is. But it's beautiful too."

"A world we haven't touched," Cutter told her. "Look at the horizon; it's clear and clean. In our time there would be a purple haze there, the smog of the combustion engine. Our world, our time, is choked half to death. We've filled the sea with plastic and gutted the rainforests. Here, it's all fresh and untouched. I begin to understand —"

He stopped.

"Understand what?" Jenny asked him.

"I begin to understand why Helen has lost herself in the anomalies. For the last eight years, she's been travelling worlds like this one, alone, shifting from epoch to epoch, using these phenomena the way some people will catch a bus. I don't know how she does it, but right now, right here, I can begin to see why."

"Would you like to do it, Cutter — lose yourself in a world like this one? See the object of your life's work not as some fossilised bones, but as living, breathing animals?"

There was a long silence. Finally Cutter looked at her. His mouth curved into a self-mocking smile.

"Nah, I'm not enough of a boy scout for that." Then he tensed. "What's that smell?"

They rejoined the others. Doody had lit a small fire and was piling dead sticks upon it. The fragrance of wood smoke rose in the air.

"I'm still not sure a fire is a good idea —" Cutter began.

"Your pal isn't in great shape. He needs to be warmed up," Willoby interrupted curtly, nodding in Stephen's direction. "Besides, we should have a hot meal, all of us, and a cup of tea. Try and maintain some civilisation in the wilderness. If we eat the meat we found, it'll save the last of the ration-packs, so we might as well make the most of it."

Stephen was shivering and wheezing for breath as he lay on a bed of bracken which Connor and Abby had gathered for him. They had opened a sleeping bag and crammed him half into it. His teeth chattered as Cutter bent over him.

"What's this?" Cutter asked gently. "Wimping out again?"

"You know me," Stephen grated. "Just one big party-pooper."

"Stay with us, Stephen," Cutter said. "I need another grown-up around."

"Jenny will do just fine for that," Stephen replied, trying to smile.

"Is it the ribs?"

"Ah, I just need a bit of a rest. A cup of hot tea — now that really would work wonders."

"Hang in there, mate," Cutter said in a voice so low he wasn't even sure Stephen had heard.

The soldiers were cooking the meat on improvised spits, and boiling mess tins of bubbling water. Cutter took Doody aside.

"What's wrong with him — he's getting worse."

Doody's face was sombre.

"Last might's march — he shouldn't have made it. I think one of his ribs has got itself poked into a lung. He's been coughing up blood for the last hour."

Cutter swore viciously.

"What's the prognosis?"

"He has to rest, propped up. His lung may be filling up with blood and fluid. I'm not sure. If that happens, I'll have to drain it." Doody licked his lips. "I've never done that before."

"There's no chance it'll come right on its own?"

"Not much. It's more likely he'll start to drown in his own blood."

"Be ready, Doody," Cutter said.

"I'll try. It'll help to have hot water on hand, too, so the fire's not a bad idea."

"Very well. Let me know if — if he —"

"I will," Doody said.

The fire, the hot food, and perhaps more than anything else, the tin mugs brimming with hot, brown tea, cheered them all. It was like a tincture of normality. As they sat under the pines and spruce which towered above them, and looked out upon the sea, they might have been having a picnic in the Scottish Highlands. Except that the sounds which completed the picture had more in common with an African game reserve.

Through binoculars they watched the Iguanodon herd return to the plain below and begin feeding as though yesterday's attack had never happened. The Iguanodon were joined by a large group of Polacanthus, like those they had chanced across in the night. These two great masses of animals mingled in apparent amity and spread out across the low-lying lands below, clustering at waterholes.

The team slept, or tried to. After walking all night, they were exhausted. Cutter took first stag. Weary though he was, he couldn't drop off with the sound of Stephen's racked, laboured coughing echoing over the campsite. He sat down beside his former pupil with an M-4 on his knee, and talked quietly of this and that, of the different strains of duck-billed dinosaurs, of herd behaviour, of the K/T event theory. Anything which kept both their minds off Stephen's ebbing battle for survival.

"I'm sorry about Helen, about what happened," Stephen rasped. "I suppose I was flattered. And it didn't seem as if you two were ever getting back together. I thought all that was over."

"Bar the shouting," Cutter said. Then he added, "She was still my wife."

"In name only, Nick." He bent over and coughed harshly, whooping for breath. Cutter took a handful of bracken and wiped blood from the corner of his mouth.

"Anyway," Stephen went on when he caught his breath again, "it was wrong, what I did. I was wrong."

"Don't beat yourself up about it, not here, not now," Cutter said, looking off into the distance. "It wasn't entirely your fault anyway."

He sighed heavily. "What Helen wants, Helen gets. She was always that way. In the beginning, it was why I loved her — that ambition, that drive. But it all went sour. She's a brilliant woman —"

"And a complete egomaniac," Stephen interrupted with a wan smile on his face.

"That's putting it mildly. Anyway, after eight years of wandering the timelines, she's become a monster."

"Oh, come on," Stephen protested.

"I don't think she'd stop at anything now to get what she wants. I sometimes wonder if she was behind —" Cutter looked across the campfire to where Jenny lay sleeping. "Behind the changes that happened after I last came through an anomaly."

"That's quite an accusation."

"Yes, it is. The Chinese have a saying: 'May you live in interesting times.' Except it's not a blessing, but a curse. I prefer the Spanish proverb: 'May no new thing arise.'"

Stephen coughed and laughed at the same time, and Cutter had to support him as he leaned forward to spit a globule of gore into the ferns. When he caught his breath he said, "You picked the wrong line of work for that one, Nick."

"So it seems."

EIGHTEEN

The Puma helicopter swung and lurched under the battery of the wind. It approached the French frigate from astern, keeping at some 200 feet, and drifted forward in a careful hover as the warship rose up and down in the heavy swells, white foam breaking over her sides.

The ground crew waved the aircraft in or waved it away as the pilot fought to position it dead centre over the bucking bullseye of the helipad. Even Lester, looking on from the rear hangar, felt a prickle of fear run down his spine as the ship rose up to meet the descent of the Puma, and one of the aircraft's wheels smashed into the steel deck with a creak of overburdened metal. The tyre blew with a dull pneumatic bang, and the helicopter rose up again.

"*Mon Dieu*," Captain Palliere said grimly beside him.

The Puma came in again, the down-blast of its rotor sending water rippling out across the deck. Lester shielded his eyes as it flared just before the pilot made his decision and committed himself.

The helicopter hit the pad with a crash that sent vibrations right through the hull of the ship. It tilted slightly to one side on its blown tyre, and the turbines were shut off. The ground crew ran out at once to lash the machine down; the wind was already making it shake and lurch upon the pad. Then the crew climbed out, one by one, and the sailors around Lester gave them a scattered round of applause.

Oh, for goodness sake, Lester thought, but he joined in. Even he thought the pilot had earned it.

The helicopter crew walked somewhat shakily into the hangar while behind them men swarmed over their aircraft. Captain Palliere shook the pilot's hand and spoke in a rapid flurry of French. Then he turned to Lester.

"We will begin the debriefing at once. Is your French good enough to follow, or shall I have it typed up for you in English, Lester?"

"Oh, don't worry about me," Lester said with a thin smile. "I'll muddle along somehow. *Allons-y!*"

At Lester's insistent request, the only people present at the debriefing were Palliere and his executive officer, a wiry Provençal called Dutourd. The pilot was given a fragrant cup of hot coffee, which he downed in one scalding gulp, and then he began to tell them of his reconnaissance.

The Puma had made two sweeps of the island, from south to north. The updraft at the southern approach had almost flipped the machine on its side, but they had managed to maintain height and ride it out. That, the pilot said, was probably what had happened to the Irish helicopter. The Scout was a much smaller, lighter craft than the Puma, and the updraft would have simply thrown it through the air like a kite.

"Did you see the crash site?" Lester asked impatiently, leaning forward.

"*Mais oui*," the pilot answered. He looked at his captain, who motioned him to proceed.

The Westland Scout lay towards the north headland of the island, not far from the British outpost. There were no bodies in the wreck, he was pretty sure of that.

Lester leaned back again. That confirmed what he already knew, but it was good to have it substantiated.

The French pilot had seen other things across the island, strange things. He thought he had seen the carcass of a large animal, but could not be positive. There was debris scattered here and there, as if left by a landing party, and a trio of strange lights had been sighted, close to the north end of the island. These were tall, inexplicable flickering phenomena, unlike anything else he had ever seen in his flying career, and he could not account for them.

Here, all the Frenchmen present turned and looked at Lester. He kept a poker face and motioned the pilot to go on.

The main door to the British outpost seemed to be lying open, and the mud around it was badly churned up, as though a rugby scrum had ploughed its way across it. That was it. In both passes, the helicopter crew had seen no living person.

The pilot was dismissed. More of the superb coffee was poured, and Dutourd left to take up station on the bridge. Lester and Palliere sat looking first into their coffee cups, and then at each other.

"I would say this was very strange, *n'est pas?*" Palliere said mildly.

Lester did not reply. It had been far too long since his last communication with Cutter, and despite the lack of bodies at the crash-site, he was fully prepared for the worst. He had a contingency plan for that, one which his superiors had approved with massive reluctance, because it entailed confiding in a foreign armed service. Something they preferred to do as little as possible.

"The Captain of the *Aoife* has officially turned over the rescue mission to *La Gloire*," Palliere went on. "His government approves. Lester, unless you have other information which you are withholding from me, then I am bound to inform you that I am taking command of all operations concerning Guns Island from this moment on."

"What do you intend to do?" Lester asked sharply.

"As soon as the Puma is airworthy again, I mean to drop a team of marines on the island, and as soon as sea conditions are suitable, I will be sending more in by boat. It might therefore be wise of you to let me know what exactly my men are going to encounter, should they make landfall successfully."

It would be the contingency plan after all, then. Lester rubbed his eyes. He had had a feeling it would come to this from the moment he had been ordered to join the French frigate.

Before he could speak, though, the French Captain continued.

"Lieutenant La Hire is a good man. When he says he sees three tall, flickering lights on the island, I believe him. I understand that your government has something to hide on Guns Island, and I can sympathise with your predicament, but the fact is that men's lives are at risk, and for me, that is the important point."

Lester studied the frigate Captain closely for a second.

"Palliere, are you not ambitious?"

The Frenchman sipped his coffee.

"Would I hold this rank if I were not?" he said.

"Then believe me when I tell you that your handling of this affair will be the making or the breaking of your career."

Palliere leaned closer. "And of yours too, I take it."

"Well, yes, of course."

Palliere gave a very French shrug, a simple movement of his shoulders.

"Ambition is all very well in its way — what professional does not want to excel in his field? But I tell you this, Lester, I have not, and I will never, purchase my advancement with other men's blood. Not in peacetime. In time of war, I will sacrifice my men to protect my country. But we are not at war, and a government's embarrassment is not worth that sacrifice."

"Noble sentiments," Lester said wryly. "A little out of place in the modern world, would you not agree?"

Again, the tiny shrug.

"That is the man who sits here with you drinking coffee. I cannot change who he is."

Lester drew a deep breath, then released it.

"Very well, Captain, in that case I have two requests to make of you."

"*Allez.*"

"I am going to tell you something you will find impossible to believe, but you must believe it. And I must be with the first of your men when they arrive on the island."

Stephen's cough grew worse as the day drew on. He sounded as though he were gargling blood, trying to force air through a flooded pipe.

"I can't leave it any longer," Doody said eventually. "I have to drain the fluid out of the lungs or he'll drown, right in front of us."

"If it has to be done, then let's do it," Cutter said, with as calm a face as he could muster. "What do you need?"

"It'll hurt like hell, and I don't even have a local anaesthetic, so I'll need people to hold him down and manhandle him. I still have a few sterile dressings, so that's not a problem."

"Get to it, Dave," Willoby said, setting a hand on the medic's shoulder. "While there's still enough light to see by."

"If I go in the wrong place, I could pierce his heart, or liver, or a kidney. It would kill him," Doody said.

"He's dying anyway," Willoby told him. "You've no choice. Set it up."

They stripped Stephen to the waist and laid him out on a karrimat. He couldn't speak, but as Doody explained what he was going to do, he nodded, fighting for air. The medic broke open his denuded medkit while Cutter, Willoby, Fox and Abby held the patient down, one on each limb.

"Don't move, no matter how bad the pain gets," Doody said. "If you move and the needle slips, it'll — it'll be bad."

Again Stephen nodded. "Get on with it," he managed to croak.

Doody took out a large syringe, and fixed to it the widest-bore needle he possessed. He pursed his lips, breathing quickly, but utterly focused. Then he stabbed it deep into Stephen's torso.

Stephen tensed like strung wire. The others held him down. He clenched his teeth and uttered a horrible, animal moaning as Doody slowly drew back the plunger on the massive syringe, and it filled with dark blood. When it was full, he withdrew it and squirted the liquid away into the trees.

"Here we go again," he said, and stabbed the needle into Stephen's other side.

It went on and on, until Cutter had to look away. In his grasp, Stephen's arm was slick with foul sweat and his own limbs ached from holding it down. The smell of blood seemed to pervade the campsite, along with the rank stink of human pain. He had evacuated himself with the very first thrust.

Doody sucked out measure after measure of cloudy blood from Stephen's lungs so that the injured man had a series of bleeding holes all along the lower line of his ribs and back. He looked as though he had been stabbed by an eccentric psycho with an ice pick.

At last it was over.

Stephen lay drenched in sweat and pale as bone, but he was breathing more easily. Doody seemed hardly less shattered. He dressed the wounds.

"Make him tea," he said. "Lots of sweet tea. He needs to get fluids down him now."

Abby dried Stephen off, tears streaming down her face. He managed to smile for her, but could not speak. Connor sat watching it all with a face of chalk, gripping Jenny's hand tightly.

"That's got it for another day or two," Doody told Cutter and Willoby, "but he has to get to a hospital ASAP, or he's not going to make it. And we'll have to rig up a litter if we're to move him — there's no way he's walking out of here."

"Anything you say, Dood." Willoby smiled, shaking the younger man gently by the shoulder. "That was a hell of a job you just did."

Doody wiped his mouth. He nodded, then broke away from them both and, running from the campsite, he bent over and was violently sick into the ferns.

As night came upon them they built up the fire and laid in a store of firewood so those on stag wouldn't have to go looking for more in the darkness. They had been lucky during the day, sighting the grazing herds of herbivores, but no predators. Once, a Pterosaur — they couldn't see clearly enough to identify it more specifically — had swooped low over the camp with its sail-like crest glowing scarlet in the sun. It had been like being buzzed by a small aeroplane.

Twice before the dusk settled into complete darkness, some kind of animal circled their camp warily. They could hear it stepping through the bracken, and they swept the wood surrounding them with the ragged beams of their head-torches, but could make nothing out in that silent forest. Whatever it was, it wasn't large in the present sense of the word and as night came on, it seemed to leave them be.

They huddled around the fire. Most had slept for several hours through the day and so the ever-present tiredness was a little less pressing than usual. Up here in the hills, the night seemed noisier, or perhaps it was the proximity of the trees around them that seemed to magnify every sound they heard.

Obsessively, Willoby did a kit and ammo check, and when this was done he subsided moodily with his M-4 on his knees. The sheer sense of wonder which had affected them all upon entering this world had begun to wane. They were more conscious now of their real predicament, and this knowledge put a damper on conversation. Plus, most of them couldn't help but keep stealing looks at Stephen as he lay sleeping fitfully close to the fire, propped up on a pillow of rucksacks.

He woke up, as though their guilty looks had nudged him out of sleep.

Cutter knelt beside him and handed him a water bottle. He drank gratefully.

"Maybe you should start a sing-along," he said to Cutter in a low croak.

"Sure thing. You break out the guitar and we'll give it a go." They smiled at each other.

"It's been an adventure, it truly has," Stephen said.

"It's not over yet."

"If I die, Cutter, I want you to bury me deep."

"Don't talk shite," Cutter snapped.

Stephen smiled. "Seriously. I've been thinking about it. If you do the job right, someone may well be digging up my fossilised bones by the time you get home. That would really put a cat in with the canaries. Can you imagine? 'Homo sapiens found alongside dinosaur'. The tabloids would flip."

"Nah, it has to be a double-decker on the moon for them to get excited," Cutter said, smiling. He leaned closer to Stephen and looked the younger man in the eye.

"*You're not going to die.* That's a promise."

"This is no good," Willoby was saying. "That machine of yours, Temple, isn't picking up a thing, and it's not likely to as long as we stay in one spot — there's just nothing in range. We have to go out and look for these things while we still have the strength."

He glanced at his watch.

"All right, here's the plan. We catch a couple of hours' kip, and then I take out a patrol with that device, and we try and cover an arc around the camp before dawn, extend our range a bit, as it were. Cutter, do you agree?"

Cutter nodded. "Take Connor along — he's the only person who really knows how to get the best out of that detector."

"Me, out there in the dark, wandering around?" Connor protested. He opened and closed his mouth once or twice, then sighed. "All right."

"McCann, you come with us," Willoby said. "Sergeant Fox, if you need us back here, fire a few shots."

Fox raised his eyebrows. "If we need you back here I'm sure you'll be hearing more than a few, boss."

The three of them set out soon after, having given up on any attempt to sleep — they were too keyed up. Before they left camp, Abby took Connor's arm and handed him a pistol.

"There's five rounds left in it," she said. "Be careful, Connor — and don't use it unless you really have to!"

"I won't. Thanks. Thanks, Abby." He looked very young in the firelight, not much more than a boy. When Abby kissed him on the cheek he blushed and stammered. It was like a scene from a school play. The only jarring note was the 9mm pistol he held in his hand.

"See you at dawn, with any luck," Willoby said as he led his little group out of the firelight and into the prehistoric night.

NINETEEN

"Brace, brace!" the pilot yelled in French as they came zooming up the mighty black cliffs.

The helicopter careered to one side and its occupants were slammed into their harnesses and then back again. The Puma raised its nose and the turbines strained deafeningly as the machine fought the updraft.

"*Merde!*" one of the marines beside Lester spat. "*Ça, c'est le bordel!*"

I couldn't agree more, Lester thought. *This is indeed a shitty place.* He kept his face carefully blank though, cultivating the stiffest upper lip he thought he had ever been called upon to wear. *It would be so typical if this thing crashed here. Such a bloody bore.*

They were above the cliff edge now and for a few minutes were flying through thick cloud. The stuff drifted in the open door of the aircraft and was salty on the tongue.

All around him, the team of marines sat stolidly, lashed to the walls of the interior with their rifles between their knees, muzzles resting on the floor. Their commander, a young Lieutenant called Desaix, looked as though he was about to be sick. Beside him, the ship's doctor, Ramis, was blessing himself.

Lester smirked a little, but not for long.

Oh, Christ.

The helicopter swung through the air like a leaf. For a moment it was on its side, and Lester, hanging in his harness, saw the ground directly below him, a desolate, sere landscape of rock and withered grass.

"*Une minute!*" the winchman shouted, and he held up one finger for the Englishman in case he should not understand. Lester smiled coldly at him and wiggled his toes in the ill-fitting boots. He was dressed in French military fatigues, something that annoyed him mightily, but he at least had possessed the presence of mind to cut the tricolour off the shoulder before leaving the ship. He was damned if he would die with a foreign flag on his arm.

The helicopter righted itself, shuddering, and swooped down with a speed that brought Lester's stomach up against his diaphragm. He opened his mouth in a wide O to make his ears pop, and then there was an almighty thump as they hit the ground.

"*Allez, allez-vite!*" the winchman shouted as the marines cast off their harnesses and leapt out of the doors of the helicopter. As they piled out, the winchman kicked their rucksacks out after them. Lester jumped with the rest and landed heavily. In front of him, a heavy green rucksack hit the ground. Another foot and it would have brained him.

He straightened, ignoring the roaring backwash of the rotor, and dusted off his hands. His ankles and feet ached with the landing. The helicopter rose, tearing away to the south as though helpless before the wind. As the roar of its engines died away into the distance, so it was replaced by the howl of the storm. Lester felt sleet sting his face, hard as sand.

Well, he thought, *I'm here at last. Perhaps now we'll be able to make some sense out of this debacle.*

The marines retrieved their gear, hefted their Famas rifles, and shook out into all-round defence. It seemed a needless precaution. The island was deserted, not so much as a seagull popping its head up to vie with the storm.

Their officer, the absurdly young Desaix, consulted his GPS, and then raised his hand in a chopping motion. The heavily armed little band of men set off at once, and Lester, wincing, had to puff as he kept up with them.

I'm a little out of shape, he thought as their fast pace ate up the ground. *I really should try and fit in a few more squash games of a weekend.*

The storm, fearsome though it still seemed, was fading. The wind was steadily slipping down the Beaufort scale and a ridge of high pressure was finally beginning to move over the island from the Americas. Had it not been for this, the Puma wouldn't have been able to effect a landing.

As the French team came upon the crash site of the Irish aircraft, Lester felt a momentary pang of pity for Jenny. *We might as well have sent her up in a bloody biplane*, he thought, staring at the remains of the little Westland Scout.

The helicopter lay on its side, the central frame seemingly intact, but the ground about it was littered with wreckage. The earth was cut up with bootprints and other tracks. The marines set up a cordon about the wreck whilst Lester, Desaix and Ramis examined it more closely.

"It is as you said. Someone came upon this after the crash," Desaix said. He had been educated at Oxford as well as Saint Cyr, and his English was correct and formal. "You see here, the seat belts have been cut with a knife, and the copilot's door has been levered open. Plus, look at the ground. There were quite a few people around here after the helicopter came down."

Lester caught sight of a perfectly formed footprint which had been made by nothing human. He quietly stood on it and ground it into the mud.

"Yes, yes, they were rescued by the team that arrived before them. There's nothing more to be done here, it seems to me. Shall we move on, gentlemen?"

The two Frenchmen looked at one another and shrugged.

"*C'est vrai*," the doctor said quietly, pushing his black spectacles up his nose.

"Very well," Desaix said. "We shall continue to this base of yours. Sergeant, *allons-y!*"

The team moved out, scanning the desolate plateau for signs of life. Up at the front, one of the marines stood staring at the ground, following tracks in the mud. The snow was melting fast, and the whole island was reverting to a kind of highland bog. Desaix fell back down the line to join Lester.

"My orders are also to investigate the site of the strange lights seen by our reconnaissance," he said.

"Of course," Lester said smoothly. "But one thing at a time, Lieutenant. You can investigate all you like once we've ascertained if any of my people are left alive. We need to locate them, before anything can happen to them."

Desaix nodded. He marched along in silence for a few seconds, before speaking.

"They should be our top priority, it's true, though I can't see what could possibly threaten them in a place like this. There's nothing here, nothing at all."

Let's hope it stays that way, Lester thought.

Connor hunkered down in the brush and switched on the anomaly detector. The little device vibrated slightly in his hand, and there was a sharp beep as it powered up. He screwed his eyes shut for a second, trying to keep his thoughts together. Never in his life before had he been so tired and so tense at the same time.

"Well?" Willoby asked impatiently.

"Give it a second." He straightened and began to sweep the detector in an arc starting at the sea shore to their left, and continuing back across the endless plain that ran from the foot of the hills.

"Nothing."

"Right, switch her off and let's be moving again. Come on McCann, lead off. Axis is that big crag down at the foot of the slope, with the trees in a line to its right. Seen?"

"Seen," McCann agreed. He brought his rifle into his shoulder and stepped off.

Moonlight flooded the world around them, revealing a vast, monochrome, quiet wilderness where anything could be lurking in the shadows and hollows where the moonlight did not reach. They were three kilometres out from the camp, and would not be able to travel much further if they were to make it back before dawn.

That's what mammals are in this world, Connor thought. *Nocturnal scavengers who creep around when the monsters are asleep.* The adventure had worn thin some time ago. Now he simply felt as if they had no place here, and the longer they stayed, the lower their chances got. Man simply did not belong here.

They descended from the hills to the plain again, to the north of the camp this time, and were swallowed by the tawny sea of ferns that extended up from the coast. There were trails through the ferns, beaten down and littered with massive piles of droppings. A truck could have been driven along some of them. Those they avoided, and they laboured instead through the tall ferns, the sharp edges of which sliced their hands and soaked their legs and feet. Connor was about to try the detector again when McCann held up a hand.

"What's that?" he whispered.

He pointed ahead. Before them the plain rose in smooth undulations to the horizon, rising steadily until it met the brim of the sky, and the fantastic, luminous masses of the distant stars. But there was another star to be seen, separate from the others. It glittered in the darkness, a spangle of distant, inexplicable light.

"Turn that bloody thing on," Willoby said, the words clicking in his throat.

The detector whined slowly to life. The battery indicator was down to its final bar, an alarming amber warning.

"It's an anomaly!" Connor exclaimed. "Honest to God it is, dead ahead!"

"Thank God," Willoby said, and beside him McCann wiped his hand over his grinning face.

Connor's own grin began to fade.

"Captain, it's a very weak signal. That anomaly is on its way out. It's fading."

"How long do we have?" Willoby demanded.

"No way of telling. Usually it's just a few hours, but the ones on the island seem to behave differently. Cutter thinks it might have something to do with the storm, that they're connected somehow."

"That's pretty much par for the course then," Willoby said through gritted teeth.

"Maybe we should go through it now, ourselves, and make sure it leads to the right place," McCann said.

Willoby studied the distant flicker for a long moment, then studied the sky. Dawn wasn't far off.

"No," he said, reluctantly. "Either we all go through it together, or we all stay put. We're not going to split up. We'll go back to the camp and get everyone out here ASAP. We'll have to run it. Ready?"

"I'm not running anywhere," McCann said stubbornly. "If we go all the way back, and then march everyone out here, that thing will be gone — you heard the boy. I say we save ourselves, while we can. We go through it now. The rest will have to look out for themselves."

"We're not going to do that," Willoby said with dangerous softness. "Your officer is back there too, McCann. You want to leave him behind?"

"It can't be helped. Besides, they got me here under false pretences in the first place. You think before we flew out to that bastard island they told us we'd be fighting dinosaurs? No way. Nobody gives a shit about us — if we don't look after number one, we won't make it. I say we go, right now, and if you won't go with me, I'll do it myself."

"You'll stay here with us and obey orders," Willoby insisted.

"Whose orders — yours? You're a Brit, for Christ's sake! What right do you have to be ordering me around? You go to hell." McCann raised the barrel of his rifle and backed away from them.

"I warn you," he said, "don't try and stop me, or I'll plug you where you stand."

"For God's sake!" Connor said. "You can't just run off on your own!"

"Just watch me. You take it easy son — once I get to the other side I'll find some way to get help for you. You'll see." He turned and began running.

"McCann, you bloody fool!" Willoby shouted after him, but he had already disappeared into the tall growth, a mere shadow in the moonlight.

A wind picked up, moving the ferns in waves and bringing in clouds from the south. It looked as though it might rain. Connor and Willoby stared for a while, wondering if McCann might change his mind, but he had gone.

"We'd better get back," Willoby said. He sounded beaten somehow.

Connor stopped him, setting a hand on his arm.

"Captain, wait. Listen."

Something was moving in the tall ferns around them — more than one something. The moon had become hidden in a rolling mass of high clouds, and now there was only the starlight to see by. They stood frozen while on both sides of them things went by in the dark, not fifty metres away. Connor saw large, swift-moving shadows. There was a grunt, and then a sharp bark, a kind of snarl.

His insides turned to water.

The creatures passed by, heading up the slope that McCann had taken. They were visible as moving furrows in the fern prairies, eating up the ground at a fearsome pace.

"Let's get the hell out of here," Willoby said in a whisper.

"What about —"

"Screw him. He made his choice. Come on, Connor. This is not a good place to be."

They took off back to the camp at a run.

John McCann jogged steadily up the incline, breathing easily with his rifle held at the slope. He felt a pang of regret about the boy, Connor — he had been a decent sort. But he hoped that arrogant SAS bastard got what was coming to him.

This whole thing, it was insanity itself, a nightmare from the moment the helicopter had left the ship. Well, he had signed up for many things in his life, but this wasn't one of them. When he got back to the island he'd sit tight and wait for rescue. The rest of those poor souls back at the camp were doomed. With Hart and Brice both injured, they'd not make it back to the anomaly for many hours, and by that time it would be broad daylight, and God knows what would be roaming these fern prairies.

No, better to —

Something moved in the corner of his vision.

He kept running, picking up the pace but bringing up his rifle and snicking off the safety catch. In his head there ran childish prayers he hadn't uttered since school, when the Christian Brothers had beaten them into him.

On both his right and left, the shadows moved up. They were loping smoothly, keeping pace perhaps a hundred metres out on either side.

McCann began to sprint. The breath tore in and out of his lungs. The bright gleam of the anomaly was above him now, at the top of the slope.

One of the things broke trail in front of him, tearing at incredible speed through the ferns, uttering a series of high-pitched squawks which sounded almost birdlike. He felt a rush of relief. They were small, these things, not more than five- or six-feet tall. It wasn't so bad after all. They weren't real dinosaurs.

Another streaked across his path, and there were more behind him. He could hear movement all about in the ferns; the starlit slope seemed to have come alive. He turned, still running, and fired a burst behind him at the shadows, the muzzle-flash momentarily blinding him.

He tripped, and went down.

For a second he lay there, heart hammering. There was almost no sound, a crackle of the harsh ferns, no more. *I've scared them off*, he thought.

He rose to his feet.

And the first one came leaping out of the air upon him with its hind legs held back, and then it slashed them forward. He saw it only as a blur before it crashed into his chest and knocked him down. As he fell, his fist convulsed on the pistol grip of the rifle, and it went off in another tearing crack of automatic fire.

The thing was on top of him, ripping, shearing away his flesh in flurries of shining claws. He screamed as the claws ripped open his belly. The thing raised its bird-like head and squawked again.

More of its fellows joined it, leaping into McCann's dying vision and starting to tear at his body as he lay twitching, his insides steaming as they were scattered through the ferns. The pack fed, crooning and squabbling and hopping up and down.

Like sparrows at a bird feeder.

Connor and Willoby stopped in their tracks as they heard the gunfire. Back up the slope behind them they saw the tiny flash of light, then another. After that there was silence.

It was daylight when they made it back to camp, a darker dawn than the morning before, with clouds building up in the sky and an oppressive heat in the air. Willoby threw his rifle down upon the ground and grabbed the nearest water bottle, swallowing gulp after gulp with his eyes closed.

The rest of the team stared at him, and at Connor, was sat down some distance away with his head between his knees.

"McCann's dead," Willoby said, forestalling Cutter's question. "He took off on his own. We found an anomaly, maybe five kays north of here, out on the plains. Connor says it's fading, so time is short."

"What happened to McCann?" Lieutenant Brice asked quietly, cradling his broken arm.

"Something got him, don't know what. We heard gunfire, and that was it."

"Did you see him die?" Brice asked.

"I didn't have to. There's something out there in the ferns, a pack of something. They're not big, but they move fast."

"Eotyrannus?" Cutter asked. Willoby shook his head, wiping water from his chin.

"No, smaller than that. I don't know what the hell they were."

"Maybe he got away," Brice said. "You don't know — you didn't see."

"Maybe he did," Willoby said. Plainly, he did not want to talk about it. "In any case, there's an anomaly out there, and we have to try and get to it before it disappears. Time to move again, people."

"Hart can't walk, boss," Doody said.

"Then we'll carry him. Fox, rig up a litter. Doody, get him ready to move. Come on people — this may be our only chance."

The team began to pack up. While they had been gone, Sergeant Fox had already broken down a couple of stout saplings and slid them through a poncho, tying the whole thing up with paracord. Abby and Cutter helped lift Stephen onto it.

"Who are our strongest?" Cutter asked.

"Me and Fox," Willoby said bluntly, "but we need to provide security. Cutter, you and Doody take the litter first. We'll relieve you if it gets too much for you — but once we're down on the plains, the soldiers need to have their arms free, so the girls will have to pitch in with the lifting and carrying."

Jenny and Abby looked at one another.

"I'm a woman, not a girl," Abby growled.

"I can walk, if I have to," Stephen protested. "I'm not a complete invalid."

"Good," Willoby said. "Because if things go really pear-shaped out there, we may all have to run for it, and the devil take the hindmost."

His tone sobered them all. Clearly, whatever he had encountered in the night had shaken him. Connor was still white-faced and silent, holding his pistol in one hand and the anomaly detector in the other. He looked as though he had forgotten what sleep meant.

"Let's do it then," Cutter said, drawing his own pistol and cocking it with a snap.

Brice looked up at the sky as the little procession left the remains of their camp, the campfire still smoking.

"Looks like it's going to rain," he said.

TWENTY

The marines advanced in fire teams across the barren ground leading up to the base. Despite his best efforts, Lester felt himself growing apprehensive. The door was wide open, and looking in, it was possible to see an American-made light machine gun lying abandoned amid a scattering of other kit. He had seen one of the SAS troopers cleaning that machine gun back in the ARC.

Desaix held up a hand, and the marines went firm. Then one four-man team approached the doorway.

"*Mon Dieu!*" Lester heard one of them gasp, and the little radio clipped to Desaix's ear crackled in a stream of unintelligible French.

"Shit," Lester murmured, sticking to Anglo Saxon.

"There are body parts all around up there," Desaix said, watching the fire team move into the base through his binoculars. "I'm afraid it doesn't look good."

"I should go forward," said Ramis, the ship's doctor.

"No one moves until the base is secured. *Monsieur* Lester — *Monsieur* Lester!"

Lester ignored him. He walked quickly and purposefully towards the base, staring at the ground as he went. There was old blood here, congealed in puddles, soaking shreds of black cloth. A black M-4 magazine lay in the mud with the brass rounds still gleaming inside it. Here was the silver foil of a boil-in-the-bag ration-pack, and there, ludicrously, a trampled tea bag.

He stopped short. A man's hand lay severed at his feet. It had been bitten off; he could see the mark of the teeth as plain as day.

He raised his head and looked up at the base, now only some thirty yards away. Two French marines were crouched in the doorway, their rifles at their shoulders. The other two had gone inside. Lester forced himself to walk on. He wasn't squeamish in the slightest, but he wasn't looking forward to walking through that doorway.

He squared his shoulders and continued, nodding at the two startled marines. "*Qu'est-ce que c'est?*" one demanded.

"*Rien,*" he replied, and waved his hand in dismissal.

The entrance to the base was a slaughterhouse. There was dried blood everywhere, and shreds of tissue plastered in pink and brown streaks of torn flesh. Empty casings rattled under his feet and bullet holes pocked the concrete of the walls.

For the first time, he began to believe that they might all be truly dead. He had not allowed himself to think it before — Cutter, that arrogant ass, always seemed so indestructible. But now the possibility was very real.

This was going to be a disaster.

"Give me your torch," he said to the marine.

"Eh?"

"*Votre lampe de poche — maintenant!*"

Scowling, the marine handed over a small maglight. Lester twisted it on and stepped into the base.

It stank. There had been animals here. Their dung reeked, and the pools of blood that covered the floor were surely too big to have come from human beings.

Stairs down.

Ahead, he could hear the other marines talking, the static crackle of their radio. He went down the stairs. More blood — it was everywhere.

The marines were standing with flashlights in their hands before a great vaulted door. This had been a lab. There was broken glass underfoot now, and wooden workbenches which had been shattered and torn into matchwood.

And something else. Lester joined the two Frenchmen and found that they were staring at the partially eaten carcass of a huge animal. There were bullet holes in its head and upper body. It looked as though it had been shot, and then something else had decided to make a snack of it. The thing must between fifteen and twenty-feet long. Lester was no dinosaur expert, but he appraised the massive jawful of teeth thoughtfully.

The marine closest to Lester rapped on the massive steel door before him.

"It's locked," he said in surprisingly good English. "Maybe they are inside." He spoke into his radio, and Lester heard Desaix's voice on the other end. Then he and his comrade went back to examining the dead dinosaur, plainly flabbergasted. They cast dark looks at Lester, as though they thought he might be responsible for it.

There were footsteps above, and more marines entered the shattered lab, their torches flicking back and forth over everything. Desaix and Ramis were with them. Desaix glared at Lester and then nudged the massive carcass at his feet, shaking his head.

"There is another one of them outside, at the north end of the base. It does not have a mark on it, but it is dead."

"Perhaps the cold killed it," Lester said. "The weather really has been shocking lately."

Desaix frowned. "Your people — any sign?"

Lester turned and looked at the great round door behind them, with its circle-lock and combination box. He touched the brass tumblers. The door had score marks all down it where the creature had clawed furiously to get in.

"If they're anywhere," he said quietly, "they're in here. Drag that gruesome heap of meat out of the way. We need to get this door open."

The tumblers ticked smoothly as Lester clicked them to the right numeral, one by one. It was a code he had been given only after a heated set of arguments in Whitehall. He had passed it on to Captain Willoby with great reluctance, but Willoby was discreet. He was a good man.

Now he was probably dead.

They swung the door open, and gaped at what they found. A Christmas tree of whirling lights at the base of a large, circular chamber with a raised catwalk all about it, and a ramp leading down. Nothing else. Just that pillar of coruscating light, turning like a slow-motion firework.

"What is this?" Desaix asked.

Lester studied the anomaly with a detached air. The chamber was empty but for its glittering radiance. They had done it — they had actually gone through. Must have. They had left not so much as a button behind them in here. He found himself admiring their courage.

Of course, when one is desperate, one might do anything.

He had seen anomalies before, and he had read countless reports on them. He studied this one now with an expert eye, and pursed his lips.

"Tell me — what is this thing?" Desaix demanded again. He stepped toward the floating lights.

"Don't touch it!" Lester snapped as the French officer approached the phenomenon, walking down the catwalk ramp like a man entranced. After his abrupt outburst, he composed himself. "Stay away from it, Lieutenant. You have no idea how dangerous these things are."

"What is it they do — is it a weapon?"

The anomaly was yellowing, and the spangled shards of light it threw out covered ever smaller arcs. It was fading. He could see that it was dying in front of him.

And Cutter, with all his people, would be trapped on the far side of it.

He stood stock still for a moment.

"Set a guard on this thing," Lester said, striding out of the chamber. "No one goes near it, and cover it with fire, you understand me?"

"The monsters are to do with this thing, are they not?" asked the doctor, Ramis.

"Very perceptive of you," Lester drawled. "Lieutenant, I need you and some of your men. We have to go to the other site, where your pilot saw more of these things, and we must be quick."

"I don't understand."

"Then stop trying, and just do as I say. *Vite!*"

Lester's abrupt authority seemed to draw the French officer after him irresistibly. Desaix called out orders to his fire teams. With four men and the bespectacled ship's doctor, they blew through the dark charnel house that was the Guns Island base until they were outside again. Lester studied the sky, and gave vent to some more prosaic profanity.

"Pick up the pace," he said. "There's not a moment to lose."

***

A hundred million or so years earlier, Cutter and the surviving members of his team made their way down out of the hills, carrying Stephen on the litter. They picked their way out of the shadow of the trees, and after an hour's stumbling march had made it to the wide, rolling plain Abby described as the Sea of Ferns.

To the north, it rose in a long series of shallow slopes up to the horizon, where it was dotted with clumps of conifers and long brakes of head-high ferns. Up there, somewhere, the anomaly stood, at least so they hoped. And up there somewhere, John McCann had been killed.

They marched steadily. Four of them carried the litter: Cutter, Connor, Doody and Abby. Willoby was out in front, Brice and Jenny walked alongside, and Sergeant Fox brought up the rear. No one spoke. It was as if the oppressiveness of the day had invaded their minds.

The sun had been hidden by an ominous build up of towering clouds, the black heads of which lowered like grey anvils over the world below. Already, they heard the first rumblings of thunder travel over the hills, and they could not help but wonder what a Cretaceous storm would be like. The air seemed charged with electricity, so that Abby's bright bob crackled like the fur of a cat stroked the wrong way, and the plains below the hills, which had been teeming with herd animals at dawn, now seemed deserted.

The big herbivores had made off in trundling masses for the lower slopes of the foothills, where they stood in patient crowds, calling to one another in bass bellows that carried from one end of the hills to the other. Of the big predators, the Neovenators, there was no sign. The air seemed hushed and still, with even the Pterosaurs retreating to their cliff ledges, as if they didn't trust what the sky held.

"We're in for a rough spell of weather," Cutter said, looking up at the lowering clouds, which shifted and jostled under the rising wind. "Still, it may be for the best. It should put predators off the scent, to some extent."

There was a beeping in Connor's pocket.

"Professor," he said, fishing out the anomaly detector, "I'm picking up the signal again. It's still there — the anomaly is still up there!"

A wave of relief swept through the group. Part of Cutter had been afraid that it would be gone, that the detector would remain dead as they approached the plains, and they would end up standing there with nowhere to go. The others must have felt it, too, though no one had said anything.

Now the revelation cheered them. They began to pick up the pace.

Cutter felt the first drops of rain slap him on the face. They were warm, and as big as pound coins. He bent his head and concentrated on carrying the litter, forcing one foot in front of the other. He tried not to think of anything else.

"I think they were Raptors, last night," Connor said, blinking rain out of his eyes. He shook drops off the anomaly detector and stowed it back in his pocket, where it clinked against his pistol.

"They were smaller than those monsters back on the island, though," Willoby said from in front. "I reckon whatever they were, they were smaller than a man."

Cutter stared at Connor, eyes widening.

"Dromaeosaurs?"

"Could be, Professor. We didn't get a look at them, but I remembered —"

"I know," Cutter said. He remembered a nighttime shopping mall not so long ago, where he and the team had battled against a mated pair of Dromaeosaurs. A single pair, and they had almost come unglued in the confines of a shopping mall.

Now they were out in the open, perhaps facing an entire pack.

"Movement draws their eye," Connor went on. "I think that's why they went after McCann. He was running, whereas Willoby and me, we were standing still."

The rain grew heavier. Quickly they became soaked through, and the wooden shafts that supported the litter began to slip and slide in Cutter's hands. Underfoot, the ground began to run with excess water, and mud sucked at the soles of their boots. Visibility decreased to a hundred metres.

"This is good," Cutter said loudly. "This is helping us."

"You could have fooled me," Doody said.

"Sight and smell, the two big senses of predators. This is covering us. It's all good, believe me."

If I keep saying it, I may even believe it myself.

An unbelievably loud rattle of thunder broke out across the sky, echoing from one horizon to the other. Out of the corner of his eye, Cutter saw a flash, and he turned his head just in time to catch the flared branch of the forked lightning as it seared an afterimage across his retinas.

"Who'd be under a tree now, eh?" Willoby shouted over the hissing roar of the rain.

The day grew dark, as though dusk had come upon them prematurely. All along the horizon, lightning exploded out of the clouds in arterial branches of unbearably bright light, and in its wake the thunder broke out in an awesome barrage, continuous now, deafening.

They trudged on through the mud, barely able to see. In the litter, Stephen lay like a waxen image, clutching his side and coughing, though the sound of his struggles was lost in the majesty of the storm.

Willoby stopped. He was staring at his compass, but the needle was spinning like a top. Disgusted, he threw it away into the ferns.

"Connor!" he yelled. "Check that thing of yours. Give me a bearing — I can't see a damned thing in front of me."

Connor checked the detector. The green light was crawling into amber. His face fell.

"It's to our right a bit. We've come too far to the left. Go right, Captain."

"How far?"

"I don't know — a couple of kilometres maybe. It's fading, the signal is fading. Professor, the anomaly is going to disappear!"

That galvanised them. They began to follow Willoby at a brisk trot, and Stephen bounced up and down on the crude litter in their midst, his face a colourless rictus of pain. Brice didn't seem much better off. Jenny had to take his unbroken arm and help him keep up with the others. He was biting his lip as he ran, and soon there was a red trickle amid the rain on his face where he had bitten it through.

It became pitch dark, except for the concatenations of the lightning, which chopped their vision up into stuttered glimpses, as though they were looking out through an old Victorian magic lantern. The thunder rendered any communication below a shout inaudible, and more alarmingly, the rain seemed to be gathering in rivulets and streams around their feet. At times they splashed through water ankle-deep, and below it the softening earth was quickly becoming a mire.

Cutter tripped, his left foot sucked in the muck. He went headlong, dropping his corner of the litter, and Stephen rolled out onto the ground.

His mouth opened in a scream as he splashed into the mud and he lay there clutching his chest. There was blood on his lips.

They lifted him back onto the litter, becoming slimed with mud in the process. Abby's bright bob was smeared black all down one side.

Then they stumbled onwards. Willoby came back down the now straggling line and grabbed Connor's arm.

"The detector!" he yelled in the younger man's ear. "I can't see where we're going!"

Connor fished it out. They stared at the fading light of the LED screen. Connor swung it round for a second and the signal strengthened. Then the battery finally gave way and the device went dead. Connor's lips thinned. He stared at the thing for a second, and then hurled it out into the rain-lashed darkness.

"What did you do that for?" Abby asked shrilly.

"I'll build a better one!" he snapped back.

"Follow me — I think it helped. I think I have an idea now," Willoby said.

They toiled on. Once, the lightning struck the ground not ten metres in front of them, and it erupted with a burnt smell and a momentary flame, drenched out by the rain a half-second later.

The water grew deeper around their feet. It was as though they were wading through a shallow river. It climbed to their shins, and then their calves, and below it the soft ground clutched at their boots so that every step forward was a battle to free their feet from the earth before setting them down again. They had to lift Stephen higher, to avoid dragging him through the water.

Cutter looked around. A strange noise had begun, a kind of distant roar that hummed below the brash staccato rattles of the thunder. It was familiar. Then he remembered a dig in Kenya, at the start of the rainy season, and realised what the sound was.

"Run!" he yelled. "Get to the high ground! Move, move, *now*!"

They began a hobbled, agonising jog, which was the best they could muster in the boggy ground.

"What is it?" Willoby demanded. "What did you see?"

"Water," Cutter told him. "Flash flood. It's building up along the plain. We have to get higher!"

Heedless of direction, they ran for the rising ground ahead, lifting the litter onto their shoulders. Cutter had never in his life before made such an agonising physical effort. But he was still able to catch the grey flash out of the corner of his eye, duller than the lightning. The ground under his feet was shaking.

They made a final, lung-searing effort, and collapsed on a low knoll that jutted above the smooth rise of the fern prairie to the north — or they thought it was north. By now, no one had any idea which direction they were facing.

The flood of water broke around them. It was as though a hungry sea had invaded the world and was intent on swallowing it. The torrent of brown water smashed round the hem of the knoll on which they stood, cutting them off from the high ground where Connor and Willoby had seen the anomaly.

It caught Brice as he scrambled to keep his footing in the soft mud, and spun him round, bearing him away. Abby launched herself through the air and managed to grasp his hand, whilst Connor and Jenny hung on to her thighs. They pulled him in, the water smashing in a savage torrent around them all, and fought their way up the knoll again. Their little hill had become an island, and around it the floodwaters foamed and gibbered in a brown and white fury, whilst above them the sky was livid with lightning.

They sat, staring dully into the rain. Once an entire tree washed past them, a straight-boled conifer, and in its branches a dinosaur the size of a turkey writhed and snapped, a tiny-headed creature with a long neck.

Stephen was unconscious, the rain sheeting down over his white face. They had lost or cast aside the last of their belongings in their haste to clear the water, and now sat with only the clothes they stood up in, and whatever the soldiers had stowed in their webbing. Willoby, Doody and Fox still had their rifles, but all the other firearms had gone by the board except Cutter's pistol, for which he had precisely four rounds left.

He joined Willoby, who was sitting staring uphill, at the high ground where the anomaly had been the night before.

"This water will go down soon — then we'll take off again. Are you sure that's where you saw it, Captain?"

Willoby wiped rain out of his eyes.

"I think so. To tell the truth, Cutter, I'm not certain. We've got turned around a couple of times, and compasses don't seem to be any use in this storm." He paused, and stared out into the lightning-shattered darkness.

"I think we're screwed," he said.

"We're not dead yet," Cutter said, almost angrily. But he was taken aback. He had never seen Willoby at a loss up to now, or anything other than positive.

"The way home is up on that high ground, and we're going to find it, Captain. Because if we don't, we're all dead — do you hear me? All of us. And I won't let that happen to my team. Not to these people. We are all going home," he said. "Do you hear me?"

"I hear you." Willoby smiled slightly. "I never took you for a hopeless optimist."

"I'm a glass half-full kind of guy," Cutter shot back. "I just hide it well, that's all."

They waited, hunkered down in the mud of the knoll while the floodwaters coursed around them. After less then a quarter of an hour, the flow began to visibly recede. Cutter stepped out into it first, finding the water up to his thighs. It was still a powerful current, but it was dwindling moment by moment.

"Come on!" he shouted at the others. "We can do this. Grab Stephen and let's get moving."

"You heard the man," Willoby said, rising. No one else had moved. "What, do you want to lie down and die here? Get off your fat lazy arses — Sergeant Fox, get that bloody litter up on your shoulders, that's an order. Doody, on your feet. We're still on the clock here. You can relax in your own time."

The team hauled themselves upright, looking like nothing so much as a demoralised nest of half-drowned rats. They moved off into the water, which was knee deep now, and splashed their way in Cutter's wake as he forged ahead into the storm. Willoby brought up the rear.

They set their faces towards the high ground, and began ascending it, foot by labouring foot.

TWENTY-ONE

The storm was easing, it was definite now. Lester raised his face to the sky and actually saw a bar of sunlight strike the black rocks of the island plateau. Ahead of him, the three anomalies weren't nearly so bright as when he had first seen them. They seemed now like candles brought into daylight, withering even as he looked.

The French marines had taken up firing positions amid the rocks surrounding the phenomena. The Puma had made another landing now that the wind was dying down, and a full platoon of soldiers had landed, with more on their way.

The sat-phone buzzed. Lester answered it.

"James Lester."

"Report," a voice said.

Lester tensed. "The French have secured the sites of all four phenomena on the island. There is, as yet, no sign of our people."

"What's the confirmed body count?"

"So far, four, we think."

"You think?"

"The bodies were in an advanced state of mutilation. In fact, very little was left of them at all. We know one was female, and from the uniforms at least one was from the *Aoife*. Forensics will be needed to give an iron-clad breakdown."

"How many still missing?"

"Ten. Eight of our own, and two Irish."

"How far up has this balloon gone so far?"

Lester rubbed his chin. "Helicopter crash on remote island, ships sent to lend a hand with a rescue under difficult climactic circumstances. Page seven of *The Times* this morning I believe." He thanked God he had called the ARC to keep himself abreast of the press reaction.

"Next of kin?"

"We'll sit on that until we have a final body count." *And until we can come up with a believable story*, Lester thought.

"Good. A pity the French got involved, but there was nothing else for it. Keep me informed."

The line went dead.

Lester replaced the headset in the cradle. His career wasn't over just yet, it seemed.

He stood looking at the anomalies, trying to put himself in Cutter's shoes once more. What was it like over there, in that world? Was Cutter even close to finding a way back? Why did the man have to be so tiresomely unpredictable?

If I lose that entire team, plus an SAS captain, then it really is all over, he thought. *I'll be lucky if they let me stay on to make tea.*

He made up his mind.

If you want a job done properly...

"Lieutenant Desaix, lend me your rifle, will you — there's a good fellow."

"What do you need a rifle for? We have the whole area covered."

"And some of those dinky little flares, you know the type." Lester didn't even acknowledge the man's question. "You snap the top off, and away they go. Come on, man, I haven't got all day."

"Monsieur Lester..."

"The rifle, Lieutenant. Ah, thank you."

"Do you know how to —"

"I know which is the dangerous end, thank you. Now tell your men to stand fast."

With the Famas on his shoulder and a pocket-full of flares, Lester walked up to the three anomalies. His heart was thudding faster as he approached them.

"Eenie, meenie, minie, mo," he muttered, and then, coolly and deliberately, he walked straight into the middle one, and disappeared.

Willoby turned around and raised the muzzle of the rifle.

Even over the chaotic roar of the electrical storm, he was sure something had been splashing through the water behind them, but in the black and white flicker of the lightning, it was like trying to recognise someone's face across a crowded dance floor. There was nothing there — nothing to be seen. What could be tracking them in the middle of this?

He clicked off the safety catch, all the same.

They were well up onto the higher ground now, and the floodwaters had been left behind. The soil underfoot was still drenched and running with rain, but it wasn't the sucking mire it had been further below. They began to make better time.

"The storm is passing," Connor said. "I think the rain is easing off a little."

"I think you're a born optimist, Connor," Jenny told him. "It looks dark as pitch to me."

"I hope your boss knows where he's going," Doody said to them.

"He always knows," Abby retorted.

Willoby jogged past them.

"Fox, take rearguard." He joined Cutter at the front of their bedraggled little column.

"Do you know where you're going?" he asked Cutter.

"Everybody seems to be asking that question," Cutter smiled. "Connor's right, the rain is easing off."

"Cutter —"

"You tell me, Willoby. Does this place look familiar?"

"I don't know. I can barely make out a thing in this —" His last word was drowned out by a rolling barrage of thunder.

"With all this lightning, an anomaly isn't going to stand out in the dark, especially if it's fading," Cutter said.

"Or if it's disappeared," Willoby rejoined.

"These things come and go. If it happens that —"

There was a burst of gunfire at the rear of the party.

"Stand-to! Enemy rear!" It was Sergeant Fox. Instantly they bunched up, facing outwards.

"Sitrep!" Willoby bellowed.

"There's something out there, boss — more than one of 'em. They're not big, but they're moving fast through the ferns."

"All right, lads. Mark your targets and conserve your ammo. Three round bursts —"

Something leapt through the air at them, visible in snatched flashes of lightning. They caught a glimpse of a snapping, sharp, beak-like head, and then it had landed right in the midst of the party, scattering them like skittles. It reached out with a sinewed foreleg and slashed left and right. Brice was caught along his back, and he went down with a cry.

Doody opened fire, the muzzle-flash yellow and blinding at close range. The creature squawked and bounced to its feet as though built of steel springs. It leapt at Doody and bowled him over, the rifle going off again as they rolled in the wet ferns and mud.

Another came tearing in at them, and then another. Cutter saw one blur past him and fired four rounds in quick succession. Then the pistol clicked in his hand with the slide jammed backwards. It was empty.

When the creature came snapping at his face, he snarled like an animal himself, and smashed the barrel of the pistol into its snout. It broke away, hopping like a monstrous magpie.

Another came at Abby, its claws ripped through her jacket and sliced the webbing belt at her waist in half. Then it sat on top of her and cocked back its head triumphantly for the killer blow.

Connor launched himself at it bodily, knocking it off her. He had a long knife in his hand which gleamed like a streak of silver in the lightning flashes. He locked one arm about the creature's corded neck, and stabbed and stabbed at it with the other, screaming wordless fury. The thing thrashed in his grip, scrabbling in the mud and squealing.

Willoby set his boot upon its neck and put a bullet in its brain.

The creatures were leaping in and out of the party's ranks, calling to one another in sharp barks and caws, the sound like an argument between a sea lion and a raven. Cutter bent and slid out one of the poles from Stephen's litter, then stood over his prostrate friend and swung the heavy stick in an arc at any animal that came close, swearing, his eyes showing the whites like a horse smelling fire.

Rifle shots here and there, in three round bursts. Fox, Willoby and Doody were firing almost blind. Two of the creatures latched onto Brice as he lay slashed and bleeding, and started to drag him away. A volley smashed through them and they hobbled off into the dark, yowling.

"Christ, they're everywhere," Willoby said.

"I can't get a shot in, boss," Fox shouted. "They're too bloody fast."

"Back to back, and face outwards," Cutter told them. "Keep them at bay. If they split us up, we'll be picked off one by one."

"Abby... Abby." Connor was on his knees, lifting up her head.

"I'm all right," she said, running her hands up and down her torso. "Just scratched."

"I see something," Jenny said. She was staring along the crest of the slope to their right. "I see a light."

"Lightning," Willoby said, dismissing her. He fired off another burst, and then shouted "Magazine!" as his weapon clicked dry. He searched for another clip in his webbing.

They came in again, three, four at a time. The soldiers fired off their weapons as the creatures leapt towards them, tracer zooming out into the storm-split dark. There were squeals of pain. Two made it through into the middle of the party. One Willoby clubbed with his rifle butt, and then Connor and Abby tackled it, Connor's knife taking it through the eye. The other was clubbed by Cutter with his unwieldy pole, and before it could rise to its feet again Sergeant Fox smashed the stock of his rifle into its head again and again, the movements made into staccato stop-motion by the lightning flashes.

"There's a light!" Jenny cried. "Look will you — off to the right!"

Breathing heavily, Cutter took a moment to stare. Out in the darkness was a pinkish gleam, guttering and flaring in the storm dark.

"That's not an anomaly," he said.

"It's good enough for me," Willoby said. "Let's move. Doody, Fox, pick up Hart. Cutter, help Brice."

Cutter bent and examined the Irish pilot.

"He's dead," he said.

"Leave him then. Come on, people, before they come at us again!"

Dragging Stephen in their midst, they stumbled towards the strange light like a battered group of Cro-Magnons, Cutter wielding his pole,

Connor his knife, and the soldiers slotting their last full clips into their rifles. The ferns were slippery underfoot, but the rain had almost stopped. The storm was passing.

It began to grow light again. They had almost forgotten that this was mid-morning. The storm had skewed their sense of things. They no longer cared about scientific enquiry, or national security, or even the bodies of those they had left behind. They were motivated purely by the desire to stay alive, to come through the nightmare. They laboured through the growing light of the day with murderous determination in their eyes.

"Here they come again," Fox said, at the rear. "They're circling us."

"Keep moving," Willoby snarled.

The Dromaeosaurs were moving through the tall ferns in arcs to their rear and to the left and right. Back down the slope they could see a knot of them feasting on Brice's body, fighting and squabbling over the fresh meat.

"God, I hate these things," Doody said with disgust.

"Shut up. Keep your eyes open. Fox, take the rear arc, Doody, you're on the left. I'll take the right. Cutter, keep them moving, no matter what. Don't stop for anything."

They charged through the ferns, their lungs burning in their chests. Stephen moaned in pain as he was pulled along by the arms, his legs trailing behind him.

The sun came out, a startling brightness that dazzled their eyes. As it did, the Dromaeosaurs moved in.

"Keep going," Willoby said calmly. He looked off to where the pink light had been, but they were in dead ground here, and it was hidden from them. He fired three quick bursts, and one of the creatures collapsed ten metres from him. The others barked at one another, weaving back and forwards in the ferns, creating dark lines through it which bisected their own trail.

They came in on the left, two of them. One leapt at Doody, and the other jinked around to burst through the other members of the party. Connor slashed at it with his knife as it whipped past him.

Doody went down, then was up again, clubbing the creature back with his rifle, yelling wordlessly. The creature got its claws around the weapon and ripped it out of his hands. It stood a moment, holding it, and then bit down on the metal. Doody drew his bayonet and stabbed it in the head. The blade snapped off. He threw down the handle and began running.

Cutter fell, and the pole snapped under him. He threw one sharp fragment to Abby and jabbed the other at a creature that banked close to him, snapping out like a gull trying to nab some chips. The jagged wood took it in its mouth, and Cutter rammed it home as hard as he could. The creature leapt away, tearing the makeshift spear out of Cutter's hands. He bent, grabbed Stephen's arm, and helped Connor drag him along.

They crested a small rise, and before them, not a hundred metres away, was an anomaly. It was truncated, glimmering, a mere parody of its full shining itself. It was about to disappear.

A few metres from it, a pink flare was lying on the ferns, burning smokily as it too began to sink. And beside the flare, James Lester stood with an automatic rifle in the crook of his arm.

"Get a move on!" he shouted, and waved his arm at them.

They ran on, the Dromaeosaurs weaving through them, snapping and snarling. Willoby brought up the rear. The creatures that had been feeding on Brice's body had left their meal and were now powering up the slope to join their fellows. Willoby halted, panting, then looked back at the rest of the party, still tottering towards the dying anomaly.

He knelt on one knee, took careful aim, and then began firing single shots at the Dromaeosaurs.

One was brought down just as it had locked its jaws around Stephen's boot. Another was wounded as it prepared to leap on Doody's running back, and it toppled, squealing and thrashing in the ferns. A third took a bullet in the leg as Abby was frantically beating it off with the other half of Cutter's stick. It fell on its side, and she stabbed the makeshift stake into its throat, then turned and kept running.

Everyone was running except Willoby. He kept his breathing steady, took careful, aimed shots, and brought down or wounded one by one the members of the Dromaeosaurid pack that were hounding the rest of the party. He saw the others reach Lester, who was also firing his rifle — though not, Willoby noted, with much effect. He saw Cutter and Connor drag Stephen through the anomaly, then Jenny and Abby went through, then Doody and Fox, and finally Lester.

He was alone.

The second group of animals was loping up the slope now, almost on him.

Cutter came back through.

"Willoby!" He shouted. "For God's sake man, come on — save yourself!"

Too late for that. He took careful aim as the foremost of the Dromaeosaurs launched itself through the air at him. The rifle clicked on an empty chamber.

Sloppy, Willoby thought, just as the animal landed on him, smashing him onto his back.

TWENTY-TWO

Cutter came back through with a face like stone. He stood blinking as the anomaly swirled and withered, and finally winked out behind him.

The other two phenomena went with it. Guns Island opened up around him, a fresh breeze winnowing the ferns and playing upon the granite of its bones.

"Where is he? Where's the boss?" Sergeant Fox asked.

"He's dead," Cutter said dully.

French soldiers were milling around by the dozen, with blankets and mugs of hot coffee. Like it was the scene of an accident, Cutter thought.

Stephen was being seen to by a French doctor and a whole team of medics. They were setting up a drip. He opened his eyes once as Cutter stood over him, and their gazes locked. Stephen nodded slightly, and then drifted off again. The medics covered his face with an oxygen mask.

"I call that cutting it rather fine," Lester said. He looked at the gasping, sweating, shivering survivors of the team as they hunkered on the ground around him, exhausted, bloody and blasted by what they had seen and experienced.

"You have no idea," Cutter said to him.

Connor was still clutching his bloody knife, as though afraid to let go of it. Cutter knelt beside him.

"Who needs guns, eh? You did well, Connor. You all did."

"What happened to Willoby?" Connor asked. "I didn't see, Professor."

"He didn't make it."

"Oh, God." Tears welled up in Connor's eyes. Cutter set his hand on the boy's head. Except he wasn't a boy, not any more. His eyes were middle-aged.

"You did well," he repeated, not knowing what else to say.

A helicopter landed not thirty metres distant, the down-wash of its rotor making them all turn away. It was a French Puma. The doctor and his team lifted Stephen onto a lightweight gurney and carried him to the aircraft, then set him aboard. It took off again, a roaring monster of aluminium and steel.

"He'll be all right," Lester said. He took a notebook out of his breast pocket. "It would seem you're missing a few people Cutter. I need their names, and what happened to them. We have to get this thing sorted out as soon as possible. For the families, you understand."

"For the families, right," Cutter said. He was in a daze. A passing French marine handed him a cup of coffee, and he stood looking into it as though it were an oracle.

"Their names," he said. "Right now, I'm not sure I can call them to mind." He handed the mug to Lester. "Hold this, will you?" Then he turned and was sick into the grass.

Lester sighed and looked away.

"I quite understand," he said, sounding anything but understanding.

Cutter wiped his mouth.

"It was good of you to come through looking for us."

"All part of the service, Professor."

"I'm surprised you risked your own neck that way."

Lester shrugged.

"It was that, or leave it to our friends here."

"Ah, the French. You must tell me, sometime, just how they got here."

"Believe me, Cutter, by the time you have written your report and I have written mine, and you've given statements to a couple of sub-committees, and hashed and rehashed the events of the last few days, you will know everything there is to know about this place, and everything that happened here."

"Why don't you settle for telling me why a bunker was built around an anomaly here, fifty years ago?" Cutter said, glaring now.

Lester looked up at the shifting clouds that were drifting across the sky. There were seagulls flying in raucous skeins below them, calling out across the island as though reclaiming the place from the storm. And the things that had been in the storm.

"Ah, now there's the little sticking point. Some things, Cutter, are better not known, not by you, and not even by the great and the good of our fine country."

"In other words, you just won't tell me."

"I could tell you," Lester said. He smiled. "But then I'd have to kill you."

He walked away, tapping his notebook against his chin.

THE END

ACKNOWLEDGMENTS

Many thanks to Cath Trechman, for her professionalism, good humour and great patience; to Tim Haines and Adrian Hodges for their invaluable insights and input; and to Nancia Leggett for keeping the whole process on track.

PRIMEVAL

SHADOW OF THE JAGUAR
STEVEN SAVILE

A delirious backpacker crawls out of the dense Peruvian jungle muttering about the impossible things he has seen... A local ranger reports seeing extraordinary animal tracks and bones – fresh ones – that he cannot explain...

Cutter and the team are plunged into the hostile environment of the Peruvian rainforest, where they endure a perilous journey leading them to a confrontation with something more terrifying than they could possibly have imagined...

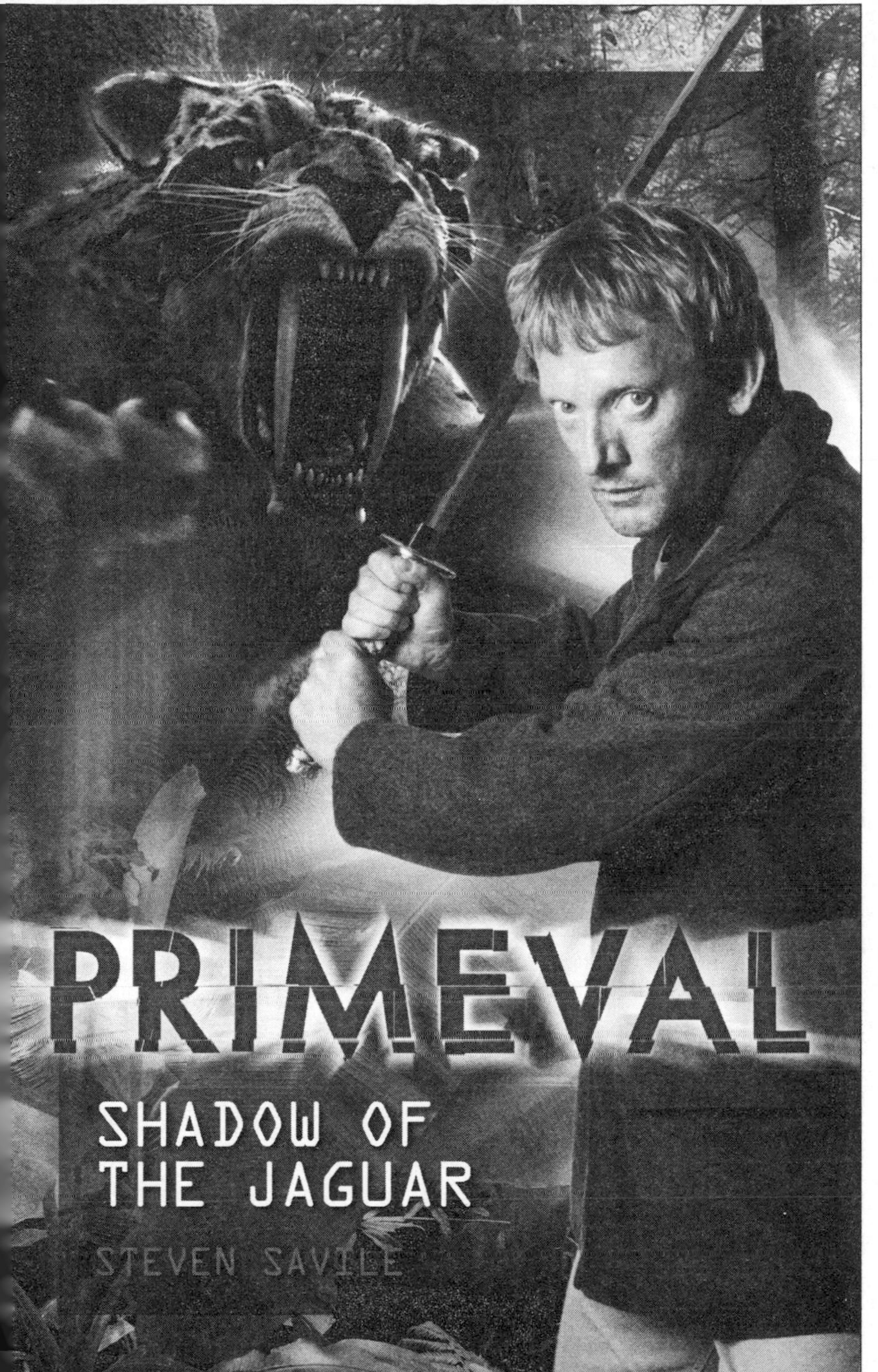
PRIMEVAL
SHADOW OF
THE JAGUAR
STEVEN SAVILE

PRIMEVAL
EXTINCTION EVENT
DAN ABNETT

An Entelodon goes on the rampage down Oxford Street causing untold damage and loss of life, and Cutter decides a new approach to tackling the anomalies is needed. When a mysterious Russian scientist arrives at the ARC, Cutter thinks he might have found the answer...

Kidnapped and smuggled into Siberia, Cutter, Abby and Connor are faced with an anomaly disaster on an epic scale... While Lester and Jenny must work together to try to track them down.

www.titanbooks.com

PRIMEVAL

EXTINCTION EVENT

DAN ABNETT

PRIMEVAL

FIRE AND WATER
SIMON GUERRIER

At a safari park in South Africa, rangers are inexplicably disappearing and strange creatures have been seen battling with lions and rhinos. As the team investigates they are drawn into a dark conspiracy which could have terrible consequences...

Back in London, Connor and Abby have been left to cope on their own. As torrential rain pours down over the city, an enormous anomaly opens up in East London...

www.titanbooks.com

PRIMEVAL

FIRE AND WATER

SIMON GUERRIER